Widow's Walk

Susan Slater

Books by Susan Slater
THE BEN PECOS MYSTERY SERIES

The Pumpkin Seed Massacre
Yellow Lies
Thunderbird
Firedancer
Under A Mulberry Moon
The Thaw
Ghost Dust
Paper Arrows
A Way to the Manger (a Christmas novella)

THE DAN MAHONEY MYSTERY SERIES
Flash Flood
Rollover
Hair of the Dog
Epiphany
Widow's Walk

STAND-ALONE NOVELS
0 to 60
The Caddis Man
Five O'Clock Shadow

Widow's Walk

Dan Mahoney Mysteries, Book 5

Susan Slater

Secret Staircase Books

Widow's Walk
Published by Secret Staircase Books, an imprint of
Columbine Publishing Group LLC
PO Box 416, Angel Fire, NM 87710

Book layout and design by Secret Staircase Books
Cover illustrations © Sergey Uryadnikov, Anthony Annese
Totah Jr., Sherryvsmith

Publisher's Cataloging-in-Publication Data

Slater, Susan
Widow's Walk / by Susan Slater
p. cm.
ISBN 978- 1649140821 (paperback)
ISBN 978- 1649140838 (e-book)

1. Mahoney, Dan (Fictitious character)—Fiction. 2. Insurance
investigation—Fiction. 3. Florida—Fiction. 4. Sea stories—
Fiction. I. Title

Dan Mahoney Mystery Series : Book 5
Slater, Susan, Dan Mahoney mysteries.

BISAC : FICTION / Mystery & Detective.
813/.54

Acknowledgement

I often get an idea for a story only to realize that I know next to nothing about the subject matter. That's what happened with schooners. They are a wonderful replica of a swashbuckling past that still captures the imagination today. But the nitty/gritty? I hadn't a clue. And that's when I met Captain Buzz Nichols. Capt. Buzz beat out Google hands down when it came to schooner knowledge! He even arranged for me to take a sail and I was hooked. I knew in an instant that Dan Mahoney would be investigating schooners!

Thank you Capt. Buzz for bringing life to this book.

Chapter 1

Monstrosity. Blight on the neighborhood. Ruined resale values. Adult Disney set—She'd heard it all, and was still laughing. She loved the design of her house, mansion really, nestled on its manicured lawn with graceful palms, all a matter of feet from the Atlantic separated from crashing waves by pristine white sand and sea oats and an endless blue-green horizon. Just because the top of the fourth floor sported an octagonal, eight-foot radius, open-air gazebo perched on the edge of the house's metal roof above a dormer, her neighbors found a reason to laugh. The old-fashioned structure acted as a look-out and faced the ocean. It called to mind days of seafaring uncertainties; lonely women longing for a glimpse of their loved ones returning safely to harbor. It had been a joint project. An idea born as a joke that gathered credence when the architect thought it was a perfect addition. Like a lighthouse, he said, the type of icon that this stretch of barren beach would call a landmark. A widow's walk— shouldn't every sea-faring man own one? A place for his land-bound love to climb to and search the sea's vastness for a glimpse of his homecoming? It was something right out of a nineteenth century romance novel—so fitting. And *so* Hank Beaufort.

Hannah loved her husband; no, adored him was a better word. How many times had she remarked to friends, "I couldn't live without him"? He was her rock, her provider, the source of everything good in her life. Hannah and Henry, Hank to his friends, philanthropists, pillars of the community, a church deacon and a Sunday school teacher. If you didn't know Hannah and Henry, you hadn't lived in this part of Florida for long. Their parties were one of a kind with much coveted invitations sought after by anyone wanting to see his or her name in the *St. Augustine Record*.

Had there been little indiscretions? Yes. But two could play that game. It was never anything serious for either one of them. Sometimes a flirtation, and even more, could only spice up what one had at home. It felt good to hear that she was still beautiful. She needed that. What was that old saying? Familiarity breeds contempt? He might be lax in showing his devotion, but he would never leave her— of that, she was certain. And she would never leave him. Hadn't she just walked away from the kind of adoration that most women only dreamed of? A man who gave himself to her body and soul, but couldn't replace the man she called her husband.

They were struggling through a rough patch right now. And as in any marriage, minor setbacks were bound to happen from time to time. It was money again. Wasn't it always money, or the lack of it? But Hank had a plan, promised her this one would work. Hadn't she heard this before? She wasn't supposed to worry, just leave everything up to him. He needed to know that she was on his side. Sign here, ask questions later, but she trusted him. He would always do what was best for both of them. Another reason he needed to see her welcoming beacon tonight, the two hundred lights twinkling from the widow's walk. When he looked toward the house, he would know she was thinking of him. She cared. She was waiting. She was his one and only, as he was hers.

She had been forty that summer they'd met. A model with a seven-year-old son, getting fewer and fewer plum job offers on either coast. This had led to a somewhat vagabond life that included international trips to small, wannabe fashion centers in countries where journalists had to grab a map and look them up just to make sure they knew where they were located. Like that summer she had graced a runway for a little-known designer in Bogota and on the way back to the states, detoured to Cancun, Mexico to give Ricky a vacation—one she could afford. And one where she would feel safe with a child in tow.

While her son played on the waterslides in the vast pool, she sunbathed before deciding she was thirsty. Adjusting the parts of the bikini that barely covered her anyway, she stepped into the water, not unaware that men who were talking to girlfriends or wives had paused to stare. Enjoy it while you can—a saying that seemed to have more and more meaning the older she got. If it was a husband she wanted, actually needed, she had to step up her game. And soon.

As if the fates were listening that afternoon, she met Hank Beaufort at the swim-up bar in the adults-only section of the Maya Hotel. Lanky, a shock of dirty-blond hair touching the eyebrow above his right eye; it was the eyes that commanded attention. A blue like she'd never seen before, icy clear, bordered by long lashes that any woman would envy, they seemed to smile all on their own. They both ordered margaritas with a mescal floater and that was the conversation opener. They finished their drinks, collected Ricky and went into the hotel for dinner. Hank assured Ricky that he would be able to order a hot dog and wouldn't have to wear a tie. That made the sale.

Dinner was lots of laughs—stories about whales tipping boats over, gulls stealing his lunch, a possum as a castaway. Ricky instantly made a friend, and Hannah decided to bait a net and cast it in Hank's direction. A fifty-two-year-old widower without children who owned a schooner and had recently established a tourist tour business in Florida—wasn't it meant to be? And he was planning on building a house—a cross between a Hilton and the Taj Mahal. Would she like to help?

His being twelve years older was never a problem. In fact, it was more of a positive, adding a degree of safety to the union. In six short months they were married. If Ricky's father had been a colossal mistake, Hank Beaufort was the best thing that had ever happened to her. She was his queen. He put her on a pedestal and extolled her modest career victories as though she were named Gigi, or Bella, or Naomi. She played along and had several still shots of her younger days enlarged to grace the hallway leading to the dining room. The kind of photos that people paused to comment on, and compliment her on what seemed to them as an exciting, bedazzling career.

Had her life been perfect? No, but it was everything she wanted. She was secure and could overlook his controlling tendencies, even his wandering eye. Recently, those were becoming a thing of the past. They were seldom apart, maybe a couple days a week when Hank's inland business trips kept him away from home; or some private party rental of his schooner where people would pay a small fortune to have twenty to forty people venture out into a calm sea for a sailing experience under the watchful eye of a seasoned mariner and his mates. Sometimes the draw was a spectacular sunset or the once-a-month moonlight sail. The excursions were billed as the perfect addition to any vacation, something for the whole family to enjoy.

There was always a party atmosphere on board with great food and drink. Waitpersons, and a chef catered the affairs to rival the best hotels in the area and served dinner onboard with utmost care. When the schooner, *Moonstruck*, wasn't rented out for private parties, it carried tourists for two-to-three-hour short trips that included a history lesson highlighting the fort, the Matanzas Inlet, the only lighthouse in the area, or the always popular jaunts to simply enjoy the scenery in the area either on the Intracoastal or close-in along the Atlantic's shoreline.

If the schooner was his pride and joy, the house was hers. They had worked side-by-side with the architect. Insurance money from a failed business venture when Hank's COO had absconded with funds gave them over four million dollars to play with, and they'd used every bit of it. What they ended up building was a six thousand square foot home complete with elevator to the roof. It had been Hank's idea to string ten rows of crystal-clear Christmas lights around the dome on the widow's walk. Lighted at night they could be seen from the harbor and Hank insisted they welcomed him home—quickened his heartbeat because he was returning to his love. Yes, shmaltzy. But that's the way they were with each other, acting out little fantasies that more often than not ended up in the bedroom. Or used to. She needed to get those intimate moments back.

She hadn't changed and tonight was no different. Fifteen years of marriage hadn't dulled the longing, the missing him when he was gone. She had never liked being alone. Ricky, now twenty-two, had opted for a vocational degree, and had gotten a place of his own. He preferred the big city and had settled in Orlando. Finally, it was just the two of them. This trip had been longer because it was a mid-week, a repair run up the coast to Savannah, Georgia. Hank had promised her that this would be the last repair to an aging diesel engine. Next, it would be an investment in a new one. She felt they were just putting off the inevitable. Money. Was there ever enough?

She checked the wall clock in the study. Less than an hour and he'd be docking. She had been surprised at the text message he'd sent just before he pulled out of Savannah. He would be a day early coming home. She had missed his call that morning and then couldn't reach him on the water. But he'd said the day before that all had gone well; repairs were complete. He was looking forward to some quiet time to talk and just be together. Things had been crazy busy lately, and he wanted a long weekend for just the two of them. They had some decisions to make. Maybe he'd get someone else to captain the *Moonstruck* on Friday night.

So, now it was time to set the stage. She couldn't help but smile. How many times had she set that same stage—made certain the rows of lights hanging from the widow's walk sent out the beacon that was expected? Well, it was probably more like a couple hundred tiny eyes twinkling in the darkness, but she couldn't let him down. It said welcome home. Something he looked forward to. Important more than ever to reassure him that she loved him, believed in him and trusted the future.

She took the elevator to the roof, flipping the outside light switch that would illuminate their private signal. Only nothing happened. It was the moon that gave shadowy illumination to the bar stools and round table in the center of the small space.

Friday night the moon would be full and she'd be welcoming twenty-five prepaid passengers for the moonlight cruise. This might be the last fully booked tour before the holidays. It was the tail end of tourist season and well into September. She couldn't imagine Hank not being at the helm of the ship himself. People trusted him, looked forward to sailing with him. It would eat into the promised alone time, but she'd be with him. She hadn't worked the last few days to miss a chance at being hostess. Deliveries had been made to the marina earlier—several bottles of a good red, a dry white, and a sparkling rose. Appetizers were varied and would be delivered right before sailing. Soft drinks and water would be added to ice chests in the morning. Everything was ready to go.

But at the moment, she needed to check the connection

where the strings of Christmas lights were hard-wired into an electrical box attached to one of the support posts. Something had jiggled loose. Four stories up, the wind often rearranged things. The bar stools and the table were all screwed to the decking. And, like everything else constantly buffeted by coastal breezes, they needed a new coat of paint.

The moon by now had climbed above the horizon, clearing several wisps of cirrus clouds that had appeared to form bars across its surface, keeping the deck of the widow's walk in the shadows. The moon's pinkish cast was quickly turning a buttermilk gold and light was rippling across the water. It was so serene. She moved to the railing to enjoy the view. She loved the remoteness of her home. Heavy vegetation separated her from her neighbors and muted any sounds of traffic. Just the way she liked to live, surrounded by nature and not people. But all this ruminating wasn't getting the lights fixed.

The anchor post for the electric box was directly above the patio. A fire pit and two stone benches below made up a favorite winter entertaining area. She leaned against the railing and tried to see the front of the electrical connection. Hindsight said she should have brought a flashlight, but going back down four floors and rummaging in the garage to find one was out of the question. Too time-consuming. She'd just have to hold onto the support post, brace her feet against the railing and lean out far enough to see if there was a possible disconnect.

So far, so good. She stepped up to the bottom rung of the white wooden-slatted enclosure. Stretching on tippytoes, right arm around the post, she leaned outward, scooting her right foot forward along the lower railing before lifting it completely off the beam to stand on the top railing, bringing her left foot up next to her right and preparing to swing her left leg around the support and straddle the post. A wobble and a correction followed the shifting of her feet.

Careful. There was no need to hurry. Then, something made her glance behind her. The moon had slipped behind a bank of clouds, leaving the small deck in near-darkness. The almost imperceptible movement had caused her to look down, then over her shoulder. What was that shadow behind the table and bar stools? She paused. Nothing. Had the movement been her imagination? It wasn't like her to imagine things, get spooked by shadows. No, she had to collect herself.

She pulled back and put both feet firmly down on the top rail. She had never been a gymnast, but the balance beam would not have been her choice of apparatus. She took a deep breath, leaned forward, and reached for the electrical box. Already off balance, it took little for the hand in the middle of her back to push her weight outward, breaking her grip on the post and propelling her body forward, literally tossing her into space. Bouncing against the edge of the metal roof of the house, there was nothing to save her from falling four stories and hitting the stone bench directly below.

Chapter 2

Here's to the newest P.I. in St. Augustine, Florida." Dan tapped his champagne flute against Elaine's before taking a sip. He leaned across to refill their glasses before putting the bottle back in its tableside bucket. A celebratory dinner which, even in late September, found them inside because of the heat and humidity. Still, it was a special occasion. His brilliant, beautiful wife had just completed coursework to legitimately become a licensed snoop. "Has it sunk in yet?"

Elaine laughed. "It probably will after I establish an office. I answered an ad today placed by the Stanley and Stanley law firm. I was surprised but I got a call back this afternoon. They want to interview me in the morning."

"They're big. It makes sense that they want their

own private investigator. Do they have other P.I.s on the payroll?"

"I don't think so. I think I'm a first based on how the ad was worded. I would be assured autonomy for one thing. For example, I would give priority to referrals by the firm but would also be able to have my own clients. Salary would be based on company workload with only a small percentage of income from my own cases going to the firm. I drove by their offices. They're really nice, on a wide corner with plenty of parking. I think it's a five-man firm, family mostly."

"Their TV ads make it sound like they're the only show in town. All those ads that fill the screen with 'size matters'.

"No comment on their taste in advertising. But, yes, I hope they're as good at what they do as they are at tooting their own horn."

"As tempted as I am, no bad lawyer jokes." Dan pantomimed zipping his lips.

"Thank you. I had hoped that wouldn't be something I had to look forward to."

"I'll try to restrain myself." Actually, Dan was thrilled to have his wife in more or less the same business. He was an insurance investigator for United Life and Casualty and had suggested she apply to his company. But Elaine was her own person and he admired that. She wanted to prove herself, by herself. He only hoped giving up a career of college teaching would be worth it once the tedium of surveilling someone's errant husband or wife possibly became the norm. What did P.I.'s do in law firms besides research, chase ambulances, and capture photos of infidelities?

But he wasn't being fair. Way too soon to judge and

way off limits to even suggest she might feel confined by less than mind-challenging situations. He just didn't want the job to become boring, or worse yet, dangerous.

"Did I lose you? I'm starving." Elaine had picked up the menu beside her plate. The Purple Olive on A1A, not far from their townhouse, was a favorite.

"Sorry, just giving into some 'what-if' thinking. I'd lie if I wasn't worried about possible dangers. We see too many examples of irrational thinking nowadays. Shoot first, ask questions later sort of thing."

"It's a worry, I know." She reached out and placed a hand on his arm. "I'm not irrational, not gullible, not trigger-happy ... age sometimes has its advantages."

"Maybe." She was younger, but he'd be the first to say that forty-eight years on her looked a lot better than the fifty-four on him. She was a head-turner—dark , shoulder-length hair; tanned, long legs; could rock a bikini like a twenty-year-old ... he was working up to cutting the evening short and suggesting his favorite dessert but that would mean putting a late-night beach walk on hold and a full moon only happened once a month.

* * *

Her appointment was at ten. Leon Stanley, senior partner, met her at the door to his office. She had prepared packets of her personal papers—resume, academic achievements, awards, community service recognition. She had briefly shared her background over the phone the day before, promising to bring paper copies of pertinent materials with details.

"Ah, Mrs. Mahoney, or is it Dr. Mahoney?" The man

standing in the doorway was probably in his early seventies but impeccably dressed, his tie picking up the exact shade of grey in his suit and combining it with several supporting shades of blue, navy being predominant. He was slightly built—one of those trim, wiry sorts who more than likely biked to work. She probably wished she had what he spent on hair stylists and product. A head of perfectly coiffed, thick, steel-gray hair parted on the right was set off by an equally perfect tan that didn't come from a bottle. He was handsome in a way that defied age and he looked like money. But, then, as owner of the firm wasn't that the image he was trying to project?

"I prefer to use my maiden name of Linden. I'll reserve using the Ph.D. for academe. I'm comfortable with Elaine, if you are."

"All right, Elaine, it is." He stepped aside for her to enter his office, and she was first amazed at its size and secondly astounded by the works of art. Bronzes on pedestals, oils, pottery from several Southwest Indian tribes—she was standing in a mini-museum.

"I see you're a collector of Acoma pottery."

"Why yes, I am. You're familiar with Native art from the Southwest?"

"Just an admirer. I lived in western New Mexico, and travel through the state always finds me checking out the wonderful museums throughout the area."

"Same here. I never tire of what indigenous peoples have to offer. Even the more modern designs are spectacular." He pulled up a shirt sleeve to show off a Zuni bracelet, an inlay design of a futuristic warrior in red coral set in black onyx.

"Beautiful. An exceptional piece."

"Thank you. My son found it for me. Now let's get down to business, shall we?" He moved to sit behind an ornate wooden desk and motioned for her to sit across from him. "I believe you've brought me some reading material."

Elaine handed him one of the packets and sat back in the chair. He emptied everything onto the desktop, separated the pages and arranged them resume first, then academic achievements second before he started reading. He wasn't a quick study, Elaine noted, but hoped a thoroughness made up for slowness. She fought looking at her watch but knew it was a full ten minutes before he looked up—not saying anything, just studying her. She knew it was juvenile, but she had to will herself not to fidget or break the silence.

"I'm impressed and I don't impress easily."

"Thank you." She knew enough to keep it simple, wait to see if he had questions before she asked any of hers.

"Do you think you'll ever go back to teaching?" He leaned back against the plush upholstery of an ergonomically designed chair, his hands resting lightly on the desk's edge.

"I believe now is an opportune time for a career change. I like a challenge. Twenty years on college campuses was time well spent; I'm not belittling it. I'm simply fortunate to be able to explore other means of employment and be able to leave before I burn out."

He nodded. "Teaching is demanding. We don't show enough appreciation for our teachers, certainly not our professors." Again, a quick look at the papers in front of him. "This might be a good time to discuss Stanley and Stanley. I'm sure you have questions for me. Shoot."

"I'm intrigued by the firm's willingness to allow me to

have clients outside of those who have come to you first. I'm hoping I didn't misread that in your advertisement."

"No, not at all. I don't believe we have the client load to keep you busy one hundred percent of the time. Our assignments will be somewhat short—research, possibly some phone work, interviews, maybe surveillance—that sort of thing. I trust an adult to be able to monitor his or her time and be able to handle more than one thing at a time. Let's see, multi-task sums it up, I think that's what they call it today. But it's not something everyone is good at."

"I know, all too well. Many students who worked and took classes really struggled. I assure you I look forward to having a choice of challenges. Have you employed a P.I. before?"

"No, we haven't. Yet, one is certainly needed. Times are changing. A private investigator would nicely round out our roster of specialists. My brother, Archer Stanley, is the money-man, investments, wills, and trusts. His son, Thomas, takes on the majority of our domestic issue cases—high-end divorces and that sort of thing. I'm the worker's comp guy or any other government compensation case. Two nephews, my sister's children, are currently mentoring with us. One is specializing in real estate, the other has a leaning toward personal injury. Miriam, Archer's wife, is our chief financial officer when she's not busy at one of her philanthropic endeavors. She's a CPA by training and is tasked with keeping us solvent and legal. She has her own office downtown. Everything else falls to Ginny, our go-to clerk, who almost singlehandedly keeps us from embarrassing ourselves when it comes to the media, in addition to keeping this place running like clockwork. If you have a question, ask Ginny."

"Sounds like a good crew."

"A little light on professional women, you might have noticed, but seasoned probably sums it up. We like to think we can handle just about anything and have been in business long enough to garner a solid reputation."

"Yes, my research attests to that. Would it be possible to see the office that your P.I. hire will use?"

"Of course. We'll take a look on our way to introducing you to the partners. I think you'd find the office and the support crew are definite pluses. May I be so bold as to assume that if offered a position, you would be in a position to accept?"

"Yes. As I said, I've done some research and feel the firm would offer exactly what I need to be successful."

"Very well, then, let's get on with the tour."

Elaine was more than thrilled, if that was possible. Getting a license was one thing but to land a job so quickly with a top law firm was a true plum. She already knew that the firm had the best reputation in St. Augustine. A solid history of fairness, which was important to her, and the firm was financially sound. They walked to the back of the building and started by Leon showing her the space earmarked for the new hire. The office was spacious and had a street view. Well, actually a view of the parking lot, but she wouldn't be buried in some windowless backroom without natural light. And the partners seemed nice. Each took time to invite her into their office and ask pertinent questions while also presenting perks of the firm. She was sold and would have their answer by the next day.

* * *

"So, if you get an offer, your answer is going to be a yes?" Dan was on his second cup of coffee of the morning.

Elaine nodded. "I'm convinced I couldn't do better and certainly not at a better price. I don't want the outlay of money that renting and staffing my own office would entail. This way I walk into a situation where that sort of thing is already taken care of."

As if on cue, her phone rang. Checking caller ID, she mouthed, "it's him", then picked up her phone and walked to the porch. A short two minutes later, she walked back into the kitchen.

"Well, you'll be relieved to know I'm gainfully employed. I have an eleven o'clock appointment to sign papers and make it legal."

"That's fantastic! Congratulations." He stepped over and gave her a huge hug. "While you're doing that, I'll be in Daytona checking on that garage fire that wiped out three classic cars. I don't expect to be late, but don't start dinner until you see me."

Chapter 3

From their condo to the office was only a short drive down the coastal highway, A1A. Usually referred to as Beach Blvd., it was just one of the things that made St. Augustine special. Elaine pulled into the driveway that led around the back of the Stanley building to a spacious parking lot. She was driving a rental but needed to make a decision on what car to buy one of these days soon.

Her beloved Mini Cooper had gone to Jason to drive back to school. She missed it, but it had been the right thing to do. She had put off replacing it until some decisions had been made about a job. Everything had hinged on getting through school and landing something full time that paid well. She guessed she didn't have a reason to procrastinate any longer. From this angle, it looked like her office was just one away from the backdoor. It appeared that she had an almost private entrance. That was a perk she hadn't counted on. And in the far corner of the lot was a charging station—that expanded her choice of vehicles; an EV was tempting. It might be too soon to take a deep breath, but everything certainly seemed to be falling into place.

The front door was on the side, complete with a portico. Maybe a little pretend-grand for a one-story building, but it offered protection from the elements when dropping someone off. Other than a fair amount of rain, it wasn't as if St. Augustine had a lot of severe weather. The double-doors with etched glass were a nice touch and Elaine entered the building to see Ginny's desk directly in front of her. Ginny rose and quickly came around the desk to shake Elaine's hand, congratulate her, and offer coffee. Mr. Stanley would be a few minutes; he was with a client. Elaine declined coffee and took a seat on an ornate bench along one wall in the foyer.

The area certainly had Leon Stanley's touch—if he was the one who decorated. Two big seascape oils graced the walls—one depicting a moon over an endless string of waves hitting an empty beach, with the outline of a sailing ship in the background. The other was a realistic rendition of the Castillo de San Marcos, the fort overlooking Matanzas Bay. There was a charm to the area that was unique.

She often referred to St. Augustine, Florida as Santa Fe, New Mexico by the sea. There were only forty-five years between the founding of the two cities with St. Augustine being the older. But both had the old-world charm of narrow streets, cobble-stone paths, one with Spanish-colonial architecture and the other with a Pueblo style of traditional Spanish heritage. Santa Fe's houses were built around a plaza with most made of adobe. She missed the ethnic diversity of New Mexico and the mountains but had to agree the ocean was a great replacement. She was jolted back to the present by male voices somewhere in the vicinity of Ginny's desk. She hadn't had long to wait. Leon Stanley nodded to her as he walked an elderly man to the door, then returned and shook her hand.

"My apologies for the wait. I'm so happy you took us up on our offer. I'm looking forward to adding you to the crew."

"I've been admiring the artwork."

"You may not have been in our area long enough to enjoy our artists' community. You need to become familiar with the local talent. It's impressive."

"I can see that."

"I suspect your job may force an introduction to St. Augustine in short order. Private investigation is certainly not a desk job. But let's get you properly enrolled." He led the way back to his office and scooted a chair up to the front of his desk. "First, let me explain these forms."

There was nothing out of the ordinary, just normal employment paperwork. Perks included the usual 401K options and health care. Elaine signed and Ginny provided copies. In the meantime, Leon Stanley explained the office setup. After six in the evening, the east side of the building including the foyer was locked. A hallway separated Elaine's office on the west side from the partner's offices. She was given keys to the entrance, the eastside suite of offices, her own office and the back door. She was always welcome to use the copy room and restrooms on the east side after hours but didn't have to be told how important it was to make sure everything was locked up when she left. They employed a guard who would check the premises twice a night—never at the same times, of course. But an unlocked door still allowed time for illegal entry if someone was watching.

He invited her to take a look at furniture and artwork in a storage unit not far from the office. He had asked the handyman to stand by to help move whatever she wanted to bring this way. They tried to rotate artwork, so he was convinced she'd find something she liked, as well as a desk and chair. The room next to her office was actually a small conference room. It already contained a table and chairs but she was free to choose any artwork that she felt was appropriate.

"That's enough to keep you busy this afternoon. I'm sure you're anxious to get set up. You strike me as just chomping at the bit to get started. Am I right?"

Elaine laughed. "I hope I'm not over-eager, but, yes, I've been looking forward to this for a while."

"Then you'll forgive me for what I did." Leon paused, twiddling a pen in front of him. "I made an appointment for your first client tomorrow morning at ten."

"But that's terrific. Thank you. I assume this is someone the firm is representing?"

"Well, actually no. After talking to the young man, I felt he didn't need the help of a law firm—at least, not yet. He needed some questions answered first. And quite frankly, there may not be anything we can help with. I felt with your university experience, especially with that age group, the two of you would be able to connect."

Parentheses reads, could use a woman's touch Elaine thought, but kept her opinion to herself. "I'm anxious to meet him—is there anything else I should know?"

"Not at this time. I want him to give you the particulars;
I'm not sure I have all the details straight. Anyway, an
afternoon doesn't really give you much time to set up
an office. I'm sorry about that but once you meet him, I
think you'll see why I wanted to offer our help as quickly
as possible. The young man's family were close personal
friends of my wife and me. I want to see him guided in the
right direction."

Elaine was intrigued. But wasn't it this problem-solving
aspect to the job that sold her on being a P.I. in the first
place? It was almost noon but she wasn't hungry. There
was too much to do. The Stanley's handyman, Andy, met
her in the foyer and said he'd brought his pickup around
and thought she might like to go to the storage unit. He
had another man who could meet them there and help load
up whatever she wanted to bring back. Perfect. She felt like
she was getting a head start.

Storage units. They were everywhere and came in
varying sizes and reasons for being. They could be simply
long strips of enclosed garages, half acres of parking slots
dedicated to RVs, or an area devoted to only boat storage.
There was a part of her that hated to see large areas of
woodlands razed to provide these somewhat unsightly
receptacles for peoples' things. Didn't it say that just maybe
people had too many 'things'?

This storage unit was about two miles from the office
and was made up of five rows of fifteen garages each with
a paved road about halfway down that appeared to run
through to the back, which looked like it was an open field.
Andy stopped in front of unit #58.

"Here's a key for the padlock. You go ahead and

look around; I'm going to grab me a sandwich out of the machine at the office up front. You want anything? Sandwich? Soft drink?"

Elaine shook her head. "I'm fine."

"I'll leave the truck here. If my friend shows up, tell him I'll be right back. His name's Rob."

Andy took off at a jog. Another pickup turned down the lane from the far end and coasted to a stop just as she was slipping the padlock from the hasp.

"Hi. I'm here to help Andy and, I guess, you move some furniture."

Elaine introduced herself and with Rob's help lifted the door to the unit upward. What a treasure trove. An eight-by-eleven oriental rug caught her attention first, next to a Ming dynasty wannabe urn on a pedestal. Several screens with Asian lettering were leaning against the wall next to the door beside maybe twenty ornate mirrors of all sizes. Had the office housed a narcissist? She could see several paintings at the very back behind two desks turned on their sides and a stack of chairs—wood with upholstered seats. A filing cabinet, again in wood, a credenza with glassed front, and more rugs were all stacked in front of the artwork.

Did she have a choice of color scheme? Or would mix and match suffice? The chair's cushions were a utility dove gray, the first oriental rug she had seen had blue as its predominant color. Those would work together. As for artwork, more seascapes added to her blue/gray theme. By the time Andy reappeared, finishing what appeared to be an egg salad sandwich—who would eat egg salad out of a machine?—she had pretty much decided on three fourths of her office furnishings.

Andy and Rob quickly loaded up everything she

pointed out and, in under an hour, they were headed back to the office. She must have set a record because Leon Stanley seemed surprised, but pleased.

"I'm so glad we're putting some of these things to good use. I hate to admit my late wife had a need to change out office trappings every year or so. I'm sure you noticed remnants of her Oriental period. And she couldn't throw anything away or, God forbid, sell it. I humored her and would sneak a few things back in if they had disappeared over a weekend, for example. Yes, it was a happy marriage. We just accepted each other's foibles." He laughed, "This rug, for instance, was one of my favorites. I'm glad you like it, too. And I'm very glad it's going to be on display again."

Arranging furniture and hanging artwork took another hour, then it was time to meet with Ginny to set up a computer, bring it up to date with software, and supply the office with any paper-goods that Ginny thought she might need. Andy was able to connect the inner-office intercom and mount a closed-circuit TV on the wall in the conference room. Remarkably, by five everything was in place. She'd bring her laptop to the office tomorrow and transfer her calendar and a few other files to her desk work station but all in all, she was ready to go—to at least get started.

She called Dan and offered to pick up Cuban sandwiches on the way home. Did he want anything else? Just her. She acknowledged the sweet answer and added a six-pack of Sam Adams to her shopping list. But all the while she couldn't get over the idea of having her very first client in the morning.

Chapter 4

Elaine unlocked the back door to her office at seven-thirty in the morning and started carrying the several boxes of necessities inside. Family pictures were first to be arranged on the credenza. Family, in addition to Dan, consisted of one son, aged twenty. Jason, the new proud owner of her Mini Cooper, was returning to school in a few weeks after studying for a summer in China—a gift trip from her and Dan.

Several Jason pictures from different stages of growing up, two of Simon the Rottweiler who was currently protecting Dan's mother, Maggie, another picture of Maggie in front of her adorable cottage outside the community of Devil's Bend, and lastly several of her and Dan in New Mexico and Florida.

Her coffee maker was a single, eight-ounce cup, espresso machine that just fit on a counter beneath overhead cabinets in the conference room. She stashed an assortment of demitasse cups and saucers above it along with a box of natural sugar and a box of sealed individual containers of half-and-half—some flavored. Just in case she needed to entertain.

There had been a bar fridge in the storage unit, and she called Ginny to see if she would be able to bring it to her office. No problem, it was hers. Elaine had Andy put it in the conference room and put a reminder on her calendar to load it with bottled water.

The time flew by. She was actually startled when there was a knock on her door and Ginny announced that her client was here, a Mr. Richard Elliston. Apparently, Andy's connection of the intercom needed some tweaking. Ginny turned to one side holding the door open, and a young man stepped into the office. Probably early twenties, clean-shaven, he sported a definite preppy look with a plaid, button-down short-sleeved shirt and chinos. He was thin, too thin really, but maybe he was a cyclist or a marathoner or, perhaps, he had been ill recently.

Elaine instantly thought of Jason. This was someone from his generation. But that's where the comparison stopped. This young man had a definite haunted look about him. Eyes that checked every corner of the room, even looking behind him before acknowledging Elaine's outstretched hand and tentatively shaking it. No, maybe it was just nervousness, the result of being in a strange place, meeting someone new. She needed to be fair, and if it was up to her to make him feel comfortable, she could do that.

"Please, sit here." She had placed a chair in front of

the desk. "I see Ginny came up with a bottle of water. Great. Shall we get started?" He barely nodded his assent and placed the bottle on the edge of her desk then sat back with both hands limp in his lap, staring at her.

"I'd like to start by making certain I have your contact information." She proceeded with the usual, correct spelling of his name, did he prefer Richard or was he called by another name? Rick? She made a note and continued with his address. He had an apartment in Orlando, a phone, and email address—did he prefer email or texting? She made another note when he indicated texting. She set the tablet aside and, after taking a breath, asked the opening question. "How can I help you?"

He coughed but covered his mouth. She noticed fingernails bitten to the quick. He sucked in his lower lip and raked over it with his upper teeth. She was just about ready to think he wasn't going to answer when he said, "I want you to find my mother's murderer."

Elaine didn't overreact. She took off her readers and put them to one side. "I'm going to need some background information. And I may need to ask some very pointed questions that might be uncomfortable to answer. Are you all right with that?"

A nod and now eye contact. "Go ahead."

"When did your mother pass?"

"She didn't fucking *pass*. She was killed. Murdered." His fist came down so hard and so suddenly on the edge of the desk that Elaine jumped as the water bottle bounced to the floor. Then, just as suddenly, he caught his breath, and with tears streaming down his face, mumbled "I'm sorry" over and over, rocking back and forth, grasping the arms of the chair, finally covering his face with his hands, shoulders heaving with hiccoughing sobs. "I didn't mean to yell. Please, don't be mad."

"Of course not. I'm not mad. I appreciate how upsetting this is. I wish I could make it easier for you."

Then Elaine did something that was probably not in her textbooks on how to become a private investigator. She got up from the desk, walked over to his chair and knelt beside him.

"I'm here to help. I want your trust—I *need* your trust to be able to do my job. I don't have enough information to comment on the cause of your mother's death. That's where you need to help me so we can work together. Your knowledge about what happened needs to become my reality, too." She left her hand on his arm and waited.

He nodded, moved his hand to wipe his face, bent down to retrieve the water bottle, and drank some before putting it back on the desk. Elaine took this as a cue to walk back around her desk and take a box of Kleenex from the top drawer. Thank God she'd added these to her list. She set the box on the edge of the desk closest to Rick, who took two tissues, blew his nose twice, and scrubbed at his eyes.

"Let's get comfortable. I vote we move to the couch by the window. I'm going to leave all my note-taking material on the desk. I just want to listen. Tell me what you think I need to know to be of help."

He nodded and seemed relieved. She wished she'd thought of a less formal interrogation setting earlier. Hadn't she picked out the dove gray leather couch with metal and glass coffee table because it would add a homey, comfy element to the starkness of a single desk and chairs? Staring at a client across a desk was off-putting especially if emotions were as raw as his. But, my God, hadn't he just lost his mother? She waited till he was settled and then sat at the opposite end of the big leather sofa.

There was more lip-chewing and wiping his hands on his slacks. And no dialogue. She needed to defuse this situation and quickly, or she suspected he'd bolt for the door. She decided to take a chance and level the playing field so to speak. Maybe if he could relate to her own jitters of doing this for the first time, he could relax and relate.

"I'm going to share something, and then I want us to do a little exercise together." He turned to look at her; at least she'd piqued his interest. "I was embarrassed to tell you earlier that you're my very first client."

"The very first?"

"Uh huh. I got my license last month. And I've really looked forward to this. I used to teach college and wanted a change. So, I'm nervous, too. And when the butterflies threaten to take over …" She pointed at her stomach. "I do breathing exercises, like in yoga."

"My mother taught yoga classes."

"Then you might be familiar with the exercise I'm going to suggest. You take a deep breath in through your nose on a count of ten, then slowly let it out through your mouth counting backwards to one. The breath needs to be deep—right from your center. Then you repeat—deep breath, count of ten, release breath counting 9 down to one, then up to ten and 8 down to one, up to ten and 7 down to one, and so on. Got it?"

"Yeah." He smiled. "Let's go." He put both feet on the floor, closed his eyes, and leaned back into the soft upholstery. She heard a deep intake of breath.

It was the first bit of camaraderie that she'd felt since

they met. Things were looking up.

She crossed her legs, closed her eyes and followed his lead, finally hearing the last whoosh of breath as he reached the end, exhaling only one time. She had finished the exercise at almost the exact same moment and saw that smile again, noticing also that his hands were resting on his thighs without fidgeting. He was really a cute kid when he was relaxed and smiling. If there was such a thing as goat yoga, why couldn't there be P.I. yoga? She only hoped that there were no hidden cameras in her office.

"I feel better. I'm afraid I do that exercise a lot." She turned to face him. "Whenever you're ready."

"It's tough to know where to start." Interesting how his demeanor had changed. He seemed really anxious to do things right.

"Think about what I need to know to help—actually the four W's—why, what, where, when and throw in a how, if needed. That will give me a good platform to build a case."

"Ok, I'll kinda start in the beginning, maybe where and when. I just got out of school, too. I was supposed to graduate from the East Coast School of Culinary Arts the first of August, but I'm taking a breather. I want to know I'm making the right decision; you know, work in the field for a while. I started interviewing for a job in this area and moved in with my mom and her husband for a little bit. He's not my father. My mom was only married to Skip Elliston long enough to get me. I never knew him. Mom and I were always best friends. Even after she remarried when I was seven."

He took a sip of water from the bottle he'd set on the low table in front of the couch. "I'd only moved up to St. Augustine to be closer to job opportunities. There are some great restaurants up here, but what I want to do is open my own. I stayed with them for a week until her husband suggested I find a place. He never liked us being so close. My mom paid for the condo I'm renting in Orlando. He wouldn't help me."

"What's his name?"

"Oh, sorry, Henry Beaufort, but people call him Hank. My mother's name is Hannah. We all got along fine when I was a kid but everything went downhill when I was in high school. Hank kept pushing sports, but that wasn't my thing. I overheard him tell someone in his office one time that I was his biggest disappointment. And he doesn't even have kids of his own. He and Mom tried but she was older by the time they married and it never happened." He twisted the cap off of the bottle of water and drained its contents.

"Another?"

"No, I'm fine, thanks. Hank travels a lot so at least Mom and I had time together. She was helping me write a business plan for a restaurant. She thought if it was good enough, Hank would want to invest. I never believed that. I think he has money problems of his own. He bought a schooner fifteen years ago and started tourist tours from the marina here in St. Augustine. Recently, he bought a second schooner but it's in dry dock. Not sure what he plans for that one. The one he operates is a money pit. But he's doing it right, you know, keeping up with repairs, adding mahogany and teak accents to make it showy. Schooners are expensive. They require years of investment and, like a house, things have to be replaced. Basics like new planking, engines, paint and staining; it's never ending. It takes a lot of tourist trade to offset costs and the bad hurricane season a couple years ago almost bankrupted him. At least this was what Mom shared."

"Has he always had boats?"

"Not always, but he's close to retirement. The plan was for him to sail off into the sunset—literally." A smile at having cracked a funny.

"Were Hank and Hannah close as a couple? In spite of money problems?"

"Mom made it look that way. I don't think she could have handled another failure—that's what she called her first marriage. No, this one was forever—even though I think she had a boyfriend. Maybe nothing really serious. Mom was always trying to help people, comfort them, take care of them. But Hank was her bread and butter—until he killed her. But I'm getting ahead of myself. I bet you're wondering how she died."

"I admit to being curious." She let the naming of his stepfather as murderer slip by. She didn't want to interrupt the flow of dialogue.

"She fell from the widow's walk on their house. There were footprints on the top railing showing that she had been standing on it. So, the cops told me we're probably looking at suicide. They decided that she'd stepped up there to jump. That's bullshit. The lights weren't working. I bet anything that she had stepped onto the rail to check the electric box."

He folded his hands into fists and pounded his thighs for emphasis. "I told them about the lights not working. So then, they decided that she had slipped and fallen. No. Trust me. That is not what happened. My mother had fixed those lights before. She was pushed. She was probably off balance and someone just stepped up and gave her a shove.

But the cops don't care. They won't even listen to me. Accidental death or suicide. Either one is a lot less messy and time consuming than murder. They don't want to do their job." He paused and looked straight at her. "That's why I'm here."

"Why do you think her husband did it?" Now was the time to slip that question in.

"He was supposed to have been out of town. Mom had told me he wasn't returning until the next day, Thursday; but I saw him that morning with his girlfriend."

"Girlfriend?"

"Yeah, Hank likes the ladies. He'd take business trips and Mom would just look the other way. Maybe she didn't really know, but I think she did. She was getting what she wanted—a house, respectability, security. I think he wanted to move on but didn't want to spend the money to cut Mom free. Maybe he didn't have the money it would have taken. Maybe he found out she had a friend. With his ego, he could never have accepted that. But I think it was about money. He upped the amount of her life insurance to two million dollars just six months ago. So, killing her gave him a big payday."

"How do you know that?"

"She told me. She wanted me to see my dreams come true and didn't want me to worry that I wouldn't be taken care of. Apparently the two of them had just recorded their wills."

"Would it be possible to see the railing? At least see the area where it happened? If it's been ruled an accident or even suicide, the police shouldn't have the scene secured."

"No, they're done. One week ago to the day and their report is in. Just like that. We can go now, if you like. I still have a key."

"Let me tell Ginny I'm leaving. Pull around to the portico, I'll follow you in my car."

Chapter 5

Dan was back in Daytona again. The classic car case was keeping him busy. Elaine left a message saying she'd call later. Then she and Rick were ready to go. She pulled around to the portico and stopped behind a fairly new BMW convertible with Rick behind the wheel. Someone had spent some bucks. It was becoming difficult to figure out who did and who didn't have the money in this family.

But as they turned onto A1A, Elaine put her thoughts on hold. This was, as always, a sight she'd never tire of. She was in awe of the scenery. The highway, a north-south coastal connection of most of the oceanfront towns in the state, stretched from Fernandina Beach to Key West. And speaking of money, the homes along the shore were spectacular. Four stories were more the norm than an anomaly. She had to admit, however, a widow's walk perched on top of floor four was a standout. She easily picked out the house from a distance and pulled into the drive behind Rick, parking to the right of a three-car garage.

Everything about the house was pretentious. Marble, never a cheap addition, comprised two columns on either side of the front entry. And the stone was a mottled pink against the house's palest of flesh colors. Ceramic tile in deep coral set off the pristine widow's walk dome to match the vastness of the house's gabled rooftop. The house was huge and beautiful, a perfect addition to the landscape of other multi-million-dollar homes along the ocean.

Rick unlocked a side door and led her through the kitchen, a pantry, two eating areas—an informal breakfast bar and a far more formal dining room that would seat forty, complete with vaulted ceiling and a Chihuly blown glass chandelier in its center. Gleaming bronze fixtures held tiers of individually crafted and colored water lilies, each with a single clear light bulb in the center. The chandelier was at least eight feet tall and six feet at its widest. Suddenly the glass flowers burst into light. She hadn't seen Rick detour to flip on a wall switch.

"Takes my breath away." And Elaine meant it. This was a museum piece; she'd never seen anything like it.

"My favorite, too. Well, maybe my next to favorite." He motioned for her to follow as he turned down a wide adjoining hallway lined with life-sized photos. Photos of a runway model strutting her stuff, raven hair blowing out behind her, gowns that seemed to reveal everything while not actually revealing anything, bikinis reversing that by leaving nothing to the imagination.

"Gorgeous." The photographer credits on the portraits

closest to her were all big names, as were the designers. "Your mother had an impressive career."

"She always thought of herself as second tier—called at the last minute to stand in for a big name, but never really commanding first class attention to start with. It was a tough business. And having me didn't help. She had to pass up some assignments. Let's go up to the walk; the elevator is right over there."

Stepping out of the elevator on the fourth floor, Elaine gazed at an azure-blue ocean in the distance, calm, only small waves breaking against the shore. It was quiet, the wind barely rustling the palms below. This was her choice of a place to be—in all of this pretentious architecture, the widow's walk was the most inviting. Thinking that a murder might have occurred up here was disquieting.

"Walk me through what you think happened."

"I think my mom was trying to fix the lights—the ones hanging in rows from the edge of the walk's roof. They must not have come on. Usually, you can flip the switch from over here."

Rick turned to the elevator and pointed to a switch on a plate beside the door before pushing it upward. "Like this." A couple hundred twinkling lights flashed. "Yeah, I think there was probably a short in the wiring and they didn't come on when Mom threw the switch. Hank didn't get home until the next day. He was the one who found the body. That night Hank and Mom and I were supposed to have dinner, but when I pulled up, the drive was full of cops. The lights were on then; that's why I think they had shorted out before."

"Who told you what had happened?"

"Hank. He just walked up and said, 'Your mother's

dead.' Just like that, no come inside, sit down, have a drink—just boom, bang it's done. Oh, then he followed up with 'When was the last time you saw your mother?' Like he was trying to point a finger at me. At least, I know he wasn't buying the suicide theory."

"Had you talked to your mother recently?"

"I'd tried to get Mom on the phone earlier, on my way here. I had been in Orlando and was running late. Traffic from Orlando was a bitch. But, of course, she didn't answer." He walked to a post closest to the edge of the house. "Look here. This is where she went over. Right next to the electrical box. It makes sense that she was trying to fix the lights. At least the cops listened to my theory about why she was standing on the railing. The lights were on when they got there, but that doesn't mean there wasn't a short in the wiring before. But they're stuck on it being a suicide and for them, that's the end of the story. I can't believe that this whole thing is just being dismissed. Over and done, get on with life." Rick shook his head and leaned against the newly painted support.

"And you've totally ruled out suicide."

"Absolutely."

"Tell me again why you think suicide is a bogus conclusion."

"Mom wasn't done with this life. She wasn't done having fun, and she wasn't done with me. Frankly, I don't think she would have given Hank the satisfaction of getting out of his way, given up her part of this fairy tale to another woman. She was possessive, feisty even, and she played the 'you're my dream come true' to the hilt. She fawned all over him. Nothing was too good for her man. I think she knew about his womanizing but it wasn't worth giving up all this. And if she could play her own games on the side without getting caught, all the better. It's how she managed to stay around for fifteen years. You want to know the truth? I'd sooner have believed they found Hank's splattered body down there." He pointed over the railing. "That would have made more sense."

The sound of the elevator being recalled made both of them turn in that direction. Just as quickly as it had descended, there was a slight pause and then evidence that it was fast returning to the fourth floor. Elaine and Rick had nowhere else to go; they stood facing the door.

When the elevator stopped, the man inside reached out, placing a hand against the elevator door and blocking it from closing; then, he waited a beat or two before stepping out, giving each of them the once over. He shook his head, shrugged, and barely concealed a snort of disgust. A feeling of 'fight or flight' washed over her and Elaine saw the muscles in Rick's jaw tense.

The word 'burly' fit the man in front of her. He was probably somewhere in his latter sixties as Rick mentioned, but he was fit, arms bulging under a long-sleeved T-shirt. Jeans and sneakers seemed at odds with the Rolex on his wrist. Barely graying hair, cut short, clean shaven; the man was handsome, and probably saw the inside of a gym at least three times a week. This was the type of man that you got out of the way for—if you blocked him, he'd mow you down. Elaine didn't have to be told this was Hank Beaufort and she wasn't expecting an introduction. The man was barely concealing his anger, squinty eyes, a slight sneer … she hated feeling cornered four floors off the ground.

"So, you're giving tours now? Showing off the place where your poor dear mother fell to her death? Callous, no? Even for you." He turned to directly face Elaine. "And here's Stanley and Stanley's newest piece of scum. You turn over rocks and this is what crawls out."

"Excuse me, I don't have to listen to this." Elaine stepped forward, but before she could reach the elevator, Hank took a step and blocked the only exit.

"Really? Aren't we a little high and mighty? Didn't think lowlifes that snooped for a living had rights. You going to take the kid's money and string him along, giving him false hope of finding some sort of murder plot just because he can't accept the fact that his mother committed suicide—or maybe just plain fell. Yeah, that's right, no secrets, no drama, nothing to uncover. For God's sake, the cops have closed the case—actually never had one to begin with. Are the two of you smarter than the cops? Archer Stanley was right, the firm is bottom-feeding. Hiring a private dick—oops, guess I can't use that term for you. But that says it all. A law firm that needs a P.I. needs to take a look at the kind of business it's attracting."

"I suggest you let me pass."

"Or what? Hey, Rick, what do you think this pretty little lady is going to do? Anybody you know believe these losers? A wannabe Dick Tracy. You need to leave what you think you're doing up to the men who know how. And, those men ruled no foul play. What part of that can't the two of you understand? What happened, you get tired of being somebody's secretary?"

"Leave her alone." Finally, something from Rick.

"Oh, look who's the big man now. Tell you what, I don't ever want to see you again. I want your keys to this house. I don't know who's going to bankroll you now but it isn't going to be me."

"I have money coming from Mom's insurance. She always promised she'd take care of me."

"Well, I hate to break it to you, but she changed her mind. You don't get a red cent buddy-boy. Talk to your friend's employer. They'll show you a copy of your mother's will. Don't take my word for it. You're on your own. You want money, you'll have to come to me and prove you're worth it—deserving of yet another handout. I hope all that crap they taught you in cooking school is going to pay off. But don't say I didn't warn you if you end up chopping lettuce the rest of your life."

Elaine took advantage of Hank's back being turned toward her to step to the elevator, push the down button, and quickly step in when the door opened.

"Running away? A little truth hit too close to home? Remember, you cause any problems around here and I know where to find you." The elevator door closed.

* * *

She surveyed her office and then stirred another packet of raw sugar into her second cup of espresso. The coffee probably wasn't doing anything to calm her nerves but she had busied herself by hanging the rest of the pictures. It was taking shape and quite nicely at that. Actually, it felt good to be back in the office. Thank God she'd driven her own car to the Beaufort house.

And Rick? She had a feeling that her very first client was already a thing of the past. Whatever hold Hank Beaufort had over Rick—and maybe that was just the threats to disinherit him—she knew they would work. Rick Elliston wasn't a boat-rocker. It was much more believable that with tail between his legs, he'd just disappear.

Now she had to tactfully tell her bosses that she was free to accept in-house clientele. She needed to be careful; it was obvious that Hank had friends at Stanley and Stanley. Was the side of him that she'd seen known to others? She guessed she'd find out; she couldn't put off a recap of her morning any longer. She stopped by Ginny's desk to see if Leon might have a few minutes to see her, and Ginny said he was finishing a late lunch in the breakroom but wouldn't mind being interrupted.

"I was told you would welcome an interruption, but I'll gladly make this later if you'd like." Wasn't she being a little pushy? What if her boss really preferred lunch time to be alone time?

But the laugh reassured her. "I'm afraid things don't wait until I've finished eating—whether it's breakfast, lunch or dinner. What can I help you with?"

"Rick Elliston took me to see where his mother fell. Mr. Beaufort joined us unannounced and voiced his displeasure at finding us there. I haven't been told for certain but I doubt that Mr. Beaufort will want his stepson to continue with my hire."

Leon had put down his fork and snapped the lid back on a refrigerator container of what looked like potato salad before looking up. "Was he unpleasant?"

"I'd rather not comment. Both men have lived through a shocking incident this last week. Grief and anger are often partners."

"So well put. And I'll leave it at that. I know Hank. He doesn't mince words and has the money to buy his way out of any trouble his mouth gets him into. My apologies to what I can imagine was Hank's strong-armed approach to getting rid of you. Can I buy you a cup of coffee? We don't keep liquor in the office even though this does call for a stiff shot of something."

"I'm afraid I drowned my sorrows in two cups of espresso when I got back to the office. A third and I might OD." She got the laugh she wanted and he pointed to a chair at the table. "I will add that I was somewhat surprised that Mr. Beaufort had been told, supposedly by someone here, that his stepson had hired a P.I." She purposely didn't mention that Hank had named Archer Stanley. There would be no pointing of fingers at law office partners— not if she wanted a job.

"That's disquieting. I would like to think we don't leak that kind of info, but I'll check. Leave that to me. Actually, I'm more than a little involved in all this as it is. Pairing the two of you was my bright idea. I feel responsible. I was the SOB who thought you would be a perfect confidant for Rick. I'm sure I don't have to tell you he's a weird child. I think his childhood was traumatic—illnesses, six months in rehab for GI tract problems; cancer was rumored. Hannah was overprotective. But under the circumstances, I doubt I would have done things differently. I frankly have been worried about how he was going to take his mother's death. There's not a lot of mental strength there."

"Then it doesn't make sense that she'd cut him out of the will."

Leon looked surprised. "I can see Hank aired *all* the dirty laundry. One month ago the two of them, Hank and Hannah, came to see me. They wanted to rewrite their wills. That is, Hank wanted to. He was adamant nothing would go to Rick unless he could prove himself, become gainfully employed, handle his own bills, and truly be on his own. He wanted any inheritance to be supervised, an iron-clad trust, so to speak, set up as a conservatorship with Hank in control."

"Graduating from a technical school would have seemed to meet that requirement if he hadn't decided to leave school and work a year first."

"Well, I'm glad to see that Rick is being truthful with you. About six months ago, he dropped out. As you know, the story was he wanted experience before getting a diploma. But there had been some incident at school. Hank and Hannah looked into suing but quietly dropped the case before we were able to get all the particulars. Apparently, there was a fight between two boys and a knife was drawn. It happened in the school's kitchen, which made it difficult to think a knife was being carried on a kid's person with any premeditation to do harm. Knives were probably everywhere. I think that's why the school backed off the charges and just expelled both young men. It was a bitter pill for Hank to swallow. He felt that keeping money from being so easily accessible would straighten Rick out. Hannah was prohibited from paying for anything."

"That would have been difficult—for mother and son. Was Rick aware before today of the extent of Hank's wishes? That Hank was in control and would remain that way? It didn't seem so."

"Maybe not, but I'm sure now he does. Hank will use it, hold it over his head. I'll be honest. I wanted you to work with Rick because I felt he'd believe you, feel comfortable with you, trust you. And I feel sorry for the kid. There's little doubt that Hannah's death was most likely an accident. I can't really buy into the suicide angle. She was the member of the Hank and Hannah duo that people liked to deal with—vivacious, yet easy-going, didn't seem to have an enemy in the world. I just don't think you would have found anything different, any reason to even suspect suicide or foul play. And the kid's hurting. He needs closure. I think his wanting to believe it was murder just gives him someone to blame, somewhere to direct his anger. Under the circumstances, what better culprit than his stepdad? Sometimes that helps to ease the grief."

"I agree. I'm sorry that my involvement didn't work out. I might have been able to help."

And Elaine felt sorry for Rick, too. But the one thing that her schooling stressed? Don't let 'poor soul' mentality take over. Objectivity created sound careers for private investigators. Always search for the truth, not try to find facts to support the way you wanted something to turn out. She wondered how many times she'd have to remind herself of that.

Chapter 6

"How'd it go?" Dan had finished setting the table by the time Elaine had gotten home and was just taking a pork roast out of the oven. Surrounded by broccoli florets and chunks of Yukon Gold potatoes, the meal was ready. "Wine, or not?" Dan had a bottle of Merlot in one hand and a corkscrew in the other.

"I'll tell you all about it, so, definitely wine." Elaine put ice cubes and water in a pitcher, grabbed two glasses and headed for the table. "Oh, don't forget a couple of those chic paper towel napkins."

Between bites, she filled Dan in on the basics: an only child torn by grief, trying to find an explanation that just wasn't there. It appeared that Hannah Beaufort might have been trying to fix an outdoor lighting problem when she fell to her death. The police, however, favored suicide as the cause. Rick was the only one entertaining murder and pointing a finger at his stepfather. Purposely, Elaine left out meeting Hank. She knew Dan would be incensed and would worry about her being in danger.

"So, what happens now?"

"I'm afraid I've lost my first client. I don't think he has a strong case and, frankly, I don't know where I would start to try to put one together. I think Rick was acting out of grief, and an extreme dislike of his stepfather, not common sense. He's refusing to see what is in front of him—absolutely no evidence of foul play, or even suicide. It looks like a simple accident—his mother simply lost her footing after placing herself in the precarious position of leaning out over the railing of a widow's walk four stories up."

"Well, it's not as though you were fired—maybe dismissed?" Dan was grinning. "Just because a client doesn't like an answer doesn't mean you haven't given them one. No one says that you have to find a problem to get paid."

"I don't think I have to worry about that either—I think my first client stiffed me."

"There'll be others—paying ones. I just don't want you to be discouraged. I truly think you'll be good at this, given the right circumstances."

"I want to believe that. The firm is going to keep me busy with some online searches—verifying employment, tracing employment history, that sort of thing. I may end up at the courthouse doing title searches. But I don't mind. It's the unglamorous work behind the scenes that needs to be done."

"Good attitude. I'd hire you. Oh my God, I almost

forgot—guess who's coming to dinner on Saturday?"

"I give up."

"Maggie."

"That's terrific. We haven't had a good visit in months." Dan's mother, somewhere in her early seventies, but known to fib a little, was fun. "I assume she's bringing Simon?"

"I don't think she'd hit the road without him. She hinted that she was meeting someone here or maybe bringing someone with her."

"A man?"

"That's my guess. Anyway, she'd like to eat at St. Augustine Fish Camp. Would you have time to make reservations for four of us at seven on Saturday? I'm back in Daytona tomorrow and may forget to give them a call when they open."

"Of course. What fun. She hasn't gone out with anyone since Stan. I'm truly glad to see her having a good time again. Maybe I'll give her a call after dinner."

Dan offered to clean up if she wanted to call Maggie. That was a deal she couldn't pass up—a chef and busboy combination. Elaine walked down the hall to the guest room. Now that Jason was in school, it was a study with two desks and separate filing cabinets. A daybed and lounger made up a reading corner with a floor lamp. A thirty-six-inch TV screen was wall-mounted across from the sitting area. The room made a cozy and inviting work area. Leon Stanley had encouraged her to work from home whenever she wanted—he wasn't going to insist that she be on the clock; she was an adult. He trusted her. Just one more welcome perk.

Maggie answered on the first ring. "Elaine how good to hear your voice. I've missed you."

"And I've missed you. I just heard that we'll be seeing you this Saturday. If you're bringing Simon, I'll make sure someone's here to let you in."

"My neighbor is keeping an eye on him. A doggy door and a half acre fenced yard, someone to play fetch with— he'll be fine. I'll bring him next trip. I never worry about leaving the house when he's on duty. He's just the best companion and burglar deterrent."

"Speaking of companions, did I hear correctly that you will be bringing a guest to dinner?"

"Oh Elaine, I've met the most exciting, caring, handsome man. It's only been a little over two months but I know a keeper when I see one. I'm really ready to fall in love again."

"This sounds serious. Where did you meet him?"

"Online, of course, but he's not like the ninety-nine percent I've met there before. He's genuine. But enough about him. You'll be able to see for yourself on Saturday. I want to hear about your job."

Elaine filled her in on Stanley and Stanley, then reiterated how excited she was to be seeing Maggie in a couple days. They hung up, both promising to make more time for family in the future.

* * *

The St. Augustine Fish Camp on Riberia Street was a bit of a best kept secret, but you couldn't have told that tonight, Elaine thought as she gazed at the full-to-overflowing parking area. There was free valet parking and three young men were being kept busy. Thank God, they had reservations. She had requested outside deck seating.

Bordering the river, sailboats tied up at a nearby dock; the view was exquisite. It might be a little warm but Elaine thought she would slip off her sundress's matching jacket and be comfortable.

The deck was already full but she instantly saw Maggie sitting at a table close to the water. Dan waved and followed the waiter out the double doors from the dining room. As they neared the table, Maggie and her date stood up and Elaine could only stare. Maggie, her usually bubbly self, had already hugged Dan and turned to introduce her date.

"This is Hank—Hank Beaufort. And this is my handsome son, Dan Mahoney, and his absolutely brilliant wife, Dr. Elaine Linden."

Hank shook Dan's hand before turning to Elaine. "Elaine, is it?"

"I prefer *Dr.* Linden." She didn't dare look at Dan or Maggie. She thought someone had stifled a gasp. Hank held out his hand, but Elaine offered a dismissive gesture in return. "I'm sure it's obvious that Mr. Beaufort and I have met before." She pulled out a chair and sat down, making the others awkwardly, but quickly, do the same.

No one broke the somewhat stunned silence until Hank leaned forward and, staring intently at her, offered, "I would be the first to say our meeting was under rather uncomfortable circumstances. This would be a good time to say that I regret that first meeting. I was a complete ass. A friend at the firm where Dr. Linden works called to tell me that my stepson had hired a private investigator to help him prove that I had murdered his mother. To say that I was angry doesn't even come close to capturing my feelings. I'm afraid I said things out of that anger that I should never have. I hope in time you can overlook my stupidity."

A waiter appeared to take drink orders and saved Elaine from commenting. She spent more time than needed on a menu she almost knew by heart—but anything not to have to interact with the man sitting across from her.

Finally, food orders were in—a fried oyster Po'boy sandwich for her, scallops for Dan and shrimp dishes for Hank and Maggie. Elaine also made sure that there would be a helping of their signature dessert, white chocolate bread pudding, waiting for her when she finished the Po'boy. At last, there was no escaping small talk.

"Coincidences always surprise me. Dan, I've been a customer of United Life and Casualty for almost ten years. In fact, I've recently been in touch with your home office about my plans to expand. It might make sense to run these plans past you. So, tell me what it is you do for the company. Maggie has filled me in a little but I'm not sure I know how your job works."

Nothing like a little bro-bonding, Elaine mused. Dan obliged but she knew he was about to burst, wanting to know about her own original meeting with Hank. And maybe she was overreacting. Losing one's wife in a violent accident would be shocking. But didn't that raise the question about the marriage? Hadn't he, in fact, still been sharing a house with Hannah Beaufort? Weren't they still married? It seemed that way. But he had been dating and wooing Maggie for over two months? Was it just another online ruse? Men pretending to be something they were not? Too many unanswered questions. And it made her more than a little worried about Dan's vivacious, but sometimes easily blindsided mother. Good-looking men seemed to be her nemesis. This wasn't the first suspect boyfriend.

The dinner was anything but comfortable. She had

never seen Maggie so quiet, or a boyfriend so attentive. He was probably going to get the third degree when they left and wanted to chalk up some positive points while he had the chance. In the meantime, a waiter was summoned the minute it looked like Maggie needed more water or another glass of wine. Was her meal too hot? Too cold? Did she also want them to reserve a dessert for her? Elaine tuned out. It was so obvious what he was up to. And the pandering seemed a bit over the top.

Finally, dinner was over. She asked for a to-go box and took dessert with her. The evening couldn't end quickly enough. She walked on to the car after promising Maggie that she'd call her. Hank and Dan stood talking for another ten minutes.

"Sorry. The guy's tough to get away from and he wants to look at insuring his newest venture with UL&C. I told him I'd take a look. Now, you want to share what happened when the two of you met at his house?" Dan didn't start the car but turned to look at her.

This time Elaine told Dan everything. "I have a problem being called 'scum' and accused of crawling out from under a rock. Though to be honest, I don't know if it was the treatment I received or how he treated his stepson. A week after the kid lost his mother is not the best time to lock a child out of your house and cut him off financially. I know anger can lead people to do and say things out of character for them, but I think Hank could have a nasty, vindictive streak. And Rick mentioned Hank having girlfriends. I always worry about your mother becoming a victim … again."

Dan didn't comment but started the car and put it in reverse. He was silent as he backed out of the parking space, turned left onto Riberia, and continued toward King Street. Dan hit the Range Rover's brakes as a group of teens stepped off the curb at the corner and, ignoring their red light, walked in front of him.

"Tourists. The only drawback to this town. At least this is the end of the summer crush. It won't be this bad again until Christmas." Dan continued east on King Street and didn't comment until they had crossed the bridge and were headed south on A1A. "I'm glad you hadn't shared Hank's comments with me before we met. I might not have been as restrained. But as you've said, grief can lead to anger and finding out his stepson had hired you to prove that he was the killer would have been a big trigger … not that I'm making excuses for him; he should have been able to handle the situation better. Empathy is not his strong suit."

"Do you really think he wants to expand his insurance with UL&C? Or is he just playing the big spender for your mother's benefit?"

"We'll see. That had crossed my mind. I'm meeting him at the schooner tomorrow to take a look at his new business plan and possibly give my recommendation to the company."

Chapter 7

The flowers arrived at exactly ten o'clock Monday morning. Elaine had been at her desk for two hours when Ginny brought them back, commenting on how she wished her boyfriend would think of doing something so sweet. But Elaine knew who they were from. Not Dan, but the man who knew he needed to make some points. The collection of white orchids—Phalaenopsis, Cattleya, Brassia—was worth more than many a worker's weekly paycheck. It screamed opulence and spoke unarticulated volumes about the sender. This was from someone who had to impress and was used to having his attention appreciated. Ginny had put the arrangement in a large, clear glass vase, centering it on the coffee table before handing her a card and returning to her desk.

The message was brief: "Can we start over?" Not even a signature. Could they? Could she put the insults behind her? She wasn't representing his stepson any longer, which would make things easier. She was a little surprised that Rick hadn't called or come by, but she supposed he had gone back to his condo in Orlando, the one his mother had been paying for.

The relationship with Dan's mother was another consideration. Wouldn't it do more good than harm to forget their first meeting and concentrate on the positive? Insuring his new business with UL&C probably meant a sizeable transaction for Dan's company. She didn't want to stand in the way of that. At the very least, she needed to acknowledge the flowers with a thank you note. Maybe something as cryptic as the note to her. She got his email address from Ginny and simply wrote: "Consider the hatchet buried." That should do it. It probably didn't require more. She pushed 'send'.

Ginny buzzed her on the intercom; there was an all-office meeting at two. Maggie had called earlier, wanting to drive up for a happy-hour drink. The day was getting busy, but Elaine liked it that way. She reached for her phone and texted Maggie, Would the Casa Monica work at four?

She knew that Maggie needed to talk and, frankly, Elaine was interested in what she would tell her about Hank Beaufort. Even though she knew no one was watching, Elaine worked through lunch, then attended the meeting, so she could leave at a quarter of four with a clear conscience.

* * *

Dan had started his day by chatting with his mother. She was apologizing again for the uncomfortable dinner they had shared with Hank Beaufort. He assured her that he thought Elaine could look past it, and she mentioned she would be having a drink with Elaine later. He liked having his mother close by, but that didn't mean that she wasn't a pain in the elbow. But shouldn't he be happy that she was enjoying life, making her own decisions, still working even, and not because she had to but because she loved challenges?

Spending a hundred thousand on an RV surprised him but in a lot of ways it fit her lifestyle at the moment. Downsizing, small houses? Those were more than just catchphrases to the over sixty-five age group. Dan needed to chill, as Jason would tell him. It wasn't his life.

He was meeting Hank Beaufort at the St. Augustine Marina at two. As a St. Johns County resident, his PayNow parking card hopefully assured him of a space in that congested part of the city. And it did. No endless circling, and he scored a spot only a block away. He was in no hurry and was a half hour early. He'd driven up the back way along A1A and over the Bridge of Lions. He never grew tired of seeing St. Augustine from the apex of the bridge— the spires of Flagler College, the dome of the Basilica, a combination of old and new—he knew of no other city like it.

If one were facing east, the marina was located on the San Sebastian River to the right of the bridge, one of several waterways that weave in and out of the area. A haven for boaters and fishermen, one waterway blended with another—rivers and the intracoastal and finally the Atlantic. Dan would be the first to admit that he had no experience of navigating on water. He wasn't even certain that he had a grasp of the terminology. It was a whole new language with new rules. For example, a local notice to mariners posted in an information bulletin he'd just now picked up at the center's office. In part, it read:

The San Sebastian River is reached from the Matanzas River and Intracoastal Waterway at ICW Mile 780. From the Intracoastal Waterway at Mile 780, pick up green daybeacon 1 and red daybeacon 2 which both mark the entrance to the San Sebastian River. Once you have cleared the entry marks, you can head upstream through the well-marked channel, and then make a sharp turn to starboard at green daybeacon 9.

Additional information could be found online at the U.S. Coast Guard website.

Greek. Absolute Greek. He had an idea of what it meant, but he needed a tutor. The head of navigation for the river was apparently the Kings Street Bridge with a controlling river depth of eight feet up to the bridge. The information in front of him also pointed out temperature, wind and tide, including both times and feet at high and low points. Having a boat wasn't a hobby, it was a way of life. Looking up, he saw Hank coming toward him along the walkway from the wharf.

"Been waiting long?" Jeans, tee-shirt, baseball cap, aviator sunglasses, and two-toned heavy rubber-soled deck shoes completed a look that was probably his work clothes. But it showed off a physique that wasn't a stranger to gym-workouts either, Dan thought.

"Got here early. Thought I'd brush up on my seafaring language. I'm at a serious disadvantage here." Dan gestured with the information pamphlet. "Yankees fan?" Dan pointed to the insignia on Hank's cap.

"Only when they're winning. Just kidding. I'm more into supporting some of the farm teams that call Florida home. I think this belongs to my stepson. He left it in my truck. Florida is a big spring training area. Baseball your thing?"

"Cubs fan. I'm originally from Chicago, but if I spend any more time in Florida, I'm going to have to change allegiance."

"I'm probably here to stay. I don't see myself moving anytime soon. I can't imagine not living by the water. I'm guessing you're not a boat enthusiast?"

"Enthusiast, never an owner."

"I'll keep it simple but I'll give you an idea of the scope of things. I moved here fifteen years ago after buying out a water-tour business down in the Keys. Now, I'm hoping to turn a single schooner into more of a multi-faceted business—a really huge expansion for me. I'm not ready to share the details just yet. There are still some things that have to be worked out, but I won't be working for someone else for a change. I'll be the one owning the operation—calling the shots. It's big; I will say that. I'll explain as we go along but everything's in writing, or will be. I'm about this close to finalizing the deal." Hank gestured with thumb and forefinger about an inch apart. "I just needed the money to come together, and finally it's there."

"I'm intrigued. Are you saying that you'll get out of the touring business?" What did the man have up his sleeve? Was this legit? Or some pie-in-the-sky scheme that was more hype than reality, Dan wondered.

"That's all I can say for now, so we'll start with what we can talk about, and that's my newest addition. That part's a reality, at least on paper." He turned and walked back into the breezeway, stopped just inside the archway, and pointed. "There, that's the public part of my tour operation. I'd been running the tours out of my office on San Marco. When this space came available, I jumped at it. I think it's going to lead to a nice increase in business, having the information booth and ticket sales in the marina itself."

The cubbyhole of space near the end of the marina nearest to the wharf had a Closed For Renovation sign displayed across a walk-up window. Was that where his mother would be working, organizing tours and selling tickets? The space was barely bigger than a walk-in closet. Dan followed Hank as he unlocked the ticket "booth" and walked in.

"This place was a pit. But a little paint and TLC and it's almost ready to go. I'll keep it staffed during the day—usually nine to five and another two hours before tours leave for last minute walk-ups, unless we're sold out for that particular event. Then we close early. It's pretty perfunctory but really all that is needed. I'll keep the larger office downtown, especially with the new business deal coming up.

"In total, right now I have two employees—one at the office on San Marco, and one here. In fact, this is where your mother will be. I'm hoping I can get by with just the two working this part of the business for a while before I might be forced to expand."

Three desktop computers looked new; two were still in boxes. A table by the ticket window held stacks of pamphlets, in addition to folded cutaway paper 'sleeves' for tickets. There was a safe, a cash register, a table fan, several folding chairs leaning against the wall, a water dispenser with a stack of paper cups on top of the inverted water jug, and a small bar fridge.

The space was small but not necessarily unpleasant. He didn't feel claustrophobic. And he felt Maggie would be safe. Someone had taken precautions by putting double dead-bolts on the door. With a safe already part of the furnishings, she wouldn't be leaving with cash to deposit. That was a relief; Still, having Simon with her would make him feel more at ease. He'd mention it to Maggie.

"Pull a chair up to the table here and I'll show you my newest acquisition." Hank had removed several folders from a nearby file cabinet. "Everything's online but I keep the originals here. I've forwarded a revised business plan for my tour business, including a budget with estimated ROI to the bank and copies to UL&C. I think you guys are going to send out your own appraiser in a week or two. I'm in close contact, but I'm still about one week from bringing my new schooner up to St. Augustine."

"A second schooner?"

"Exciting, isn't it? I still can't believe it. I was able to buy my second schooner in a bankruptcy situation. I've had to do a pretty complete renovation on it. I won't be using it in the tour end of things, but rather as a hauler adding a new dimension to H&H Enterprises. As you look through all this, let me know if I'm missing some paperwork that UL&C might need. Or if the hauler might need something to bring it up to UL&C standards."

Dan set up a folding chair but first helped himself to a cup of water out of the cooler while Hank spread out maps and legal documents.

"I'm in a great position here in St. Augustine to expand. You're going to laugh but I tried to buy the *Black Raven*, the pirate ship."

"Pirate ship?"

"Yeah, one of those tourist staples. A local favorite for kid's birthday parties as well. But it's a floating theatrical playhouse. Singing, mock saber fights, story lines that include treasure hunts, damsels in distress—a bit juvenile, but popular. I just couldn't see staffing up to the level that's needed to make it all work. So, I came up with a plan that promises to pay for itself and then some. The *Moonstruck* is my love, but I've found it's a precarious way to make a living. No tourists, no income. The last couple years have been a challenge. Two hurricanes, two years in a row, were disastrous. Things have picked up over the summer but not to the extent that I've been able to recoup all of what I've needed to. I think I've found a solution by adding a hauler—a second income that's not so fickle. Here's what I've decided to do."

Dan knew he was a captive audience but that was all right. He'd been an insurance adjustor before he became an investigator so he had a pretty good idea of what to listen for. Apparently, the plan had passed muster with the bank, which must mean the boat was in good shape if a bank loan had been secured.

"I hope I don't sound too mercenary, but money is driving this plan. As I mentioned, I've had the schooner that I picked up in the Keys modified to haul—for the most part, I plan on delivering only non-perishables. The area will include the Bahama Outer Island resorts. Areas within a 10-15 hour sail from here, depending on conditions. But that doesn't mean I can't extend the territory. Right now, I'm working with an agent on contracts with a Margaritaville, Sandals, a Hilton, and several others covering resorts as far south as the Turks and Caicos."

"Tell me more about the schooner."

"Overall length eighty-two feet, with length on deck of seventy-two feet, length at waterline sixty feet. Draft with centerboard seven point five feet, beam twenty feet, rig height ninety-two feet. The hull is wood, displacement tonnage is one-forty-two. Sail area is thirty-five hundred square feet. There's a diesel engine for auxiliary power. The spec page should be the first page in the folder. In short, she's a gaff-rig, topsail trading schooner or cargo hauling schooner capable of carrying one hundred forty-two tons. First couple trips down will be all building materials for local businesses."

"Do you have a crew in place? Sounds pretty demanding."

"It's rigged to require only one crew member in addition to the captain and still meet U.S. Coast Guard regulations for commercial vessels. Of course, the captain and mate are responsible for supervising the loading and unloading. This can be a little challenging, in that the load has to be distributed in such a way as to maintain the integrity of the schooner. It has to be safe so the captain has to have specialized knowledge as a load master."

"I'm assuming that's you? You'll be the ship's master?"

"When I can. I'll be bringing on a friend in a permanent position. He's currently overseeing the repairs on the hauler but everything should come together in another couple days. He's helped me out before and knows the drill. The two of us will divide duties between the *Moonstruck* and the *Nomad*. I even like the name. While he'll be in charge of the *Nomad*, I'll continue with the tourist tours on the *Moonstruck*. Here are some photos of getting her ready to sail. I don't have to tell you how excited I am. In a lot of ways, this is a dream come true. I know you may not understand, but I believe that Hannah would want to know that she had contributed to my dream. We were great together for many years, supportive of one another, had the same goals … I let her son come between us. He has lots of problems."

"Mixing families can be difficult."

"Yeah, more than I realized when I signed on. I wanted to tell you personally how sorry I am that I let my temper get the best of me when I found that Rick had hired a P.I. to try to prove me a murderer. As I said the other night at dinner, I lashed out without thinking, just gave into anger. Finding them up on the widow's walk just fueled the fire. I know how much Maggie admires your wife. I don't want to cause friction."

"You'll find Elaine is pretty level-headed and understanding."

"Good. Maggie and I look forward to more dinners with the two of you."

"Probably safe to say that can happen."

"I hope so. I'm looking forward to a friendship. Then, I'm going to tell you a couple things that I'd like you to share with her—might make a difference as to whether she continues to represent my stepson."

"I don't think that relationship has continued, but I'll share whatever it is you'd like me to tell her."

"Just this—I'm convinced that Hannah committed suicide. Our marriage was pretty much over. I had hoped to have had time over the weekend to discuss some basic issues with her. Money being at the top of the list. I've got a lot of irons in the fire at the moment—investments, new business ventures. To support this latest wild hair of mine, we were going to have to sell the house, and I know that would have crushed her. I'm not sure she could have faced it. I don't think she realized that she didn't have much to say about it. The house is in my name. And, I would have seen that she had a place that she could afford, but social position was everything to Hannah. She hadn't had a lot growing up, so her place in this community with a grand backdrop for parties—well, it was her identity. She was somebody."

"That would be difficult to walk away from." Or lose by having someone turn you out, Dan thought, but he didn't say anything. There was something petty and selfish about Hank—a 'my way or no way' approach to life. But maybe he was selling the man short.

"But what is most confusing is why she would be on the widow's walk trying to turn on the lights in the first place when I wasn't scheduled to come back until the next evening. It was a welcome home gesture; one she'd been doing for years. On the night I was expected, she would switch on the strings of lights around the widow's walk as a beacon of sorts. I could see them as I sailed into port. It was one of those thoughtful things we shared. But that's the problem. There, see the calendar?"

He pointed to the wall behind Dan. "That shows my departure and estimated return. I was coming back on Thursday, not Wednesday. And one more thing. When I first drove up to the house, the lights weren't on. But when I took the police up to the walk after I'd found her body, I switched the lights on without a problem. So, this idea of her standing on the top railing next to the electrical box trying to fix a loose wire or whatever and then accidentally slipping—it just doesn't hold water. Her footprints prove she was there, on the top rail, and I can think of no other reason for her being there than to jump. I've shared my thoughts with the police, and I think they finally agree with me."

"That makes sense. I can see why the police would change their minds and lean toward suicide."

"I know Rick can't accept that. Maybe when the shock wears off, if it ever does, he'll be able to accept the facts. I don't wish him ill. Believe me, he has enough of his own problems. The kid isn't stable; he's having a tough time growing up."

"Thanks for sharing. I'll tell Elaine. Like I said, I'm not certain that she's currently representing him but this is helpful information."

"I appreciate that. Do you have any questions about the plan?" Hank gestured toward the table of scattered papers.

"I'd like some extra time if that's possible—any chance I could take this set of papers with me? I need to give your plan more than just a once-over before I make any suggestions."

"Not a problem. I appreciate your time—whatever amount you can give to it. Just as a thank you, here are a couple tickets for the *Moonstruck*'s next cruise. I think you and Elaine would enjoy an evening on the water. The five-forty-five afternoon cruise highlight is what usually turns out to be a spectacular sunset. Of course, I'm ruling out cloud cover. And in Florida you never know. We have wine, a few select mixed drinks and heavy hors d'oeuvres. Don't eat beforehand."

* * *

Miraculously they were able to snag a table outside on the terrace. The day was warm but there was a certain safety to sitting outside where they were unlikely to be overheard.

"This is perfect. I'm so glad you were able to take the time to meet. You can only imagine how I've wrestled with what came out at dinner. I had no idea about a lot of things."

Maggie ordered a La Paloma and leaned against the back of the wrought iron chair. "I honestly didn't know that his wife had just died—or that she was still his wife. Or that the circumstances of her death were so awful."

"How are things now?" Elaine had ordered a New Zealand Sauvignon Blanc and paused when the waitperson returned with their drinks.

"Iffy, as you can imagine. I really felt I knew the guy. We'd met three times before last Saturday, and, of course, talked a lot. I thought things were developing nicely."

"He'd never mentioned his wife?"

"Never—at least, not in any detail. I knew that he had been married fifteen years but he said he had separated from his wife. I didn't know that they were still living in the same house. And I was totally surprised by the discussion of a stepson."

"Had you ever been to his house?"

"Never, not even invited. I wondered why, but guess I know now."

"Are you still comfortable with the relationship?"

"Yes and no. We were on the brink of adding a business partnership. I think I'll go ahead with that."

"Business project?" Elaine willed herself to ignore the red flag and listen to an explanation before commenting.

"Hank is buying out the water excursion agency at the marina in St. Augustine. He'll have two schooners in operation soon—one is the current tourist tour schooner, and the second is one that he just purchased and is having converted into a commercial hauler. Plus, he's involved in another maritime project—something big. I don't have all the particulars yet, but I'm going to invest in the project if my investment broker looks into it and gives me a green light. It will be a nice addition to my portfolio. And it will be nice to have something hands-on to relate to. I honestly think working with Hank will be exciting. I'll help with tours and manage the office. I'll be honest, spending my life reading Tarot cards might not be as fulfilling as I had expected it to be."

"That does sound like fun. I can see how it might have more appeal than card reading. Does that mean you'll be moving this way?"

"I'm beginning to think I should leave my bags packed and the majority of household belongings in storage. I've really been bouncing around the last few years."

"I'm interpreting that as a yes?"

Maggie laughed. "A big yes. Dan's going to have kittens but I've been looking at RVs. There are lots of great RV parks along the ocean in Flagler Beach. I've found one I like. And I already have the cottage in Devil's Bend rented."

"So, I don't have to worry about you driving cross-country with your house in tow?"

"Goodness, no. I think I've decided on the model I want. There's a great dealership in St. Augustine. I'll have it towed to the campgrounds. I'm even allowed a small fenced area for Simon. It's an adult park, you know, over fifty-five, and everyone has a dog. The grounds are kept up and patrolled at night. I'd feel safe there. Being directly across from the ocean, Simon will be in heaven with morning walks."

"You always amaze me. You make things sound easy, changes that would give most of us heart failure just working out the details. As always, it sounds like the planning is done and only the execution of the plan remains?"

"Pretty much. I was able to snag the spot at Lazy Daze RV Park because of Hank. And a good friend of his is the sales manager at the Ocean Way RV dealership and I'm pleased with the deal I'm getting. I'll put my furniture in storage and cut back to just the necessities—I've even pared down my closets and shoe collection. Two of my favorite thrift stores in the area are really cashing in. But isn't it amazing how we collect mounds of things—most of which we seldom use? I'm looking forward to living small."

"Instead of 'iffy', it sounds like your relationship with Hank is moving forward."

"I don't ask that you understand it, but, yes, we're going to continue to see each other. There were things he probably should have shared with me and didn't. For example, he was afraid that I wouldn't understand how he could be estranged from his wife and still live in the same house. At our age so many decisions hinge upon money and convenience. I'm certain he still had some feelings for Hannah and was as shocked as everyone else by her death. But he firmly believes that it was an accident and isn't buying into the suicide theory the police are suggesting. But murder? That was the supreme insult. To have his stepson hire you to see if he could be proved a murderer caused an already estranged relationship to totally deteriorate. Apparently, he's paid for the young man's schooling, his apartment, his car … this was more than a slap in the face, it was a betrayal. I hope you can see that."

"Of course, I can. I'm sure finding me in the house, looking at the accident scene was a shock, too. Still, I would have liked a little more professional behavior. If it doesn't bother you that he can be so blasé about his wife's death, I suppose I shouldn't be overly concerned either."

"It's my understanding that the marriage had been over for some time. I don't think that they had a true friendship even, at least not mutual respect. She appeared to be very judgmental. I think he felt he was being used; that he was necessary to her keeping up appearances. The big house, the parties … these were what was important to her. I know there's going to be a celebration of life at the church they attended, but Hank is adamant about life moving forward and not getting stuck in the past with what-ifs."

"If you're comfortable with his reaction to his wife's death, I'm willing to move on, too. Anger and grief can be a volatile combination. We never know how we will react until it happens to us."

"Oh, Elaine, I just knew you would be understanding … forgiving even."

Elaine let it go at that and changed the subject. What a weird position to be in—she had been hired by the son of the man who was dating her mother-in-law, a really recently widowed man who was a client of her husband's employer, and the charge to be proved was murder. Wasn't that a good definition of conflict of interest? She guessed she should be relieved that her first customer had in all likelihood, ditched her.

They finished their drinks, caught up with a report on Jason's travel in Asia; then, it was time to go. A hug and a kiss on the cheek ended her time with Maggie with the promise to get together again soon.

Chapter 8

The celebration of life for Hannah Beaufort was held in two places—those in attendance first gathered on the beach for eulogies and a ceremonial scattering of ashes before meeting again in the community room of the Episcopalian Church on King Street for a pot-luck supper. Because actual human remains cannot be put in the ocean closer than three nautical miles from shore, flowers and wreaths were floated closer in, and the *Moonstruck* carried Hank and Rick, their family minister, plus a handful of close friends out the specified distance to officiate at the actual spreading of the cremains on the water. A thoughtful, heartfelt ceremony and a perfect seaside celebration.

Dan and Elaine had decided to meet at the church. Elaine had spent the morning at Stanley and Stanley, and he had spent the greater part of the day giving Maggie his two cents' worth of advice concerning her RV purchase. He was still mulling over her decision. Not that she'd listen or that he could change her mind. Independent thinking didn't even come close to describing his willful mother.

He was pleasantly surprised that the pre-owned RV really was a good buy—refurbished, had always been under cover when not in use, low mileage on a barely used engine, lots of extras that could have cost a small fortune if added separately—all in all, it was a sweet deal. And he really wasn't opposed to this newest life change. He could see the plusses—a completely set up home across from the beach, maybe five miles from her new workplace. He hoped she wouldn't decide to tour in it and would stick to her plan of living in it.

Arriving at the church a bit late, he had been afraid that he wouldn't find parking close by. But after twice circling the block, he had literally pulled into one of the last two parking spaces in the church lot. Walking inside, he estimated that a hundred and fifty people had crowded into the church's community room and spilled over into the breezeway and garden. Dan was amazed at the number of people who were at the church. Sometimes a person needed to see that kind of support while they were still living. It was only four thirty in the afternoon but several men in suits and ties sat at a table prominently up front. Dan guessed that he might be looking at the entire office of Stanley and Stanley.

Elaine's casserole dish, which had once held her famous 5-cheese macaroni and ham looked like it had been licked clean. Even the dessert table had been reduced to crumbs forty-five minutes after the doors had opened. Dan helped himself to a soft drink and a helping of scalloped potatoes and bar-b-que ribs and found an empty spot at a card table close to the kitchen. Finally, the crowd began to disperse.

He was getting ready to leave when Elaine motioned for him to join her. She was standing next to an older man whom she introduced as her boss. A handshake and a few niceties, both of them agreeing how lucky he was to have hired her, and Leon Stanley rejoined what must have been the office contingent. Elaine had volunteered to help clean up. It had been a good idea to come in separate cars; Dan was able to leave whenever he wanted. He once again offered his condolences to Hank and Rick, waved to Elaine in the kitchen, and headed out.

* * *

Elaine slipped on the apron that was handed her and began carrying plates to the kitchen to begin scraping leftovers into plastic bag-lined trashcans. A group of street people had shown up, checking to see if there might be hand-outs but the table that had once held a hundred or so dishes of food looked like it had been attacked by locusts. Elaine had even missed out on a piece of a chocolate torte that had come highly recommended. However, she had thought ahead and slipped a truly decadent looking brownie into a plastic drink cup and put both in her purse.

It was a meager helping, but she hadn't attended for the food and she was glad she hadn't missed the service. The minister had offered a eulogy before everyone started eating, and mentioned that anyone who wanted to could share anecdotes about Hannah as he passed around a hand-held mic.

The stories were heartwarming. A picture emerged

of a thoughtful, caring individual who never turned away anyone who needed help. Her current Sunday school class sat together at one table and several children sweetly offered a tribute to their teacher. Stories of church summer camp art classes, such as the one where all the paper mâché projects were eaten by mice because someone left them in the breezeway to dry overnight . Or the time when the lamb in the live nativity scene in front of the church bolted and ran into traffic on King Street. It was Hannah who had chased after the errant animal and brought him back. The laughter felt good and lightened the mood.

Finally, every dish was washed, dried, and placed in the church's cupboards or set out for its owner to pick up; paper plates separated from plasticware, empty water bottles bagged to recycle—it was time to go home and enjoy that brownie with a cup of coffee. Elaine promised to return the apron after she'd laundered it. She folded it and put it in a bag with the now-clean casserole dish. Someone had even swept the breezeway and picked up trash in the parking lot.

As she neared her rental car, she could see someone leaning against the hood. "Rick. I was hoping I would see you. I think the service was lovely, heartfelt, and a wonderful tribute to your mother."

"I'm glad you could come. My mom would have liked this."

"Did you get something to eat? I didn't see you in the dining room."

"I wasn't hungry."

"You really missed out on some good food."

"Yeah, the kitchen smelled really good. But I just wanted to talk to you."

"Ok, I have time now." Elaine unlocked the car and put the bag in the back seat. "Do you need a ride somewhere?"

"No, I've got my car here. I just needed to tell you that Hank is lying to the police. He's telling them that mom committed suicide and trying to prove it by saying the lights weren't broken so she wasn't standing on the railing trying to fix them. Plus, he says that she had the wrong day, that he wasn't supposed to return until the following day. I found mom's phone at the house and made a copy of a screen shot of Mom's text messages. Here's the one from Hank telling her he'll be a day early. She thought he was coming back on Wednesday because he told her that." Tears pooled at the corners of his eyes and started to run down his face. He paused to wipe his nose on his sleeve. "I hate him. He's lying. He's covering up the murder—his murdering my mom. But the cops believe him."

Elaine dug a package of Kleenex out of her purse and handed it to him. "Have you shown the screen shot to the police?"

"No. I thought it should come from you. They don't want to pay attention to me. They asked me to not interfere."

Which means he's probably hounded them to the point that he's not welcome at the station anymore, Elaine thought. This was tough. How involved did she want to get, especially since Dan had shared the information from Hank? But proof that Hannah thought he was coming home early put the suicide theory in question—gave her a bona fide reason to be on the widow's walk and adjusting the lights if needed.

"Let me see what I can do." She took the screen shot and quickly read the message: "Hey, sweetie, change of plans. Finished here early and I'll be home this evening. Already on the way." The time of the text was 4:15 in the afternoon on Wednesday.

"See? He set her up. This is proof."

"I'll talk to the police and let you know what I find out."

"Thanks." Rick stepped away from her car and waved as he headed toward the back of the lot. She hadn't seen his car but maybe he'd had to park on the street. Early on, the church lot had been full.

What was she going to do? He still thought of her as available to work on his case. Was she? Technically not without compensation. She shouldn't have promised to go to the police. She needed to discuss this with Leon Stanley. And if she showed the screenshot of the text message to Dan, it made the information from a UL&C client out as a lie. How could she prove that Hank had really sent the message without having his phone?

She needed to drop the case, tell Rick that the conflict of interest was just too great for her to continue. But then she felt sorry for him. He was truly one of creation's lost souls. That didn't mean that she had to try and save him, but she wasn't known to walk away from anyone needing her help.

* * *

Elaine decided that she wouldn't say anything to anyone until she'd talked with the police. At nine o'clock the next morning she was waiting outside of Chief Rob Mitchell's office on King Street in downtown St. Augustine. She trusted the man. The year before he had been helpful in solving a human trafficking case that had included relics stolen from the Basilica—Church artifacts insured by UL&C. She knew Dan respected him.

The place was busy. She'd passed on a tepid cup of coffee and opted for a bottle of water. The receptionist made excuses for the wait, saying how glad she was that summer was finally over. Every illegally parked auto, stiffed restaurant waitperson, lost piece of luggage, or even lost child was a problem that came their way.

They would have a couple months of relative quiet before the throngs of tourists would descend for the holidays. St. Augustine's Christmas lights that decorated every inch of the plaza, rooftops, trees and shrubs had made magazine covers and nationally they were becoming known as a must-see tourist destination. The trolleys and horse-drawn carriages only added to the appeal. In addition, who could pass up the usually comfortable weather and a pristine beach?

Actually, the wait wasn't bad. Within fifteen minutes, Chief Mitchell opened the door of his office and walked a visibly upset man and woman to the hall door before returning and holding his hand out to Elaine.

"Impounded car. But I've arranged a trip to retrieve it. Another problem solved. Let's grab a little privacy and move to my office. So, how has Ms. Mahoney been?" He held the door open and motioned to a chair in front of his desk.

"Probably not as busy as you seem to be."

"Tourists. I don't need to say more, do I?"

Elaine caught him up on her new title and position with Stanley and Stanley and accepted his congratulations. He added, "We need good people in the field. You're a welcome addition. Are you working on something with Dan?"

"No, not this time. Leon Stanley set me up with Rick Beaufort—"

"Let me guess, the kid has been relentless in hounding you to accept his mother's death as a murder, right?"

"Yes, he's absolutely adamant that his stepfather is to blame."

"I know. But the evidence just doesn't lead in that direction."

"As I'm sure he's told you, he's convinced that his mother shouldn't have been on the widow's walk to begin with—she had the wrong day. Yesterday, he shared proof that she'd been misled." Elaine handed the copy of the screenshot to the chief.

"Interesting. The origin of the message would be easy to prove if we had his mother's phone. I'm assuming he would be willing to let us take a look?"

"I couldn't say for certain, but if he wants answers he needs to let you have it. I won't take up any more of your time. I've added Rick's contact info at the bottom of the page in case you don't have it."

"Thanks. I'll try to connect with him this afternoon and check out the phone. I'll keep in touch. Don't work too hard—leave a few investigations for my men to handle. And say hello to Dan."

Chapter 9

Finally out of dry dock with all repairs completed, the *Nomad* was supposed to dock in St. Augustine at two in the afternoon—at least according to Hank when Dan had called him that morning. After looking at the hauler's specs, Dan had a couple of suggestions, additions that he knew UL&C would insist be done before finalizing and issuing an insurance policy.

The schooner wouldn't be going anywhere until full coverage could be assigned, so he was eager to not hold up Hank's maiden voyage. The schooner wasn't making money sitting in a slip. The additions were small things—a larger handrail on steps leading below deck, non-skid rubber matting in two places that would get the most foot traffic, two extra security cameras fore and aft for use when in port, and a better, newer alarm system—something sensitive to natural phenomenon like fluctuating water levels, as well as unwanted human intervention. Other items like proof of age for the diesel engine, including copies of the manufacturer's date of production, and a complete annotated list of upgrades and costs which could be easily obtained.

Hank had suggested meeting at the dock mid-afternoon and either going over paperwork onboard or going back to the office. Dan opted for onboard the schooner. He'd seen the sketches and photos but, of course, hadn't actually been on the ship itself. When he arrived, the gangplank was in place and Dan started up the steps to board when suddenly his way was barred.

"That's far enough." Arms crossed and feet wide apart, the guy was six foot and sinewy, not an ounce of fat, just athlete-solid. The kind who could climb Everest and never need oxygen. Or in this case shinny up a mast pole and mend a sail without a safety net. His jeans were stained and the tee-shirt had seen better days. Unkempt hair and a straggly beard helped give his scowling face a sinister look. Still, cleaned up he probably made a nice appearance. This was just a man not afraid of a little hard work.

"I'm Dan Mahoney with United Life and Casualty. Hank and I are meeting here to look at some insurance requirements for getting a policy on the *Nomad*."

"Didn't say anything to me." The guy wasn't moving.

"Give him a call; he'll vouch for me." Two could play this game of not giving way and the guy was irking Dan. "I don't think I caught your name."

"Because I didn't give it to you. Now, I'll thank you to step back."

As tempting as it might be, a fistfight never solved

anything and wasn't he getting too old anyway? He probably had twenty years on the guy guarding the entry. Those were not the best of odds. Dan swallowed the retort he was tempted to say and followed directions. He stepped back and turned to retrace his steps up the walkway when he saw Hank waving to him from the back of the marina.

"Just had a chat with the pit bull who's guarding the *Nomad*."

"Ron Carter. The man's going to get me in trouble someday. But the bark's worse than the bite—trust me on that—he's only following my orders and I probably did forget to tell him you were stopping by. A pronounced lack of people skills will keep him on the *Nomad*. He's pretty much no nonsense. I can't see him handling a boat-load of tourists on the *Moonstruck*. I had hoped we might share duties but that's out of the question. He's a good skipper and a great guard. We ever get in trouble on the water I'd trust him with my life. I can put up with a lot to get those qualities."

"I can attest to the guard part. And that's pretty high praise for his ability as a sailor."

"Not easy finding knowledgeable people today, willing to work hard. Ron came my way via the islands. A lot of young men from down there grew up on boats. A friend wanted me to give him a chance. Ron had a few missteps as a youngster, but he's paid for them. He's clean now but an ex-con rep follows a person to his grave. Makes getting a job a challenge."

"Has he been with you long?"

"Just since the first of the year. He's been babysitting the *Nomad*, even helping with some of the repairs. Well, here we are. And as you see, we're open for business."

Dan noticed that the 'closed for renovations' sign was absent and it looked like the entire space had a new coat of paint since he'd been there. A cheery baby blue interior with white appointments—a new desk, table and chairs—and a huge, four-foot by six-foot seascape on the back wall, with a very real rendering of the *Moonstruck* sailing under a full moon. Nice. It looked inviting and probably sold tickets for their once-a-month full moon tours.

"Place looks a little different than when you first saw it."

"I like the changes. The oil painting is spectacular."

"Local artist. Even got a nice write-up in *The Record* with a couple photos. You may already know, but your mom starts tomorrow."

"The last time we talked she'd just decided on an RV and snagged a spot in an oceanside park between St. Augustine and Palm Coast."

"You're pretty much up-to-date. I'm insisting she take time out from moving and have a little fun. I've got you and the wife down for the sunset tour this Friday. I've invited your mom to come along."

"I'm looking forward to it."

"Eventually, I'll set her up to hostess the tours. She's a natural."

"You're right, she's good with people. And while I'm thinking of it, what are the chances she could share this office with a dog?"

"Ah, the trusty sidekick, Simon?"

"You've met Simon?"

"Yes, and was impressed. I think it's a good idea. No one will even be tempted to harass her if he's by her side."

"Thanks. They'll both be happier."

"Now let's see what kind of hoop that company of yours wants me to jump through."

Dan handed Hank a list of requirements. "Not too much to do. Ron might be able to make the changes himself. Once they've been made, I'll inspect and verify with photos."

"Not a problem. Now let's walk back down and take a look at the *Nomad*."

"By the way, good choice of name."

"I didn't change it—it does seem fitting."

Hank proved to be a superb guide, well-versed on retrofitting a schooner to haul. And there was a lot to learn, Dan realized. A throwback to the golden age of sailing, a schooner was uniquely designed to navigate hard-to-reach ports. Perfect for serving coastal or river and lake settlements. For example, Hank pointed out the fact that the schooner with its keel not far below the waterline, could navigate shallow water yet the hull and sail designs assured speed. And when in port, it was paramount that loading or unloading was done efficiently. Time in port could be a deal breaker when it came to making money.

"So, when's the first trip?"

"Coming up pretty quick. Depending on UL&C, Ron should be taking her down to the Bahamas by the first of the week. We're scheduled to deliver building goods to a Hilton that's adding a string of cabanas on its oceanside. She'll be full to the gills with lumber, pre-dyed canvas, fake thatching for roof accents ... we signed a contract over thirty days ago and they're getting a little antsy."

"What's left to do, other than having UL&C's policy in place?"

"That's about it. The Coast Guard issued a Certificate

of Inspection after repairs were completed. Everything's in order. Logistic specialists that I've used in the past will handle transportation and disposition of cargo. I guess that leaves a couple dry runs and I'll be satisfied that we're ready. I want Ron to be comfortable. He's experienced, but the kid who's signed on as first mate needs some seasoning. There's no way that I can get away. My house goes on the market Monday. I may find having two schooners to be more of a challenge than I bargained for. But I'm slowly putting together a good crew. I'm determined to make this work."

"I'm assuming you'll continue to live close by?"

"Made an offer on a condo about two miles south of here. I'll be glad to get out of the big house—too many bad memories. I'm going to squeeze into eight hundred and fifty square feet, and, frankly, it's about time. It won't be ready for a couple weeks. I'll put some stuff in storage and rent a garage for my truck; it's all doable. In fact, I'm looking forward to a change in lifestyle."

Chapter 10

The text came from a burner." Chief Mitchell had called her on her cell and thanks to Bluetooth on the rental car, she hadn't had to fish her phone out of her purse while driving.

"Guess that doesn't prove anything. Hank could have used a burner but highly doubtful. Can you, at least, verify the vicinity where the call was placed? All calls have to go through the service provider in the area that they were placed, don't they?"

"Yes, but we've closed the case. I don't think this is enough to get my office to reopen it and serve a T-Mobile or AT&T with a friendly subpoena requesting they share records."

"Have you talked with Rick?"

"Yeah, and he basically hung up on me. I feel for the kid but he's got to give this up. It can't be good for his mental health."

Elaine agreed. Rick seemed vulnerable and totally unable to walk away and accept what authorities were telling him. She thanked the chief and promised that she would continue to encourage Rick to face the truth. She pulled into her parking spot at Stanley and Stanley and just sat there. How was she going to do that?

Rick was convinced that his stepfather had set up and then killed his mother. He could be persuasive, she could attest to that, but did it change the way she believed? At this point she thought the police were correct. Hannah must have suspected Hank had a new love interest. She supposedly knew that he was going to sell the house. Elaine had a mental picture of a very depressed woman. Someone who feared losing an entire way of life.

One thing that she'd meant to run by Leon Stanley was whether the life policy on Hannah had a suicide clause. Once again she found him in the break room, this time with a cup of coffee and an Egg McMuffin. Didn't the man ever eat at home? But then, he had referred to his wife as having passed. Elaine felt a surge of compassion for her boss.

As always he welcomed her with an offer of coffee and pointed to a chair opposite his at the table. "A good question but strict, long-term suicide clauses are becoming a thing of the past. A policy might cost a little more but under certain circumstances can be worth it—just for peace of mind. The Beauforts updated their wills six months ago and each policy contained a suicide clause stating that the manner of death would not impact payout if said death happened after the two-year grace period when the clause was in effect. Their policies were nine and ten years old respectively so the suicide clause restrictions had been met. As I shared with you earlier, the main addition to both policies was the conservatorship governing Rick. I have to admit that Hannah was unusually verbal about her distrust of this. She wanted one half of the two-million-dollar policy on her to simply be handed over. I didn't interfere, but I thought Rick's receiving one million carte blanche wasn't the best of ideas. The kid has some growing up to do. Are you still helping him?"

"Yes and no. Officially, I'm not pursuing a case. Unofficially, I worry about him; he's hurting."

"I appreciate your concern, but try to stay out of Hank Beaufort's way. He can be rather forceful when crossed, but I think you've already found this out."

No one had to convince her of that. She hadn't said as much to Maggie, but Elaine worried about her continuing a relationship with the man even if it was predominately work related. It wasn't much, but she was silently pleased that the RV Maggie had chosen would really only be comfortable for one occupant.

She thanked Leon and walked back to her office. Were there any other pieces to the puzzle that hadn't been explored? There just didn't seem to be a case. Hank Beaufort wasn't even in town that Wednesday. Hadn't he said he was the one who had found Hannah's body a full twenty-four hours later? On Thursday, the day he was supposed to have returned?

Wasn't there something that she was forgetting? Something that Rick had said about seeing his stepfather ... seeing him with a girlfriend, that was it. On *Wednesday*, that's how she knew that Hank was in town early.

She picked up her cell and texted a quick message: "You told me you saw Hank with a girlfriend on the day your mother died. Where was this? And when?" Her phone rang five minutes later.

"Rick, thanks for getting back. I don't have any new information but I'm feeling a need to close all the gaps."

"Yeah, I appreciate that. I was at One Daytona that afternoon. You know that place with all the restaurants and a movie theater?"

Elaine didn't but made a note to check it out later. "What time was this?"

"It was late maybe six o'clock. I'd had a late interview at Rock Bottom Brewery. I hoped to be hired in their kitchen, but they were looking for someone with experience. That's where I saw Hank. When I left the restaurant, I just walked around. He was with some woman—probably close to his age. He didn't see me; they were having ice cream at Ben and Jerry's."

"No promises, but I wanted to check this out. I'll keep in touch."

No getting cold feet now; she needed to make sure Rick had his day and time right. She punched in Maggie's number.

"I'm going to feel like the inquisition but did you have ice cream with Hank at One Daytona on the fifth?"

"For heaven's sake, Elaine, what's going on?"

"I'm just trying to prove that Hank Beaufort was nowhere even close to home on that Wednesday. I'm trying to discourage his stepson from continuing with what is probably a hopeless case."

"Then I'm not going to be of much help. Hank had brought the *Moonstruck* into the marina at Daytona for a minor repair—something electrical, I think. He'd called me and because I was only thirty miles away, I agreed to having dinner at One Daytona. And, yes, we followed that up with ice cream."

"Was he using a rental car?"

"No, he borrowed someone's truck from the marina."

"Did you guys make it a late night?" Elaine hated to pry into her mother-in-law's private life, and the pause on the other end of the line made her realize that Maggie was just as uneasy.

Finally, Maggie answered, "Couldn't, he had to get the truck back. I was home by eight or thereabouts."

"What about later after you got home? Do you know if he took the *Moonstruck* on up the coast to St. Augustine that night?"

"I know he didn't."

"How so?" This was embarrassing. For a moment she felt Maggie was about to say something, then thought better of it. Maybe she was going to tell Elaine to get lost; she'd had enough of a third degree, but after an audible deep breath, Maggie added.

"He texted me later in the evening to say he was stuck overnight and wouldn't get away until the next afternoon. I passed up having breakfast because I was already scheduled to open the office early for the guys setting up the computers, and lunch was out because I was meeting the new renters to sign a contract."

"Maggie, this has been helpful. I'm not sure where or how it all fits together but it's answered some questions. And I'm so sorry that I had to ask them. By the way, Dan and I are really looking forward to the sail this Friday. It's going to be fun."

A few more niceties as to how the move was going, was the RV in place, would she have time for dinner sometime over the weekend, and Elaine hung up. What had she learned? Basically, that Hank Beaufort could have easily run up the coast on Wednesday evening. Instead of ruling him out as a suspect, Maggie had just placed him front and center. The question was what could she do with the information? Was it really helpful? It put him within forty-five miles of his home but that was about it. It did not put him on the widow's walk.

There was one last thing that she'd thought of doing—canvass the neighborhood and see if any neighboring house had a security camera that might have picked up something. A car in the driveway, someone on the widow's walk or just wandering around the exterior. There were two houses that might have surveillance cameras that could have picked up movement at the Beaufort home—the three-story house directly in back and a house to the side separated only by an empty, narrow lot of overgrown vegetation. This second house was four-stories tall. It was such a long shot. She couldn't imagine having cameras aimed toward one's neighbors, but there was a chance.

Chapter 11

Friday evening was perfect—a few wispy clouds, slight breeze, low humidity, calm waters. Dinner was at the Athena and it was gyros all around with a Greek salad to share, extra dressing, extra olives. The pita was warm and the baklava was perfection. Just her kind of laid-back evening, Elaine decided.

Maggie had met them at their townhouse and ridden downtown in Dan's Rover. Simon was left in the care of a neighbor, and Maggie would pick him up on the way home. She had been able to close the ticket office early as the tour had sold out by four. Elaine smiled, all local Mahoneys were present. Dan had found a parking spot a block from the marina and a brief walk got them there with time to spare. Elaine kept any mention of Rick or his stepfather out of the conversation, and Maggie didn't ask for follow up on the implications that Hank had been close to home the night of his wife's death. Elaine was relieved. It was good to get away from suspicion and innuendo—at least for a little while.

Hank met them as they boarded and had roped off a bench and two deck chairs close to a young woman playing a guitar.

"Best seats in the house. I'll join you once we set sail. My sidekick is at the wheel tonight; so, I'm going to get that rare treat of simply enjoying the cruise. I'll send a waitperson over. We have a nice selection of beer and wine. Anything stronger is pre-mixed—Mimosas or Bloody Mary's."

Once everyone was onboard, a young woman announced several safety features, the location of restrooms, and rules of etiquette—share the binoculars provided when possible. There would be sea life to view. Yes, there were life jackets for everyone and would be distributed by the crew, if needed. She assured her audience that a checklist for the number and condition of lifejackets, the expiration dates on flares, and tests of crew's overboard training were all done yearly by the Coast Guard. On board, the restroom or 'head' was a little tricky to reach in that the stairs taking you below deck was really a ladder. She encouraged passengers to move about the deck but be ever-mindful of crew. Help raising the sails was welcome. No, there was no real path or destination. Everything depended upon the wind, weather, and time of the sail.

Then Hank took the microphone and gave a brief history of the *Moonstruck*, her origins and capabilities, which included a briefing on nautical terms. His presentation was actually well done, Elaine thought. He divided the audience up into two groups and asked questions, kept score and awarded a prize to the side containing twenty or so winners, a twenty-dollar voucher toward dinner at O.C. Whites, a favorite St. Augustine restaurant. Tonight, there was a bonus prize to the person who could give the exact overall length of the vessel or come close, and the composition of its hull. The answer of seventy-six feet and steel won a moonlight tour.

After everyone had been served drinks and hors d'oeuvres, Hank asked Dan if he'd be interested in taking the helm. He commented that it wasn't something he offered that often but thought Dan would enjoy a first-hand feel for what his company was insuring. Elaine almost laughed out loud. Interested? Try and keep him from giving it a try. This would be the highlight of the evening for him.

Elaine didn't know why she thought the cruise would be more festive, more party oriented, but it certainly wasn't. A few men had moved to help with the sails, others had moved closer to the music, but overall, the group was almost reverent. And the schooner was quiet. What had she expected to be noisy if there wasn't an engine? Sailing was maybe the most relaxing thing she'd ever enjoyed with thirty-some people, including children, all in the same place. They sailed as far as the Matanzas Bridge to the south and enjoyed a pink and gold sunset that somehow was prettier from a position on water. There were some cameras and lots of iPhones capturing the scene. She could see why this was one of the most popular tourist events St. Augustine had to offer.

* * *

In the meantime, Dan followed Hank to the helm. He was having to adjust his opinion of the guy and ease off being worried about Maggie's involvement. The man was leaning over backwards to share a fun time with his family. Dan could chalk up the man's outburst on the widow's walk to anger probably brought on by shock. It was obvious that he was trying to smooth things over. And Dan was willing to drop his guard a little and enjoy the offering.

Just knowing that this type of sailing was steeped in history led to a lot of questions. For example, sharing facts about the steering gear of 18th and 19th century sailing ships, Dan was adding a new vocabulary filled with words like spindle, tiller rope slots, barrel—to name a few. And savoring every minute. Hank knew his sailing history.

And Hank didn't seem to think there were any dumb questions. How could you tell the exact position of the rudder at night in the old ships? There were extra grooves in the handles or spokes at the tips of the king spoke used by the captain or helmsman steering in the dark. When the king spoke pointed upward, the rudder was supposed to be in a straight line with the hull. Hank was a walking encyclopedia.

When needed, a diesel engine guaranteed maneuverability if there was no wind. Hank admitted to hating to fire up the engine—it seemed an imposter on a sailing cruise, but often needed to return to port in a timely and safe manner. At the end of an hour and a half, bringing the *Moonstruck* into the dock for people to disembark required firing up the diesel engine. Almost effortlessly, Hank lined up the vessel with the gangplank, and several tie-offs. Reluctantly, people stood up to leave, placing tips for the crew and musician in a bucket beside the exit. Judging from the relaxed atmosphere of the crowd, this had been a successful evening. Dan knew he'd recommend it.

Maggie wanted to show Elaine her office so they walked back through the marina breezeway. "It's small. I hope Simon won't feel too cooped up."

"He's six now. It's time he took on a little responsibility and started paying his own way." Both women turned to look at Dan. "Ok, just a joke. Maybe only one or two days a week, he should be fine."

"I know I'll feel better with him here. The entire corner from the back of the building to the intersection of King Street and Avenida Menendez is usually filled with homeless people by late afternoon. It's a mini-park with benches and a water fountain—luxuries if you live on the street."

"Is the area patrolled at all?" Elaine asked.

"As well as can be expected. I have seen a patrol car cruise the area but only once during the evening hours."

"Well, keep Simon with you and make use of the locks on the door. Is there an alarm?" Dan asked.

"No, but that's a good idea. I'll mention it to Hank."

The three of them walked back around the building, past the restrooms. Elaine paused, "I'm going to stop in here. I'll catch up with you at the car." She pushed the heavy door inward and took her place behind two other women she'd seen on the cruise. She didn't have to wait long. But by the time she'd stepped out of the stall, there was now a line of five women. One soap dispenser was out of liquid but otherwise the restroom was clean and well stocked. She washed her hands, pressed the dryer button, touched up her lipstick, and left.

Walking toward the intersection, the path cut across a section of grass littered with sleeping bags, blankets, laundry baskets of belongings and bodies—some asleep, some sitting on benches dozing, talking with others, eating—three came toward her with their hands out, one held a sign requesting help in buying food for their baby. Another man yelled out that his dog was hungry.

She wasn't sure what had caught her eye but she found herself staring at a person sitting on a bench wrapped in a blanket maybe five feet from the sidewalk. Even turned away from her, she recognized him. Rick. Why was he on the streets? She called out to him but he seemed reluctant to respond. He looked toward her, then glanced at the ground.

"Let's talk." She tried again. She knew he'd heard her. The man next to him looked her way and then leaned toward Rick and said something before getting up and motioning for her to take his place on the bench beside Rick.

He looked terrible, puffy eyes, sallow skin, and he smelled. His clothing was stained and wrinkled from constant wear. His hair was dirty; he was wearing mismatched sneakers, and his hand shook as he unwrapped the blanket and let it fall to one side.

"What do you want?"

Not menacing, just tired, sounding like someone who was giving up on life. "Where's your car?"

"Hank had it repossessed."

"And your condo?"

"Kicked out. Hank stopped paying when mom died. I only had it until the end of the month."

"Have you eaten today?"

A shake of the head, eyes once again not meeting hers. "I can't do anything right now, but let me see if we can't change this somehow. Do you still have your phone?"

"For two more weeks."

"Then I'll call you. I promise we'll talk tomorrow." She stood and stepped back on the sidewalk. "Please take care."

A shrug was the answer. The man who had given her his seat quickly sat down again. A bench seemed to be a prime space and much coveted.

All the way back to the car, she couldn't get the pitiful situation out of her mind. Once again, it made a bully out of Hank. Absolutely no compassion, but worse, he was putting a young man in danger. She knew exactly what she had to do in the morning—talk to her boss.

* * *

She was making a habit of cornering her boss in the lunchroom. When she mentioned it, Leon just laughed and invited her to join him.

"I hate to take up time when you're working. Somehow eating doesn't count."

Leon laughed. "I do seem to eat less when I'm talking. I think I'll just make you my new diet. Seriously, I don't want you to be shy about coming to my office, but this seems to work fine. Now, how can I help you?"

"I'm worried about Rick Elliston. He appears to be in poor health and is living on the streets. Hank has apparently had him evicted from his condo and had his car repossessed. In my opinion Rick's conservator should be doing more—at least safe-guarding his life, not putting it in danger. There should be some way to pay for better care—*make* Hank take better care of him by using Rick's share of the life insurance policy. It's not like there isn't money available."

"Rick is over twenty-one, too old to be a ward of the state and assigned to a foster home. At this point Rick would have to sue to have the conservatorship overturned; and he would have to prove he's a discerning adult of sound mind and intent in order to sway a judge to release him from the legal agreement involving his stepdad. Do you think he could do that? Prove that he's able to care for himself by providing shelter, food, even to being actively employed?"

"No, he probably couldn't."

"I worry that Hank will institutionalize him. He probably hasn't, so far, because of the money. Hank has invested the one million that was set aside for Rick and doesn't want to spend a penny that he doesn't have to. But further sleuthing to prove he's a murderer, and Hank isn't going to be kind. He'll want the kid put away, out of reach from hurting him, ruining his reputation at the very least. Believe me, in return, Hank could do a smear job on Rick that would force him out of state if he ever wanted to work."

"When you put it that way, I'm surprised that Hank hasn't taken action before. Hank has a lot of good qualities but also a vengeful streak that scares me."

"Even after saying what I just did, I think he's harmless. He's been more into controlling Rick than hurting him."

"Until now. Depriving him of any comforts and forcing him to live on the street is harmful."

"Ok, I agree. I would bet Hank would excuse this extreme behavior as just trying to wake Rick up to the consequences of pushing falsehoods and not finishing school in order to work toward a goal like any law-abiding adult."

"Can anything be done?"

"At this point, Elaine, I don't see how things can be turned around. Keep encouraging Rick to face the truth about his mother's death—I have every reason to believe that the police have it right. I believe a very depressed woman simply chose to end her life."

"You could certainly be correct." Elaine decided not to share the latest twist—learning that Hank was not only in the vicinity a day early but could have easily driven to St. Augustine and set up the murder. And she probably needed to cease and desist, not in any way encourage Rick to believe that his theory could be true. But wasn't she now, herself, needing closure? Or was aimless curiosity about to maim the cat?

She wasn't going to tell anyone what she was about to do. Her idea to canvass the neighbors in the probably farfetched possibility that a camera had caught any life-threatening activity, or even Hank driving by, would be the last thing she would explore. That she promised herself. Then she would have closure, be finished with any conspiracy theories.

Nothing really conclusively pointed a finger at Hank as a murderer. To be honest she could think of no other even remote possibility to look into. She would check it out. Then, she could be adamant and simply insist that Rick give it a rest, give up trying to prove something that didn't happen, and get on with his life. She grabbed her purse and headed to the parking lot.

* * *

It was only her second visit to that area along the coast. The houses were all monuments to an opulence that seemed a perfect addition to the shoreline. Each had manicured grounds of palms, sea grapes, fountains and statuary depicting everything from angels to dolphins. Two and three car garages, gazebos, balconies facing the ocean, the community was grand, but inviting. She drove past the Beaufort residence and turned down a street that would take her to the houses behind it.

The house directly in back wasn't as tall, only three stories, making her inquiry a real long-shot. Standing in the driveway, it didn't seem possible that a camera could have caught anything useful. Still, if someone was prowling around the area between the properties, that might have been captured.

She rang the doorbell and waited at the request of the housekeeper who needed to find her employer and bring him to the door. Elaine ended up handing one of her cards to a very taciturn man who looked like he'd just been awakened from a nap. He took her card but said he couldn't help. His outside cameras had been out of commission the past month and he had just been lax in getting them fixed. He expressed how sorry he was about Ms. Beaufort and then indicated that he was needed back inside. He, rather abruptly, said good-bye and shut the door. Not in a brusque manner, just a final, don't bother me way.

Elaine wanted to walk around the back of the house but doubted that anyone would give her permission. There were some things she'd like to know; such as, did the two yards meet? Or was there a path between the properties? Was there a clear view of the Beaufort residence or mainly vegetation that allowed cover? What could be seen from the second and third floors? But all was a moot point if cameras weren't working. And she was at the mercy of the owner.

She walked to her car, backed out of the driveway and retraced her steps to return around the block to the mansion next to the Beaufort's. This house was equal in size, the same height but with an overgrown lot separating the structures. There was a For Sale sign on the lot and even though long and narrow, Elaine bet the price tag was well over a hundred thousand, probably closer to two.

Standing in the driveway, it was difficult to see what a camera might record—certainly nothing at ground level. But starting with the second story, depending on the quality of camera, the Beaufort house was in plain view—second story, third story and fourth. The widow's walk was directly across from this house's fourth floor. Maybe, just maybe … but what person would situate cameras to record their neighbors? Literally point cameras at them? Wasn't that a kind of, maybe illegal, voyeurism? And she'd be lucky to have them own up to it.

The woman who opened the door introduced herself as Nancy Hunt. Petite, blond ponytail and lilac crushed velvet jumpsuit over a purple sports bra. Had Elaine just interrupted a workout? At least there were no servants answering the door. Nancy appeared to be the owner.

"I really want to apologize for just stopping by like this but I'm representing the Beaufort's stepson, Rick Elliston." Elaine handed her a card. "We're just tying up loose ends and making certain that we haven't overlooked any possible source of evidence. It's still unknown whether Ms. Beaufort's fall was intended or simply an accident."

"Oh, I miss her so much. We belonged to the

Beachcomber's Turtle Preservation Club. She was great fun to be around. My husband and I were just shocked at what happened. I hope Rick and Hank are both well. But come in. I was just finishing a run—treadmill, way too hot still to run outside."

Elaine stepped into the foyer. It was difficult not to just stare at her surroundings.

The stairs in front of her reached two stories. It was a movie-set staircase taking little to imagine women in flowing ball gowns drifting down the polished wood steps. The entryway was marble and a chandelier just inside the door was magnificent—at least thirty glass-encased lights balanced on the ends of brass arms. Did most of the houses along the beach have such opulent furnishings? She recalled the glass artwork at the Beaufort house.

"Would you like something to drink? I was on the way to the kitchen for a bottle of water."

"No, thank you. I'll try to make this quick. Because of the close proximity of the houses, I was hoping you might have security cameras that would have caught something—movement around the grounds or drive? Perhaps, some activity on the widow's walk?"

"Oh, I wish I could be more helpful. My husband is the IT guy. We have a room of screens monitoring every corner of the house and grounds. But he doesn't always check them on a regular basis—he travels a lot. We were having problems with garbage being dumped and scattered. That proved to be a family of raccoons. We were able to have animal control capture them and rehome them inland. So, I'm not even sure which cameras were activated. He's out of town now, but I'll check with him when he returns. I'm so sorry I'm not being helpful."

Elaine thanked her and asked her to call if she remembered anything from that evening that she might have noticed, or if her husband found something captured by a camera. Even if the image was difficult to discern. Elaine asked that Nancy allow her to decide what was useful and what might not be. Nancy promised to do just that and reiterated how much she'd like to help.

* * *

The first thing she did when she got back to her office was call Rick. Twelve rings and no answer, plus the voicemail box was full. She knew what she wanted to offer but wasn't a hundred percent certain that it was the right thing to do. On a short-term basis, she wanted to literally bring Rick home for a couple nights—long enough to get some good food in him, clean him up, dress him in some of Jason's discarded gym-wear, and let him sleep undisturbed in a comfortable bed. Would Dan agree? That remained to be seen. But she couldn't imagine her loving husband to be anything but supportive. She had a feeling that she could count on him.

Chapter 12

Scare tactics. Dan changed the car's radio station to one of music without news breaks. Five days out there was supposed to be a hurricane forming in the Atlantic. Zena. Every news program opened and closed with an update. But five days? That was a long time to watch the spaghetti map of possible paths the storm might take, but already there were lines at gas stations and basic necessities were flying off the shelves at Publix.

Elaine had already devoted a corner of the pantry to four cases of water and had purchased two new flashlights. Did they need a generator? There one waiting for pickup at Lowes in Palm Coast. As Elaine said, if they didn't need it there was room in the garage to store it. And hadn't he seen three, twenty-four roll packages of toilet paper in the linen closet? But weren't they overreacting? Generators, toilet paper, water? Did they need all of that?

If St. Augustine was involved in the storm, it would be something new. The city was somewhat protected by the curve of the shoreline and was seldom a target for a direct hit. But ominous threats preceded this storm—unprecedented flooding, record high waves, winds of Level Four strength ... even if the storm just tucked in and followed the shoreline, damage could be catastrophic. Especially if it hit at high tide.

To be on the safe side, he called Maggie and insisted that she plan to evacuate to their townhouse. The three of them could hunker down together, and he wouldn't have to worry about her. She was now living in the RV and the winds alone would be threatening enough without the accompanying flooding. Mobiles were always sitting ducks. But she was a step ahead and had already prepared to move inland. She was having the RV driven back to Devil's Bend to be parked beside her house. The new occupants were from out-of-state and wouldn't be moving in until the first of next month. Other than possible high winds, she thought she'd be perfectly safe some forty miles inland.

Dan was more concerned about Hank and the two schooners—the newly renovated *Nomad*, and the tour cruiser, *Moonstruck* were both in St. Augustine at the moment but the *Nomad* was scheduled to deliver goods to the Bahamas as soon as possible. An agent for the Hilton chain had commissioned the hauler to bring building materials as far down as Harbour Island.

Dan guessed it could be a ten-hour trip from St. Augustine in good weather but with a hurricane threatening, who knew? Originally, the delivery had been planned for the weekend. Had storm warnings changed the itinerary? He probably needed to find out and offer his help, if needed.

He found Hank and Ron both at the wharf behind the marina. The ticket office was closed when he walked by, so he could assume that Maggie had taken off work a day or so to move her RV.

Dan wasn't sure what he'd expected but Hank was treating the impending storm as 'no big thing'—take precautions, but don't stress over it. Maybe that was the attitude one should take, but Dan was finding it difficult to keep the dire warnings of newscasters from overriding any calm. The Midwest had tornados and the warning was far less than five days. So, was this buildup and extended warning any better? He didn't think so. He'd almost prefer a tornado.

"Heard from UL&C this morning. We're good to go; your suggestions were in place and no new requests were made. I appreciate your help. Couldn't have gotten through the red tape without you."

"Just my job. I'm glad things worked out so quickly. So, what's the next move?"

"I've got cargo waiting at the Daytona marina that needs to be loaded and inspected. Zena has stalled out to the east of us and may fizzle—it's too early to tell but I'm tempted to keep to the original schedule. We'll load and take off tomorrow."

"I'm assuming the 'we' means you and Ron?"

"Yes. Under the circumstances, the plan now is for me to close up shop here and go with them. I think this trip calls for a seasoned crew even though Ron has a group of men he's crewed with before. Trip down takes a little over eight hours—depending on conditions. We should be able to make this a three-day round trip. Everything's in place at the hotel to unload and get us back out of there quickly. We'll be turned into a garbage scow for the trip back."

"Garbage scow? How so?"

"Need the weight, can't really safely bring her back empty. There's always garbage to be taken off the islands. And it makes the trip just that much more lucrative—coming and going."

"What about the *Moonstruck*? I see you've canceled tours for the next few days but would she be able to ride through a storm if Zena came early?"

"I think she'll be fine here. If I change my mind, I'll be back in time to make adjustments as needed. I'm counting on St. Augustine again being a safe destination during a storm. However, if Zena picks up intensity and comes this way along the shoreline, I may have to rethink whether I want to 'ride at anchor' or take the more desirable path of fastening the schooner to ground."

"Not sure I understand what that entails."

"Taking her out of water for one thing, and there may not be time for that. In a perfect situation, I should be able to down-rig—take sails and spars off and leave just the bare masts to face the wind. If I left her in the water, I'd secure her with at least five anchors. Both scenarios have drawbacks. Even though fastening her to ground is more stable, you take the chance that other boats may not have been properly secured and flying debris can rack up some real expensive damage quickly."

"When will you make your final decision?"

"The weather report this evening should be an indicator as to which plan might work best. And the rest is up to Zena. And need I say, women can be fickle."

* * *

Dan ordered another drink and listened to Elaine plead the case for having Rick live with them at least until the hurricane scare had passed. He wasn't going to say no, but his sixth sense was trying to tell him that this might not be such a good idea. But wasn't he letting his work with Hank get in the way of obviously doing the right humanitarian thing? Could offering a safe haven to a young man very much in need really interfere, even jeopardize, a client's business? He didn't know. It was a unique position to be in—with questions he'd never had to face before.

"I can't imagine him not having shelter—being on the streets during a hurricane."

"Elaine, I think the armory and several churches take in people who don't have any place to go."

"It's not the same. We can provide food—even hand off some of Jason's old clothing. He'd have privacy, a bath of his own. I think you'd have to admit that we're a cut above the armory. Dan, he needs human interaction, sympathy even. I hate to see a young person struggling without support."

"Ok, we'll give it a try. But he has to understand that it's not forever. We'll all get through this storm and then reassess. Sound fair?"

Elaine nodded. "There are so many reasons why I love you."

* * *

When she ran her plan for Rick past her boss, he surprised her. Leon had been working on a plan of his own.

"It's not much but I'd like to offer Rick a job as office courier—maybe three days a week to get started. Right now, I have Ginny running around in her spare time and it doesn't work to take her away from the office. I have my son's Yamaha scooter in the garage that I could give to him. The only catch would be I'd like him back in school— at least part-time at the start of the spring semester. What do you think? Will he be interested?"

"He'd be foolish not to be."

"I'll pay for his tuition and there will be a salary. He knows the area and cleaned up he makes a nice appearance, but I'm thinking of coming up with a uniform of sorts. Even if it's just a cap with a logo, it's one more way to advertise Stanley and Stanley. If he says yes, we'll start him as soon as possible. I definitely want him on board after this weather scare passes."

"I love your plan. It's perfect. Rick needs something to take his mind off of what's happened this last month."

"Keep him safe through the storm—if we have one. I have an apartment unit coming available on the first that might work but we'll see. He needs to agree to these other offers first."

"I'm sure he'll be appreciative of what you're offering."

"I hope you're right. I'll have the scooter here in the morning. Here's the key to the ignition. If he has any questions, have him call. His mother and my late wife were inseparable. I know my helping is what Marilyn would have wanted. She always worried about Hank being too tough on the kid. Not being compassionate. It was always easier for Hannah to look the other way and not rock the boat. I'm glad to step in where I'm needed."

* * *

Finding Rick proved to be more of a problem than Elaine had anticipated. She checked a group in the park and one that hung out as far from town as the Outlet Mall. People knew who she was looking for, but no sign of Rick until one man volunteered that several people were working with the county to set up a temporary storm shelter at the armory. He might be there.

But by the time Elaine was back downtown on San Marco Avenue, cots were in place, chairs and tables folded and leaning against the wall. Local churches were providing blankets, and those would be delivered later. All was in order and just waiting on what the weather would do. Those helping had been dropped off at the soup kitchen on Riberia Street. Elaine got back in her car and drove back across town.

Rick was carrying two large plastic bags of garbage to the alley behind the warehouse used to feed the homeless when Elaine pulled up.

"Hi." He immediately dropped both bags in a dumpster and walked over. Elaine thought he honestly looked better than he had in a week.

"Do you have a minute to talk?"

"Yeah, but just a minute. I've promised to wash dishes."

Elaine didn't even get out of the car, just quickly ran through the offers by first inviting him to stay with her and Dan at the townhouse during the storm; then, she laid out the opportunities being offered by Leon Stanley … and waited. At first, Rick looked like he was in shock.

"Is this for real? I mean, even a scooter?"

"Absolutely."

"Wow. I can't say yes fast enough. Can you tell Leon? And thanks to you, too. This is great." He leaned in the car window and squeezed her arm. "This is the best thing to happen to me in a long time."

Elaine didn't need him to say anything else to know her decision had been the right one and that Leon's was truly a life-saver. She asked him to meet her at the office in the morning and they could go over particulars. In the meantime, she'd get fresh sheets on the daybed in the office and do some grocery shopping.

* * *

Rick was waiting in the parking lot behind Stanley and Stanley at seven-thirty the next morning. Now that's excitement, Elaine thought. And then she saw it. Tucked up against the building was a red scooter—not just any one, this model looked like a mini motorcycle. Plush upholstery on the driver's seat and backrest, large saddlebags with the Stanley and Stanley logo—now, how had he gotten that done so quickly? And finally, a large wire basket directly behind the driver with a locking cover. What kid wouldn't be thrilled? Even one who was twenty-two.

"Wow. That bike is way lit. I wonder when Leon will let me have it."

She was pretty sure that 'lit' was the new 'cool', but the look on his face said it all. Was it possible to fall in love at first sight with a scooter?

"I just happen to have a key here that should make it yours right away. Get your stuff together and meet me at the townhouse at four. Plan on dinner with us." Elaine stood back and watched Rick start the scooter, then after two turns around the parking lot, wave and head down the drive to the street. This was such a great, fresh start, she could only hope he didn't blow it. Thank God he'd be able to keep the scooter garaged at night and not run the risk of it being stolen.

Chapter 13

Dan was running late but had called ahead and told them to eat without him. There was a neat French bakery on Granada and he'd pick up dessert on his way back. Thanks to his job and now hers, time together was limited. Dinner was burgers and a veggie medley all on the grill. Originally, the suggested dinner had been a couple buckets of oysters from the Commander's Shellfish Camp on A1A, but Rick ever so politely turned up his nose. She needed to think adult-kid menus for the next couple weeks. But he was helpful—filled water glasses, set out condiments, kept an eye on the burgers.

She'd talked him into a shower, laid out jeans and a pullover sweater from the slightly worn but definitely outgrown stash that Jason had left. Elaine had luckily been lax in taking them to Goodwill. Lastly, she insisted that he take an advance on his salary—twenty dollars from her—to get a haircut in the morning. Cleaned up, he really did make a nice appearance. Leon had been right to hire him on as a courier. It was changing his life.

The highlight of the evening was Dan taking the scooter for a run down the block and then helping Rick move boxes to make a corner for it in the garage. Finally, she had Dan all to herself, dessert on the deck while Rick closed himself in the office to watch TV.

"I have to hand it to your boss, the courier job was a great idea."

"And it isn't just a handout. The firm does enough business to warrant someone in charge of everything from shipping and receiving to running errands. Rick will be kept busy. And he's agreed to getting back into school second semester."

"Do you think he's gotten past wanting to blame Hank for his mother's death?"

"He hasn't mentioned it recently, and I'm not going to bring it up. I haven't heard anything from the Beaufort's neighbors. I imagine that's a dead end, so, the less said, the better."

"If Hank and Ron get away tomorrow on the *Nomad*, I'll help them secure the *Moonstruck* when they return. If the storm continues on its present track, we could be in for a rough time. I think they are counting on finding a safe harbor for the *Nomad*—something south of here on the way back from the Bahamas, maybe Daytona or closer to St. Augustine at Palm Coast. That would leave him with only the one schooner to try and stormproof when he gets here. I still don't know if he's going to want to batten her down on land or leave her at anchor. So far, the storm's trajectory is to follow the coastline, not actually cross it. The storm's eye will travel parallel to the coast. There's lots of possibilities and unfortunately decisions may have to be made last minute. Whatever the outcome, I've signed on as crew."

"Sounds dangerous."

"I can think of things I'd rather be doing. Hard to say now; it's tough to second-guess a storm that's threatening to become a Cat-3. In fact, I'm thinking of bringing Maggie and Simon up here. The RV's probably safe but I wouldn't have anything to worry about if they were with us."

"I think that's a great idea. Call your mother. I could run down and pick them up in the morning."

* * *

But Maggie opted to drive her own car, bringing Simon and his very own orthopedic dog bed, plus his freeze-dried meals and treats. The dog was spoiled, Elaine decided. Still, it was fun to have a full house.

Rick graciously insisted that Maggie take the office turned guest room and have some privacy. He insisted that the living room couch was perfect. Simon considered the couch his go-to for daytime naps but Rick seemed to not mind. Three times a day Rick took Simon to the ocean for a run, even coming home at noon to do so. The dog was in heaven. Had Rick ever had a dog? A pet of any kind? He was making up for it now and Simon was loving it.

"When I mentioned that I was riding out the storm with you and Dan, Sue Ellen, the woman who runs the corporate office downtown, asked if I could help her. She didn't want to close down the office until she absolutely had to, but she wanted to have time to get over to the panhandle to be with her family during the storm. I'm glad to help. It'll only be for a couple days. I was going to take Simon with me to the office, but I don't want to separate him from his newfound friend. I swear if he were small enough to fit into that basket on the scooter, he'd be going everywhere with Rick."

"Every kid should have a dog." Elaine recalled that there was always a pet of some kind when Jason was growing up.

Hank had called Maggie to say he was safe. The *Nomad* was on schedule to offload cargo and take on the load of garbage in preparation for coming back. In the meantime he had business to attend to. No, he couldn't say more about it now. It needed to be kept a secret. At the moment he was thinking of the *Moonstruck*. He would let her know if he decided to seek out a safe port and move the ship from St. Augustine. The plan to take the *Moonstruck* inland was still in place and he was counting on Dan to help. In seventy-two hours the storm should have settled into its final path and preparations needed to be in place.

Chapter 14

The corporate office of H&H Enterprises on San Marco Street was an older building that housed a restaurant with patio seating downstairs and three small offices upstairs. H&H Enterprises shared a floor with a law office and a CPA who apparently was only there during tax season. Maggie loved that part of St. Augustine, or the ancient city as it was called.

The parking garage was only a couple blocks away and good restaurants surrounded her. She met with Sue Ellen in the morning, before the woman took off for Pensacola. Her family was thrilled that she was getting out of harm's way and would entirely miss the storm. There were several stacks of papers that needed to be scanned, placed in electronic folders, and the originals manually filed in office cabinets. Not difficult work, just redundant and time consuming.

A quick look through one of the piles revealed invoices, records, and appraisals concerning everything from the latest schooner's purchase to its repairs, and even Hank's house. It was going to be necessary to separate these and file like-paperwork in the same folder. She had no idea how anyone could find anything now. But didn't Sue Ellen say that these were all papers that Hank had kept at home?

Now, with the house on the market, he needed to clear that office, empty the safe, and have important papers safely in one place. Sue Ellen apologized profusely for leaving Maggie with such a mess but it had just been dumped on her and she hadn't had the time to organize it. She insisted on Maggie allowing her to buy lunch.

Finally, peace and quiet. Maggie separated invoices and then divided them into piles according to subject matter. One pile set aside for miscellany contained costs incurred by Hannah's death—interment and celebration of life— alongside an invoice for a few thousand dollars for rather expensive dental work which included two implants for Rick.

But the record that stood out was literally written on a bar napkin—an IOU from Hank to Leon Stanley for two million dollars. The transaction was already almost three months old. The fact that it was stapled to the title for the *Moonstruck* made her wonder if the ship had been used as collateral. But more importantly, would an agreement on a bar napkin really hold up if contested? It sounded like something out of the movies.

The other rather startling fact that unfolded as she worked through the thick stack of papers that pertained to Hank's home was the fact that it was mortgaged to the hilt. It appeared that he had used it as his private bank. Selling it would only allow him to wipe the slate clean and not owe the bank that held the deed. He had been given an extension in lieu of foreclosure by putting it on the market after falling behind in mortgage payments. It was a do-or-die situation—he had to sell the house or risk hefty penalties. And he would be forfeiting a sizeable amount of equity.

It was dawning on Maggie that she probably wasn't supposed to see any of this. Had he even gone over what he was bringing to the office before he left the papers for Sue Ellen to file? Maggie wasn't sure why she felt this was important, but she quickly got out her phone and took photos of any document showing something owed or borrowed. It seemed like everything he owned had a lien against it. But why the need for so much money? It appeared that the insurance company would be paying Hank some two million over Hannah's death and the house was on the market for over four million, which would put him straight with the bank possibly allowing him to borrow against the business; and, of course, the napkin loan.

If that was for real, it was evidence of another two million from Leon Stanley. She hadn't found evidence of any luxurious purchases—condos, yachts, cars—nothing stood out. And hadn't he sent some proposal to her own investment broker? This was frightening. Where was all the money going?

And then she found the answer. A thick folder on the bottom of the stack was marked, 'Boatarama'. She scanned the first page, a business proposal including a list of already committed investors in a Limited Liability Company.

Based on the highly successful Cargurus, Carvana, and CarMax companies that sold and delivered cars via online, Boatarama would do the same with boats.

Was this what Hank had hinted that he might be working on? The 'something' that needed to be kept a secret?

Touted in an article from *Marine Life*, bringing e-commerce to the world of boating was a first of its kind and way overdue. According to the article, the number of marine enthusiasts had simply exploded this past year—and caught a market off guard. The opportunity for investors seemed over the top. Maggie kept reminding herself that if something seemed too good to be true, it probably was.

Still, the information contained in the folder in front of her extolled the praises of this new addition to the marine world and hinted at a fortune to be made. Hank could become very, very rich. Was United Life &Casualty a part of this plan? Insurance was always necessary to conglomerates of this type. She'd remember to ask Dan. It was a lot to think about.

She finished scanning all the documents and made a fresh pot of coffee before beginning to file them. Some of the documents belonged in the safe. A quick call to Sue Ellen, explaining why she needed access, and the combination was hers after she promised not to write it down and to 'forget' it when she no longer needed to put anything into the safe.

Built into the wall, the safe was an older model with a rotary dial instead of electronically programed numerical buttons to push. Signage on the door's inside panel listed fire protection as up to, but not exceeding, one hour. The inside was approximately two feet deep by two feet across divided into three shelves from a height of four feet. The top shelf was full to within an inch of the edge with packets of thousands of dollars, each made up of one-hundred-dollar bills and banded with a bright blue strip of paper secured with a narrow piece of tape. She gingerly picked up the nearest packet and counted its contents—thirty, one-hundred-dollar bills and it appeared that some of the packets were thicker in size. She was looking at a lot of money. But what was it doing in the safe? Where had it come from?

Did keeping such an amount of cash on hand ever make sense, even if one had a crew to pay or cargo to transport? This shelf of money left questions, knowing Hank's mortgage woes and the needs of the new corporation. Maybe this money was slated to be applied to the new project. But cash? Weren't most money transactions done electronically? Bank transfers or computer withdrawals? Who would carry this much cash around and not put it in a bank?

And Maggie wasn't sure she agreed with Hank's priorities. She thought of Rick and the stories Elaine had shared—repossessed car, withholding rent money—basically kicking the kid out on the streets. Not a picture of a nurturing, loving parent even if he was the stepfather.

There were three revolvers on the floor of the safe along with two boxes of spare ammunition but the middle two shelves were empty. She started there first, separating folders of private documents from business ones and placing them in neat stacks, securely closing the safe when all were inside. Each bundle was bound by a rubber band, and a brief note listing contents was stapled to the top folder. Finally, she was finished. She felt relieved. That wasn't the kind of information that anyone would want circulating.

And it made her give some thought to her relationship with the man. The incident with Elaine had put a check on her feelings. And hadn't she recently suspected that he was back on Match.com? She would remain a friend but there wouldn't be any benefits, not any more. She'd have her broker check out Boatarama, but maybe it would be wiser to just walk away now? She had just gotten up to get another creamer when the office door opened.

"Sue Ellen?"

"She's not here. I'm Maggie. Can I help you?" Maggie walked to the counter that separated the room into two parts, and kept just anyone from walking back to one of the two desks. Hank had said he used the office for interviews, storage—there was even a back room—and deliveries that couldn't be left at the ticket office. Was this man leaving something?

"Yeah, I'm here to pick up the package."

Fingers staccato-tapped nervously on the counter as he looked around the room. He was tall and lean—wiry better described him. Maggie noted the deeply tanned arms, this was not a man who worked in an office. Grizzled hair and a stubble of a beard aged him probably beyond actual chronological years. He was maybe in his forties, and looked late fifties. Still, he was handsome in an outdoorsy sort of way. But it was his voice that caught her attention—that beautiful lyrical cadence that belied a home in the islands. She could listen to him all day.

"I'm not aware of any package. I'm just filling in for a couple days. Sue Ellen didn't mention anything would be picked up."

"Sounds just like Hank. Stiff me for wages anytime he can. How do you like working for a real SOB?"

Maggie chose to ignore the insult to Hank. "Let me check and see if there's an envelope in the back. What was your name?"

"Ian Fredericks. Here's an invoice if that will help." He handed her a creased paper that indicated wages of two thousand five hundred dollars were due and owing. A description of the work and the date completed were stated briefly and both Ian and Hank had signed what was basically a work order with parts and labor itemized.

Pelican Electric, Palatka, Florida. Apparently, Mr. Fredericks was an electrician and had done work on the *Moonstruck*. She didn't doubt that it was an honest request. When a look around the back room and the desk drawers of the lone piece of furniture there proved fruitless, she checked the desks in front before calling Sue Ellen, only to be forced to leave a voicemail.

"I'm sorry. Is there a way to reach you if I hear from Sue Ellen?"

"Yeah, use this number." He scribbled a number on a post-it note that was on the counter next to the office phone. "Depending on the storm, I'll either be around here or at a marina down south. Leave a message if you miss me."

"Let me scan the invoice; I'll email a copy to Mr. Beaufort as a reminder."

She scanned the document into the computer, then made a paper copy for the work-related files. "Here you are. I'll call if I have any information. I expect Mr. Beaufort back in a couple days." She handed the original invoice back. "Do you live in the area?"

"Sometimes." He folded the paper and put it into a shirt pocket. "Depends on where the company wants to send me." He picked up his baseball cap from the counter and pulled the cap's bill low on his forehead before walking out the door.

No mention of thank you, I appreciate your help; he just left, and Maggie was glad he did. There was something about him. Maggie walked to the window and watched him go down the steps along the side of the building and walk up the street. Unsettling. That was the best word to describe him. She moved to lock the door, something she should have done when she first got there. She'd bring Simon tomorrow.

* * *

The evening was uneventful; it was just the three of them. Rick was out, said he might go to the movies. The discussion over the dinner table centered on the storm. Elaine had left the TV at the end of the kitchen counter on with the sound turned down, and Maggie found it difficult not to watch. She had never been in a hurricane before and it appeared that Zena was intent on gaining strength and rolling up the coast. Warmer coastal waters assured high winds and dangerous rip tides. But the scary part was the possibility of flooding. She realized that she was feeling anxious. It had been a good idea not to ride out the storm alone. Even inland wind and rain could inflict untold damage.

Everyone seemed to have a job in preparation for what might happen. Dan had volunteered to fill sandbags with the local fire department and help hand them out. He said the lines of cars after lunch stretched around the block. Elaine joined the phone bank sponsored by the county and had spent the day at the armory sharing advice on storm preparedness and answering questions.

Maggie marveled at the fact that Elaine seemed to step right up and do all the right things. She had added a checklist to the county's website, including a list of do's and don'ts hoping the gravity of the situation would be taken seriously and that people would adhere to curfews, and other rules in place within the county. Reaching out online was a great way to get attention. Maggie was proud of her daughter-in-law.

But she was secretly relieved that even with all the volunteering, preparing the townhouse hadn't been forgotten. Dan seemed to have a handle on how to make it storm resistant and had spent the late afternoon putting everything in place. He'd ordered two-layer, corrugated plastic window inserts that upped glass resistance by two hundred percent. Supposedly. The inserts hadn't been tested by one-hundred-plus mile an hour winds. With the front windows facing east, he shared that he was afraid that they might be during this storm. Maggie tried not to think about consequences if the glass failed. She had already lost her appetite for Elaine's pot roast.

She was letting all this talk of possible impending doom override any calm, rational side that she used to have. On top of everything else, she was worrying about the *Moonstruck*. Hank should be back by tomorrow afternoon and he would begin preparing the *Moonstruck* to ride out the storm. She was somewhat relieved to know that Dan was going to help him. When she questioned him, Dan still didn't know if the ship would be anchored at the marina or brought inland. He relied on Hank to know the best way to keep her safe.

Waiting for the storm to hit was nerve-wracking. Elaine offered her a glass of Merlot and Maggie found herself wishing it was something stronger. Wasn't this a whiskey moment? She helped with dishes and then excused herself to retire for the night. But she wasn't sleepy. She watched some television in the office—turned back into a guest room, now her bedroom—before setting her phone alarm for seven-thirty and going to bed.

Chapter 15

Maggie opened the blinds on the windows in the office. The day was gray, and seven-thirty seemed especially early, even though Dan and Elaine were already out the door, and Rick was fast asleep on the couch. But she hadn't slept well—new place, new noises, and Simon had divided his time between trying to squirm onto the couch to sleep with Rick and scratching at the office door to join her.

Around two o'clock, she had dragged Simon's orthopedic foam bed into the hallway and sternly commanded him to stay there before firmly closing the office door and getting back into bed herself. It was always amazing what that dog seemed to understand, and he didn't bother her again.

When she finally got dressed and made it out to the

kitchen to start coffee, Rick and Simon were just leaving to go for a run on the beach. Kids and dogs were made for each other. She hoped the run wouldn't be long; she needed to be at the office before nine. She turned on the weather channel and waited for the coffee to finish brewing while she viewed with some relief the strings of brightly colored spaghetti on the weather map. At least they seemed to be in the exact same position that they had been in the night before. There was the US string almost in line with the European model. Still looked ominous, but there were no surprises.

Rick and Simon both showed up ravenous. Maggie fleetingly thought how simple it would be if they both could eat perfectly proportioned, calorie enriched, vitamin and mineral enhanced kibble. Just open a bag and scoop it out. Instead, six eggs, sausage, minced bell pepper and onion went into two fluffy omelets, toast on the side and a pitcher of juice on the table. Even Simon absolutely inhaled his scrambled egg treat.

"Any chance you could give me a ride into town, drop me off at Stanley and Stanley? I missed getting a ride in with Elaine and Dan. I promised to help set up the shipping and receiving area today. Leon's letting me use the area as my office once I get it cleared and organized. The wind isn't bad now but I don't trust it not to get a lot worse by the end of the day. Not exactly scooter-riding weather."

"Not a problem. I'd planned to take Simon in with me. Just meet me back at the office by four. Maybe you could take Simon for a walk before we come home."

"Sure. That'd be great."

* * *

Finally, Rick had been deposited at the law firm; she'd purchased a cup of her favorite cold brew at Dunkin', her car was in the parking garage, and now she was unlocking the office door. Sometime in the middle of the night between hassling with Simon and then trying to go back to sleep, she remembered that she had left the copy of the invoice from Ian Fredericks on the copy tray of the machine, and it really needed to be added to the house folder already in the safe. Was there anything else that she'd overlooked?

A lack of sleep made her feel sluggish. Her extra-large, Dunkin' Donuts vanilla flavored cold brew was doing its best to help her wake up but not exactly getting the job done. She didn't want to miss anything; she wanted to leave the office like she'd found it. Sue Ellen would be back on Friday, depending on what the storm did, and everything needed to be in order.

She picked up the invoice and walked to the safe. Luckily memorizing six numbers wasn't a problem. She certainly hadn't had to write the combination down, but when the safe's door swung open, she couldn't stifle a gasp. The entire top shelf that just yesterday had been filled to capacity with bundles of one-hundred-dollar bills was empty. Absolutely cleaned out. In addition, one of the revolvers was missing.

It appeared that someone had pulled out the stacks of receipts and personal papers that she had organized, but not seeing anything of interest just haphazardly thrust them back onto the second shelf. She found the house's account folder, added the Fredericks invoice, separated the stacks by category once again, closed the safe's door, and spun the dial.

What should she do? There was no sign of a break-in. Someone who entered the office had a key *and* knew the combination to the safe. Other than Sue Ellen and Hank, who would that be? It wasn't as if she could report it. When asked what was missing, what would she say? Money, but how much? She had no idea. A gun, but what kind? Again, guns weren't her thing. This was hopeless, and she had been left in charge. She felt sick to her stomach and suddenly the overly sweet coffee was making it worse.

Had they been burgled? She looked around. The tidiness of the office made that seem far-fetched. Nothing was out of place. So, why did having a lot of money on hand seem to indicate something criminal? Probably because most people used banks.

Maybe he did have salaries to pay, cargo to purchase, or space to rent; but would you do that without a paper trail? In business, didn't you need proof of various transactions? Businesses paid taxes; accountants demanded accountability. Of course, no honest businessman would disperse funds without a way to trace where they went. So, what legitimate reasons would there be for someone to have that amount on hand?

There had to have been upwards of fifty thousand dollars on that shelf. Maybe more. Now, it was gone. She realized her hands were shaking. Mentally she retraced her steps from the day before. She'd locked the safe, and locked the front door behind her when she left. She was positive of that. Once again, she assured herself that they had not been burgled. This had been an inside job. Would she be blamed?

She walked to the bathroom—it might be a small office but, at least, it had its own amenities—and dumped what was left of her coffee and then scrubbed out the sink. She was too upset and every swallow of the sticky-sweet liquid threatened to not stay down. In addition, the weather was becoming an issue. The wind was picking up and the rattling of the front windows was unsettling. Wasn't the storm still at least forty-eight hours away? That is, if you could trust the weathermen.

"Anybody home?" She didn't know what was the loudest, the door blowing shut or Simon's explosive barking. Luckily, he was behind the counter.

"Hank?" Maggie stepped back into the main room just as Hank walked around the end of the counter. "Great to see you back. Did the *Nomad* have a good trip?" She shushed Simon but left a hand on his collar.

"A perfect run. The guys in the shop did a bang-up job on the hauler. Handles like a dream. I think those Hilton folks must have been shocked to see their delivery made on time. Not everyone would defy nature and make a trip that close to a storm coming in. But how does that saying go? 'A smooth sea never made a skillful sailor'? A challenge is good for a sailor now and then. Keeps everyone on his toes."

"Sounds scary. But I'm glad the trip was successful."

"I see you've got your four-legged protection. Where's Sue Ellen? You pulling double-duty?"

"She wanted to be with family over in Pensacola during the storm. I'm only here for a couple days."

"Thanks for stepping in. Anything exciting happen?" Hank held out a hand and let Simon sniff.

"Actually, yes." She had to tell him, own up to being in the safe and seeing the money gone. She turned to face him. "Sue Ellen had left the paperwork that you brought in from home for me to sort, scan, and file and to put the originals in the safe. She shared the combination but you wouldn't hurt my feelings if you changed it. In fact, I think you should." She paused, "Hank, when I put the folders in the safe yesterday, there was money on the top shelf. This morning when I went to add an invoice that had been left out, the money was gone."

Hank paused. "Oh baby, I should have left you a note, but I had no idea that you had access or were even here. Sue Ellen's used to my coming and going at odd hours. I got back into town around midnight and needed to pay off the crew at the Daytona marina, settle up on a few repairs and pay for a week's rent. Took them half the night but they did a hell of a job cleaning up the *Nomad*. Got rid of the load of garbage and scrubbed everything down. I drove on up here and looted my own safe."

"Thank God. I've been so worried." She didn't mention the gun.

"By the way, kiddo, I got a chance to look at the folders. That was a lot of work. Here I was thinking that Sue Ellen would be wanting a raise."

She laughed. "She might need one, but I didn't mind doing a little organizing."

"Job well done. Let me buy you a drink after work. I've got about a half day's running around to do but maybe two-thirty or three? Will he be ok here by himself?" He pointed at Simon.

"I'll walk him at lunch and he'll be fine."

* * *

She went back and forth a couple times between offices

stocking up the ticket office with supplies such as an extra stapler, colored pens, extra copy machine paper; then took the time to sync the computer there with the one at the main office by downloading matching software.

Simon was thrilled—car-riding was his favorite thing to do, and she let him hang his head out the window. Always a much relished plus. But even keeping busy, she found it difficult not to wonder about all that cash.

Was it possible she was overreacting? Questioning intentions when there really was nothing to make her suspect wrongdoing? Hank had explained everything. Had she really totally lost trust in him? And did she really know how the shipping business was run? The situation might be perfectly normal. She had no way of knowing.

Still, taking thousands of dollars out of a safe in the middle of the night didn't seem normal. Was he really making payments on the *Nomad*'s mooring at that hour, or even early this morning? There didn't seem to be any corresponding paperwork to support any of his claims. She hadn't run across one bill of lading, or receipt of goods loaded for this recent trip. She sighed. She needed to let go; it really wasn't her business. And, thank God, he wasn't blaming her for any possible wrongdoing.

Hank called a little after two to beg off getting a drink that afternoon. He had changed his mind about how he wanted to safeguard the *Moonstruck*. He and Dan were going to take her up the Intracoastal waterway north to the St. Johns River and travel south until they found safe anchorage somewhere along the ICW. He had a place in mind but didn't know if that was going to be available for certain. He had some calls to make before taking off and once moored, of course, the work would begin.

She understood completely and felt a little relieved. There was no doubt that the romance had cooled. Wasn't she old enough to trust her gut? And her gut seemed to be bombarding her with red flags—from his stepson calling him a murderer, to his less than professional treatment of Elaine.

She was in the middle of mopping the bathroom floor, giving into her overly fastidious self, when the phone rang. It was startling. The thing was more of a fixture than an actual piece of useable equipment or at least seemed that way until now.

"H&H Enterprises. How may I help you?"

"I'm the assistant manager of the Hilton hotel at Deadman's Reef, Grand Bahama Island. We were told to be expecting a load of building materials that should have been here yesterday at the latest. Do you know if Mr. Beaufort decided not to make the trip at this time? With the impending storm, I, frankly, didn't expect him to risk it. But I'm wondering if the delivery has been rescheduled?"

Maggie's heart pounded. She took a deep breath. She had to say something …

"I'm just sitting in for the office manager and don't have answers for you. Mr. Beaufort is not here at the moment, but I'll leave a message for him."

"I'm certain that communication got screwed up somehow. Everyone gets a little crazy during hurricane season. Tell Mr. Beaufort to call me when he has a chance."

Maggie took down the man's name and direct number along with his cell and offered her apologies before hanging up. Then she just stood there. Who was the crazy one? Had she misunderstood that the cargo run to the Bahamas to deliver building goods to a Hilton hotel had been successful?

Granted, Deadman's Reef didn't ring a bell and she hadn't known exactly where the *Nomad* was going, but it had been loaded at the Daytona Marina—or, at least, she thought it had—and it was going to a Hilton in the Bahamas. Again, hearsay, no proof. She picked up the phone and dialed Hank's cell but it went to voice mail. She left a brief message to call the hotel manager at the Deadman's Reef Hilton hotel, and included his phone number.

Then, just to make doubly sure Hank would act on the message, she pulled a piece of paper out of the copier and wrote a detailed note as to why the man had called and taped it to the front of the safe—if he came back to the office, he'd see it. And then, she called Elaine.

"What are my chances that you'd have time to talk if I closed up here in another half hour and came over to your office?"

"I'd say really good. It's been slow, which is to be expected. Lots of appointments have canceled for the partners and I'm just helping Rick where I can. Come on over."

Chapter 16

Maggie pulled into the parking lot behind Stanley and Stanley to find that she pretty much had her choice of spots. There was Elaine's car and a couple that probably belonged to partners, a delivery truck, and a single car in one of two handicapped slots. The town was battening down. Elaine met her at the door to her office and after a quick hug pointed to the couch.

"Make yourself comfortable. I promise I won't be long. Since we're on our own tonight, I'll make sure Rick has money for his dinner and the two of us can share some oysters at the Commander's Shellfish Camp. Sound good?"

"Sounds perfect. We haven't had a girls' night out in forever."

"I have some follow-up phone calls to make. Ginny went

home sick. The stress is getting to everyone. I promised to reschedule several appointments for her, clearing the rest of this week because of the storm. Shouldn't take over a half hour, then we're out of here."

"Tell me where shipping and receiving is, and I'll take Simon over to see Rick."

"Down the hall and to your right."

The minute Maggie knocked on the door and turned the knob, Simon pushed it open and rushed toward Rick. Simon was absolutely beside himself to see his new friend, but Maggie wasn't sure who was happiest. Rick was down on his knees hugging the big dog and getting some pretty slobbery kisses in return.

"Why don't I take Simon back to the house with me when I leave? I mean, if you're with Elaine, maybe I could take your car? I'll get a couple burgers on the way home—does he like McDonalds? Or Culvers?"

"Good idea. Here are the keys. I don't think he has a preference as to burgers." Maggie was waiting for Rick to laugh but realized that he was deadly serious. He honestly wanted to satisfy the dog. "Go with what's closest on the way to the townhouse."

"Will do. Right now, I think I'll give him a couple turns around the parking lot, maybe play a little fetch. Some kid left his toy football here the other day." He reached in a desk drawer and held up a rubber football for Simon to see. "Look what I have. Want to play fetch? That'll be fun, won't it, boy?" Simon was barely containing his excitement, bouncing up and down in place and making little yelping sounds.

"Great idea. He's been cooped up for most of the day." Rick shut down his computer, took Simon's leash from Maggie, clipped it in place, and they were off. It was amazing to see how happy Simon was; he even carried the rubber ball in his mouth as they headed toward the door. Maggie was feeling a little neglected as she walked back to Elaine's office like she hadn't been chosen first for games at recess, passed over for a kid with a rubber football.

"I'll be finished here in fifteen minutes—just a couple more calls. Don't let me forget to turn off the coffee maker and do a quick clean-up in the conference room before we take off."

"I'll do that. Just finish your work here."

* * *

The restaurant wasn't crowded at four-thirty and they chose a table in the back along the windows looking out over the wrap-around deck. Two dry whites and a bucket of oysters each; this was the good life.

"Now, tell me what's going on. You sounded a little anxious on the phone. Are you having problems at Hank's office?"

"Yes, and no." Maggie proceeded to tell Elaine first about the money and Hank's explanation for it disappearing out of the safe, and then shared the call from a man at a Hilton in the Bahamas who said his paid-for cargo hadn't been delivered as promised. And Hank had raved about how well the *Nomad* had done on its maiden run. Who was lying?

Elaine was left shaking her head. "That's odd—all of it. A pile of cash in a safe? To be paid out as part of your business? No one does business by the seat of their pants—not anymore, at least. No one can afford to. Even handshake policy doesn't hold up in court. Today, everyone is lawsuit-crazy. You have to have a paper trail; prove your every move. And then the delivery they've talked about for days, maybe longer, didn't happen? How can you load a hauler with building supplies and then what? Leave them sitting somewhere? Have you talked with Hank? Asked him to clarify what happened to the Bahamas delivery?"

"No. I called his cell but missed him. I left a message but suppose I should try again. To be honest I'm sure he'll have a plausible sounding excuse, but I'm beginning not to trust the man. And that's just for starters."

"Let me do some research. I have programs, software, to trace just about anyone I'm curious about. It'll give me good practice. I'd thought of seeing if Ron Carter had anything in his background that might be of interest. Didn't he go with Hank to the Bahamas?"

"Yeah, as far as I know, it was just the two of them. No, I take that back. I think the Ron person had some mates with him. If I remember correctly, he's been partners with Hank for a year or so. It might be interesting to find out about him."

"My sentiments exactly."

"I'm still having problems trying to rationalize Hank's treatment of Rick. On any level, it's absolutely unacceptable. By the way, how's Rick doing? The shipping and receiving area looks great. Did he put all those shelves in himself? I saw tape dispensers, scales, work tables, a computer all within easy reach. The area looks ready to go. He's done a good job."

"He really has and thanks to Simon, he's exercising and just in general, coming out of his funk and being a real contributing member of Stanley and Stanley. I overheard

Leon congratulating him on his work."

"Have you given up on proving foul play in Hannah Beaufort's death? I guess my question is, has Rick moved on from wanting to implicate his stepfather?"

"I all but have, and I think so has Rick. At least, he hasn't mentioned anything recently. My last hope of any concrete evidence turning up depended on the neighbors and the long shot that one of the nearest houses might have a camera that picked up something. One man's cameras weren't working and a woman who lives to the south of the Beaufort's was going to check with her husband when he got back into town. But I haven't heard anything. I'm hoping Rick has decided to let it drop. A job and a scooter seem to have helped his state of mind immensely."

"Do you know when Dan and Hank are taking off on the *Moonstruck*?"

"I thought this afternoon, but I'm waiting on a call from Dan. This will be dinner." One bucket of oysters had already disappeared. "There's some mac an' cheese and ham, so Rick won't starve if he gets the munchies later. A pitcher of margaritas and a movie might be on the agenda for the two of us. How does that sound?"

"Really good." And Maggie meant it. She was just a little tired of being tied to the office. It would be good to think about something else for a change instead of disappearing money, missed shipments, and people demanding to get paid. An evening of just being with family would be a relief—if one could relax in the face of a storm.

"Then it's a go. I'll have to pick up Simon at the office and give Rick a ride home."

"Oh, I wasn't thinking; I should have mentioned Rick is going to take my car and stop to get a couple burgers for the two of them on the way home. But text him, mac and cheese might sound better than McDonald's."

"Are you ok with Rick taking your car? He was wise not to ride the scooter to work. I don't like the way the wind is picking up."

"Not a problem; I trust him."

Chapter 17

Unless a person had a map of the state of Florida in front of him, it was difficult to even imagine the number of waterways that crisscrossed the peninsula. Rivers like the Apalachicola, the Suwannee, the St. Johns, not to mention the lakes or the Intracoastal. It was truly a water wonderland—whether you had a bass boat, a yacht, or a jet-ski.

Dan didn't know for certain where Hank had decided to take the *Moonstruck* to ride out the storm, he only knew the plan was for Ron to meet them at the final destination, help strip the schooner's deck, and then bring them back to St. Augustine. He was looking forward to helping and, supposedly with the three of them, the work would go quickly. Even then, they would barely get home before the brunt of the storm would hit if it followed the most recent predictions.

Tomorrow would mark one day out from the hurricane traveling along the coast, possibly touching land. He knew that up-to-the-minute weather reports were a necessity and would be the final decision-maker as to where Hank and his crew ended up. Time was already oozing away and wasn't any longer on their side.

Ron and Hank were already on board when Dan reached the gangplank. Dan knew a few things about the schooner; the *Moonstruck* was a gaff-rigged, topsail ship with twenty-four hundred square feet of sail area. They would be taking sails and spars off leaving bare masts to face the wind. Still, she would be vulnerable. And whether or not Hank would have a schooner in good shape to bring back to St. Augustine after the storm depended upon decisions made in advance. There was no room for error; wind and flooding could wreak havoc. Storm surge alone could raise water levels well above normal heights, lifting boats above docks and pilings. Dangerous high tides could reach outward from the storm's center for up to twenty, even fifty, miles.

Dan knew what he'd signed on for, and it was a lot of responsibility. Rigging, canvas, and deck gear had to be removed, if possible, and then the schooner's bow turned to face the greatest exposure if she was left in the water. Hank looked like he hadn't slept for a couple days, and he probably hadn't. Ron nodded in greeting before continuing to wind a mass of rope into a useable, coiled pile.

"At least my policy with United Life & Casualty has a Named Storm Haul-out Clause. It's making me lean toward getting her out of the water altogether if I can. I've never used it, but if I remember correctly, the policy reimburses fifty percent of the hauling cost to professionally remove the schooner from the water and strap her down on land. It's probably my preference, being more secure and predictable than riding at anchor. Of course, there's always some danger from blowing debris but if the yard is patrolled and maintained, that danger should be minimal. It all depends on what facilities I find. Not everywhere is going to accommodate a haul-out of a seventy-six-foot ship. It may be too late to find somewhere close enough to get here in a few hours."

"Have you contacted marinas?"

"Yeah, just got off the phone. There are a couple marinas in Florida that have tie-down eyes embedded in concrete in their storage areas but no one has space available. The storm is now under a 'hurricane watch' which means it's less than thirty-six hours out. So, from now on, every minute counts."

"Sounds like time for a Plan B."

Hank was making him nervous by dithering around this late in the game. Granted, Hank had been out of pocket the last couple days, but plans should have been in place before he left. This was leaving too much to last minute decision-making.

"I agree."

"Am I allowed to say you're making me nervous?"

Hank laughed, then playfully punched Dan's arm. "Hey, I don't mean to give anyone a stroke. Looks like I'll have to come clean. I hinted earlier that I had a deal in the making. I couldn't say anything until it was completed—my life signed away on the dotted line, so to speak. But I've had an alternative up my sleeve that gives me safe mooring not far from here. Finally, it's a done-deal which also means I'm not going to waste any more time in trying to find a place to get her out of the water. That might have been my preference but I'm going to commit to securing her *in* the water. That will take the least amount of time to do it right. And I might as well take advantage of what's literally in my own back yard. We're going to be able to do just that at my very own, newest acquisition and not be bunched up like sardines getting chaffed from being buffeted against other boats."

"Not sure I'm following. I think you lost me." Dan felt like he'd missed part of the conversation but he couldn't mistake Hank's Cheshire Cat grin. What was up?

"The ink isn't even dry yet on my newest venture. As of late yesterday, I, along with a number of stakeholders, own the old SeaTrac boat manufacturing plant. The one down in Palm Coast with its five acres of seaside land, including slips for forty vessels of varying sizes—maybe what's most important, there's two hundred and twenty-five thousand square feet under roof of repair or building facilities. We'll be able to get her leeward of the tallest building that's closest to the water. I'll drop five anchors and she should do well, ride it out without a scratch."

"Wow. That's great news about investing in the SeaTrac place. Congratulations. Will you be building or just repairing boats?"

"Neither. I'm bringing a new concept to the marine world—on-line buying and selling with delivery right to your door. I'll be the CarMax of the boat world. And there isn't any type of boat that I'll turn down. There's a terrific market out there right now for a little bit of everything. It's time to take advantage of it. I've been hiring on the sly. I got six guys down there today to help us out. Two of the guys will sleep at the facility and be there through the storm."

"Sounds like a good investment."

"And not for just the original stakeholders. We should be ready to go public with an IPO in a few months. Might be something you'd want to look at. I heard from your mom's broker yesterday. She's in. It's a hundred grand minimum with a ten percent return guaranteed first year. Eventually we'll offer some repair work and up our workforce to a hundred or so. But that's a ways off—need to get off the ground first. All this has been in the works for the last three months. It's been worse than herding cats to get everybody to the table and keep it under wraps. The final countdown had to be kept secret. We weren't the only ones vying for that particular bit of real estate. But it's done. You're looking at the owner and CEO of Boatarama, the newest full service boating enterprise for the investor, as well as the enthusiast."

"Congratulations. That's exciting. I like the concept; it's been a winner for car sales." And Dan wasn't lying. Situated along the Atlantic coast with easy access to the Keys, Bahamas, and Gulf of Mexico, the new business was in a prime spot. Hank and his stockholders stood to make a lot of money.

"Enough of this chit-chat; we need to get a move on. We're looking at an hour and a half to get to the barn as I like to call the boat house in Palm Coast; so, let's get started."

* * *

Six men made short work of mooring and stripping the *Moonstruck* until only bare masts were left to take on the wind's fury. Five anchors held her securely. All her trappings were safely stored inside the repair facility. Hank had Ron bring an ice chest full of beer in the bed of the truck and a Dos Equis was a good way to end the afternoon.

Dan even volunteered to help get the *Moonstruck* ready to sail again after the storm. Depending on the amount of damage done to the marina in St. Augustine, Hank would bring her back up the coast in three days or leave her moored in Palm Coast for longer. Owning the facility gave him the luxury of not having to move the schooner until her old home was in top-notch shape. If Hank were lucky, the storm wouldn't cost him more than a week's worth of tours. It was tough to base your salary on something as uncertain as tourism. Weather and the whims of vacationers—two fickle entities for sure. Dan was glad it wasn't his business and he could fully understand why the Boatarama idea had such appeal for Hank.

It was comforting to know that the *Moonstruck* was secure. Of course, plenty could still go wrong. Dan decided that it was this 'wait and see' that would drive him nuts if he had a boat in the path of a storm. The TV weather channel was now predicting Zena would skim the shoreline, buffeting St. Augustine full force at high tide. It meant water and more water, exactly where it wasn't wanted. Not a good scenario. He was anxious to get back to the townhouse and be with Elaine and Maggie.

Chapter 18

Why did storms always strike at night? At least Dan had gotten back in time to finish placing sandbags in front of the garage door. He'd helped Rick put the scooter up on a pallet against the wall shared with the house and braced it upright using a tool chest to keep it from toppling over. He fully expected to get water in the garage and maybe as high as the lowest step leading up to the porch in back. But water was always tough to predict.

By late evening the electricity was out. The transformer at the end of the block had literally exploded, sounding like a bomb going off. The fact that Elaine had snagged a generator from Lowes and had filled two five-gallon gas cans meant their freezer and fridge would remain in operation. Even though he'd questioned the need for a generator at the time, it had been a good call.

Dan brought out the radio he kept in the garage and tuned in the weather emergency station. They'd had what might be their last take-home meal for a day or two. Most restaurants were already closed and, depending on damage, would remain that way for a few days. Elaine had filled the cupboards with snacks and meal items, including lots of peanut butter, bread, and tuna. They wouldn't go hungry. Three cases of bottled water were in the pantry and the bathtubs were full. Simon had two full, one-gallon buckets.

Whoever said that changes in barometric pressure affected dogs knew what they were talking about. Simon paced back and forth in front of the sliding glass doors to the patio porch and refused to eat his supper. He sensed something abnormal was taking place.

Everyone went to bed at his or her usual time but no one was sleepy. Rick helped Dan pull the king-sized mattress off the bed in the master bedroom and lean it against the sliding glass doors with the frame of the bed snugged up tight to hold it in place. It meant that bed, at least for that evening, was going to be sleeping bags on the floor.

Simon stayed in the living room with Rick, but wouldn't budge from his post where he could see outside. A brand-new smoked cow knuckle sat untouched on the kitchen floor. The dog stuck to his priorities and number one was to protect the house, at least to stay on alert. Dan was impressed with Simon's single-minded attention to safety. There was no doubt that if water came in under the door or if a tree fell on the house, Simon would make sure everyone knew about it.

The wind came first, gusting to maybe fifty or sixty

miles per hour—still within the definition of a tropical storm. Dan knew that as the storm intensified, the wind could reach seventy-four, hurricane strength, gusting to more than double that. The townhouse's roof had received a wind mitigation inspection when they bought it and was certified to withstand winds of up to one hundred and ten miles per hour. Dan was just hoping that the roof wouldn't be tested.

Finally came the worst part—sitting and waiting, not knowing what was happening in the city and surrounding area and no way of finding out. Another transformer blew, a block over, and something big hit the garage doors. Dan checked the garage and discovered water seeping in under the sandbags, not a flood, but a steady trickle had formed a puddle. Water had also reached the bottom step of the porch.

He stepped outside to find the side yard was already filling up with palm fronds, leaves, branches, and they'd inherited two stray lawn chairs. The street had turned into a somewhat fast-moving stream. Dan counted seven large plastic garbage containers bobbing along single file about a block away. Why didn't people take things inside during storms? Of course, many of the town houses were owned and occupied as second residences—some owners only coming to Florida for holidays or a summer vacation, relying on property managers to take care of things in their absence.

Someone's lanai screening was sitting in the middle of the street in front of him and several blow-up Halloween decorations had floated up to get caught in the mesh—a seven-foot, white ghost, a witch on a broom, and a monster that was supposed to be Frankenstein. A macabre meeting of the surreal even if it was already October and Halloween was the next holiday.

Water was already up to the tops of tire rims on cars parked on the street. Striking at high tide, the storm really exacerbated what was already promising to be one of historical proportions. Weren't weathermen calling it 'the storm of the century'? Years of the city having been missed by ocean-fed hurricanes was coming to an end.

Dan closed the door to the porch after convincing Simon to follow him back indoors. He kept a hand on his collar as he led him toward the couch. "Hey, big guy, you need to keep Rick company."

Only there wasn't any Rick in the living room. Strange, maybe he was in the bathroom. But a quick check of the hallway guest bath and no Rick. He called out—no response. Dan continued down the hall to the garage. He'd just checked the garage. Had he missed something? No, a quick look around revealed everything in place with a small stream of water continuing to puddle at the back of the double sized metal door.

Odd. His sixth sense was kicking in—something was wrong. Where would Rick go in the middle of a storm? Without transportation and slogging through ankle-deep water in the dark?. Dan rushed back to the living room. Rick's jacket was gone but his billfold and phone were on the coffee table. The phone was open to the messages screen—**Meet me outside in back**. A cryptic, if not ominous message in this kind of weather. What was going on? Was this some friend trying to get in touch? But Rick could have brought the friend back inside to safety.

The time on the message was ten twenty-five—only fifteen minutes ago. Did Rick walk out the back door while

Dan was standing on the front porch? It appeared that way. Dan's first instinct was to throw on a windbreaker and boots and try to find him. But where would he look in a blinding rain storm? Best to just hope for the morning revealing some logical reason that he'd left the safety of a house to venture out. The weather station was projecting the passing of the storm to be complete by six a.m. but the next four hours were supposed to be the roughest.

* * *

Dan hadn't expected to get much sleep, but most of the night was spent listening for a door to close which would mean Rick had returned. There were lots of noises—debris hitting the glass patio doors, windows rattling from the force of the wind. The top half of the neighbor's forty-foot-high pin oak crashing against the metal garage doors had shaken the house earlier and now littered the driveway. Intermittent growling by Simon. The morning was shaping up as a work day. He'd be able to put his almost-new chainsaw to work. And finally, after what seemed like eight hours instead of four, there was calm. But no Rick, only an empty couch in the living room. He kept telling himself, Rick is not your kid. He made his own choice.

He started the generator and Elaine made coffee. He pulled a stool up to the breakfast bar and then just leaned on his elbows realizing how tired he was. It seemed like a better idea to start his morning off with a cup of coffee instead of rushing back outside to view more damage. Plus, he was hoping that the morning would shed light on Rick's disappearance

Elaine was obviously distraught. "I can't believe that

he walked out in the middle of a storm. What could have been so important to have risked his life? Who could have messaged him? I certainly don't know of any really close friends. He supposedly went to the movies night before last with someone he'd known from school. He hasn't lived in St. Augustine for over a year. I don't think he's made a lot of friends locally."

Dan didn't have a way to reassure her. He was just as much literally in the dark.

"Maybe we should check his backpack. As far as we know, all his belongings are here."

"I don't know, Dan, that seems like an invasion of privacy. And we don't know that he won't come walking through that door any minute."

"I'll just make sure it's here." Dan walked back into the living room. "I don't see it. Maybe he left it in the office when he was staying in there. I'll check when Maggie gets up."

He couldn't put it off any longer; he needed to check the perimeter of the house and start to clean up. The water was receding quickly. He had to remind himself that Florida was really just one big sand bar. Drainage usually wasn't a problem. Dan swept what little water had seeped in under the garage door back down the driveway before he started hauling debris out of the front yard and placing it on the curb. He counted ten shingles and several pieces of maybe five more. He hoped patching would take care of any problems and that they wouldn't need a new roof. Maggie's car had a sizeable dent in the hood with the limb from the neighbor's tree still resting on top. But it could have been worse.

The weather report was sounding the warning to stay

inside unless travel was absolutely necessary. A curfew had been placed in effect for six p.m., but local travel was discouraged. City cleanup crews were out clearing major intersections and it sounded like downed electrical cable was a real danger. Dan cleared the yard and drive of as much as he could, bagging small branches and leaves before going back inside. He broke the news to Maggie about her car's dented hood and said he'd go out later and take pictures that she could send to her insurance company.

He insisted she come out to the kitchen for a cup of coffee. He didn't want her to worry. The car was something that he'd get taken care of. The important thing was they were all safe—hoping, of course, that Rick was included in that assumption.

Pulling a stool up to the breakfast bar, he felt like he was part of a Norman Rockwell painting—three adults huddled around a radio having a cup of coffee. In fact, he was so intent on the forecast that the first knock on the front door didn't register—other than it reminded him that the electric was still out.

"Sounds like we have company." Dan headed toward the door.

"I bet Rick forgot his keys." Elaine turned the radio down. "I wish the news was better. Sounds like King Street was badly flooded. I can't imagine what that means for the marina."

Dan pulled the door open. "Chief Mitchell." Dan was surprised to see the police chief standing on his doorstep.

"Got a minute? I'd prefer it if you could step outside. Is Ms. Mahoney available? I'd like to speak to the two of you."

"Sure. Let me get Elaine."

"Are you certain you wouldn't be more comfortable inside?" Elaine stepped onto the porch and pulled the front door closed behind her before moving to stand beside Dan.

"I won't take long but what I have to share, and my concerns should stay with the three of us."

"Of course." Elaine nodded.

"I'll just get to the point. Rick Elliston's body was discovered about three blocks from here earlier this morning."

"Oh my God, what happened?" Dan put an arm around Elaine as she reached out to him for support.

"He's going to be counted as a storm death, but frankly, that's still conjecture. Initial cause of death is electrocution. He apparently stepped off the curb into water just as an electrical power line came down. As far as we know he was simply in the wrong place at the wrong time; I got a call from the coroner saying there was a sizable contusion above his left eye with pronounced swelling and bruising along his right shoulder and upper arm—probably the result of falling branches or even debris blowing around. It was dangerous out there, but right now, we have more questions than answers. Maybe the big question is—why was he outdoors during the height of the storm?"

"Horrible. I can't believe that he's gone. You know my history with Rick. I've been so pleased to see him take on the courier job for Stanley and Stanley. He was even going back to school, already bought the books for next semester. Leon Stanley was helping him turn his world around. His death is so untimely; he had so much to look forward to for a change." Elaine took a Kleenex out of her shirt pocket and wiped her eyes. "And within weeks of his mother's shocking death. This is so sad."

"I know he hasn't been with you long, but has he had any friends over? Commented about meeting anyone? Do you know of any activities outside work?"

Elaine shook her head. "Nothing. We were talking about that earlier. For the most part he was a loner. He told us that he and a friend took in a movie the other night, but that was the first we knew of any local friends. Recently, he put in some extra hours at work revamping the shipping and receiving area at the office. He did a great job. He hadn't even mentioned the death of his mother for days. He seemed to have a great outlook and was excited about planning his life going forward."

"I've left a message for his stepfather to call me. I'm sure he's been tied up, keeping his schooners safe. The storm wasn't kind to the marina."

"Chief, if you have a minute there's something I want to show you. I'll be right back." Dan went into the house and returned with Rick's cell phone. "I was up around ten forty-five to check the garage and back patio. When I got back in the house, Rick wasn't there. He'd left the house but hadn't taken his billfold or phone. Here's the message left only fifteen minutes before I got up."

The chief looked at the message, repeating it out loud. "Meet me outside in back. This supports my feeling that there's more to this than what we know. I'm going to need to take his phone with me. If there's anything of interest, our guys will find it. You didn't notice anyone? A car, maybe, when you checked the house?"

"Nothing. The water was already pretty deep in the streets. And the bad thing is that with the electricity out, our house cameras weren't working. Believe me it was dark out there. I have a battery-operated motion detector on the garage but the light wasn't on. It's programmed to remain lighted for ten minutes after being triggered, but it was dark. I don't think anyone had been out front."

"I'm going to head out. Call me if you come up with anything. There could be a simple explanation to all this, but something doesn't feel right." The chief slipped Rick's phone into his jacket pocket before turning and going down the front steps.

"I agree with the chief, Dan. Something just isn't right. I'm going to do some checking, see whether anyone at work noticed if he had visitors. Ginny, the receptionist, would know if he'd gotten calls through the company's landline, or had made any calls. I'm sure he used his cell for everything, but it's worth checking. It's just so incredibly sad; I'm having a difficult time accepting he's gone."

Quickly, Dan filled Maggie in on the chief's information, and she was as shocked as they were. "I need to take a quick look at his backpack. Is it still in the guest room?"

"I haven't seen it. I don't think he left anything other than some clothing in the closet and a couple pairs of shoes. What isn't hanging up is in boxes, like his school books."

"I'm most interested in his backpack. He took it everywhere." But even looking in closets, under the desk, behind the daybed, turned up nothing. Dan walked back into the living room. "I know he kept the thing close." He looked behind the couch, then took the covers off and pulled off the pillows. "Wow. Look at this. This *is* interesting." Dan held out a packet of money bound with a strip of blue paper. "Anyone know where this came from?"

"Oh no. I know." Maggie stepped forward and looked

closely at the packet. "This matches what I found in the safe at Hank's office. Only there was a top shelf full of them and most of the packets were a lot thicker. Hank insisted he'd come back in the middle of the night to empty it. I have no idea how one packet got here."

"There's three thousand dollars in this one. I wonder if he had any others, maybe stuffed into his backpack and this one fell out." Elaine was trying to make sense out of the find. "Or he could have left the backpack at work."

"Not full of money, I bet. Hank told me he was the one who emptied the safe. Maybe this was running money for Rick. Maybe he felt sorry for how he'd treated Rick after all."

Maggie knew she didn't sound very convincing, and she actually didn't believe her own words. More likely, Rick had helped himself to a packet. But from where? From the safe? And when would he have had that opportunity? Why had Hank lied—maybe he hadn't? Maybe he *had* given the money to Rick. But this much? And for what purpose?

"Do you have any idea how to find out where Rick could have gotten the packet of money?" Maggie turned to Elaine. "It might explain all this."

"I'm going into the office tomorrow—mid-morning. The streets should be cleared by then. I'll see if I can take a look at the office Rick just set up. I'll take some boxes and gather up anything that Hank might want to give to Goodwill. I'm pretty sure he left his good leather jacket there. And maybe I'll find his backpack. Not sure we'll find answers, but it's the logical place to start."

"Good idea. That'll save somebody some extra work. I'm headed toward the marina about the same time; let me know if you find anything. Maggie, let's go see what has to be done to your car. I think the dent is cosmetic and not a threat to operating it."

Chapter 19

Stanley and Stanley opened at ten with exactly three people—Leon, Ginny and Elaine. Archer's house had received some flooding and he would be out until next week. No reasons were given for the rest of the crew other than storm related damage to property. Breaking the news of Rick's death was unpleasant. Ginny burst into tears. Leon appeared stoic. Without comment and only shaking his head, he abruptly excused himself to go to his office.

People react so differently to shock and grief. She thought Leon had brushed away a tear but wasn't sure. He had certainly known Rick for the longest time and recently had been the one most vested in helping him turn his life around. Maybe it wasn't unusual to want to digest the information alone.

At least a quiet office would give Elaine time to question Ginny about any contacts Rick might have had and do some snooping. She doubted anyone had even been in his office since he left yesterday. She hoped she wasn't stepping outside boundaries by wanting to help clear his office of personal effects. Maybe Hank or someone at the office would have a favorite charity for donations; she'd ask. If not, she'd offer to take anything she found to Goodwill.

She obviously wouldn't give something away without checking with Hank first. But his involvement might be limited, due to dealing with the aftermath of the storm. She could keep things in her garage until Hank had been contacted. That was probably the best plan.

Ginny was still dabbing at her eyes when Elaine sat down next to her desk. "I'm trying to find friends or family to contact concerning Rick's passing. I know his stepfather will be too busy the next few days to give it much attention. Did Rick ever have visitors here? Friends or family?"

"No, not really. When he first joined the staff last week, several street people hung out in our parking lot, even attempting to spend the night in our lobby. Leon put a quick stop to that. As you can imagine, three or four filthy sleeping bags and their itinerant owners dozing in the foyer wasn't the image that the firm wanted people to associate with us."

Elaine stifled a laugh. She could just see Leon's reaction to having the lobby of the prestigious Stanley and Stanley law firm defiled by the unwashed. Chasing poor unfortunates back out to the streets wasn't exactly part of the Christian image that Leon tried to project, but there was a distinct snobby side to the man. But who could blame him? As senior partner, it was his money that started and backed the firm. Nothing wrong in protecting one's investment.

"Any calls? People who called more than once or seemed to have a personal relationship with Rick?"

"His stepfather called twice. Rick took the calls here in my office. Neither one seemed to be very pleasant—more of a lecture on how he would be expected to keep the scooter in top shape, take care of it, and not let it be stolen. He actually told Rick not to embarrass him and to get off the streets. That's when Rick shared with his father that he would be staying at your house."

"They really didn't have the best of relationships."

"That's putting it mildly. It was almost like his stepfather didn't want him to succeed."

"And to tell him to stay off the streets but refuse to pay for a place to stay is setting him up. Were there any other calls?"

"Chief Mitchell called a couple times. I have no idea what that was about. Oh, then someone with an accent—he was so difficult to understand that I put him through to Thomas by mistake and the guy was livid."

"Any idea what his first language was?"

"Oh, I'm not good at that, but I think Spanish. He was so hard to follow—even his English was sort of sing-songy, you know, like he was from the islands."

"Doesn't sound like a close friend."

"No, I just thought it was someone Rick knew from the streets. And that was about it. In the short time he was here, he spent most of it making deliveries or picking up packages. And then the last couple days were spent setting up the shipping and receiving office."

"Do you know if the shipping and receiving area is

open now? I thought I'd pick up any clothing or personal items that he might have left here. I know I didn't see his leather jacket at home. I thought I'd help Mr. Beaufort out. I can't imagine that he's going to want to come in here and pack things up."

"Great idea. No, I can't imagine his stepdad even offering to help. I'm sure I was going to be the person stuck with boxing things up. Before I forget, I'm sure it's too early to know if there will be a service but let me know if you hear of anything, and I'll get the word out here."

* * *

Elaine took the keys to the room housing a newly dedicated area of business that hadn't been emphasized before, and let herself in. Rick had taken such pride in pulling the office together and making it useable. He was so proud of Leon placing such faith in his being able to set up a workable space that would meet company needs. It was so unfair to think Rick wouldn't have a chance to prove himself further. There was no doubt in her mind that he could have been successful. And if foul play had robbed him of his life—she couldn't even think of that. Who would kill a young man who had just lost his mother and was struggling to make his life work?

The first thing she saw was his leather jacket on the back of a chair just inside the door. Funny, but the pockets had been turned inside out. Maybe Rick had been looking for his keys. What looked like a stack of school books and notebooks sat on another chair beside the desk. Pegs on the wall behind the door held a shirt and a couple ball caps. She took a deep breath. It was all so incredibly sad. She put the cardboard boxes she'd brought on the floor, folded the shirt and jacket putting them in one of the boxes and tossing the caps on top. She put a second box beside the books.

She'd only brought three boxes and it might be a good idea to check the desk first before she filled the boxes and ran out of room. There were a couple posters on the wall, one of Harley Davidson bikes and another of antique sailing vessels plus framed photos on a credenza behind the desk of him with his mother—five to be exact, from what was probably a school picture from kindergarten to high school graduation—and one 8 ½ by 11 of his mother alone on a runway in the heyday of her modeling. A well-worn sleeping bag, a pillow and two blankets were stuffed under the desk along with shirts, jeans and underwear. Once again it struck her how sad his life had been lately and how close he'd been to his mother. He'd had a home.

After pulling open the first drawer, she was glad she'd checked the desk before filling the box. What a jumbled mess. A cell phone with a cracked screen and missing a back, several packages of plastic cutlery from various take-out restaurants, at least a dozen ball-point pens, a calendar with a number of dates X'd out, a corkscrew, a church key, a couple unopened Kleenex packets, a dog leash, a bag of dog jerky treats, chap stick—it looked like a typical junk drawer. But it also looked like someone had haphazardly gone through the drawer, maybe pulling some things out before just tossing everything back in. It was something a kid in a hurry would do if he was looking for something.

It was difficult to tell from the mess what was useable and should be kept. A lot of it was throw-away stuff but she needed time to go through the rest. She picked out things that were obviously Rick's but didn't spot her house keys among the mess.

The other drawers in the desk were all filled with work related items—a fan, iPad marked property of Stanley and Stanley, screen cleaner, a ream of printer paper, a replacement ink cartridge—these drawers she could ignore—they would be used by the next person hired for shipping and receiving. But they also looked like someone had rifled through them.

The top of the desk was neatly laid out. She wasn't certain who had provided the desk blotter, pencil box, and cup-holders that all matched, but she'd leave them and ask Ginny. As she lifted the blotter, a piece of paper floated to the floor. Without giving it a second thought, Elaine quickly put it in her pocket. If it was important enough to hide, it might be important enough to read. And she'd not found anything else the least bit suspect.

Suddenly, the door banged open. "What are you doing in here?" If looks could kill, she would be dead. Her usually pleasant, never-say-a-cross-word boss was glowering at her.

"Leon, I'm only trying to save an overworked Ginny some time by boxing up Rick's belongings. And, I'm hoping to find my house keys."

He slumped against the doorjamb and covered his eyes with both hands, then collected himself and stepped into the room. "Of course, of course, Elaine, I'm so sorry. I'm not myself. Losing Rick has just torn me up. I so wanted him to succeed. I always sort of thought of him as my son. Of course, I should be thanking you. You're very considerate to take on emptying this office yourself and saving Ginny and others the work. I guess seeing the office empty just makes the loss sink in. He's not coming back; I have to face that."

"It's been a shock for all of us. It always is difficult to lose young people. I understand your grief."

Elaine smiled reassuringly and got a wan smile in return. Then Leon excused himself after apologizing one more time for yelling and left the room. Elaine filled the boxes and moved them to the hallway before bringing her car to the front for easier loading. It was close enough to lunch time that she opted to take everything back to the townhouse, unload, and grab a sandwich before facing the rest of her day. Dan was going to be spending most of the day at the marina, but Maggie should be free for lunch.

* * *

"So, you didn't find anything out of the ordinary? I mean most of this stuff is what I'd expect to find in an office. Well, maybe not the dog treats, but he was so crazy over Simon—always prepared if he happened to visit."

"I know. Simon's going to miss the extra attention. I think he was Rick's best friend, maybe only friend. He didn't have many calls at work—a couple from his stepfather and some guy from the islands whom Ginny thought he must have known from the streets. But the funny thing was I had the distinct feeling that someone had gone through his things before I got there. The desk drawers were a mess."

"Did you get everything?"

"There was so little to get. But, yes, between the little bit I brought from the office and what he left here in his room, everything that belonged to Rick is in those boxes."

Maggie picked up the box of desk items and walked to the garage. "Will there be help in returning the scooter?

Maybe someone from work with a truck?"

"More like one of the partner's sons coming by and riding it back to their house."

"I did take the time to check the saddlebags. I found a much-worn sweater and more school books. Oh, and a couple notebooks. Hadn't he enrolled for the spring semester at Flagler College?"

"Leon made it a prerequisite of taking the job as courier. Rick agreed and even seemed excited about going back. I'm not sure he was going to stick with culinary arts. Thanks for thinking of the saddlebags. I hadn't given them a thought. Now, I'll have to remember to ask Leon to have someone pick it up."

"Makes me wish I was fifty years younger; I'd volunteer to ride it back to the office. But they are dangerous."

Elaine looked at the small stack of Rick's possessions. "It doesn't say much for twenty-plus years of life. Oh wait, I did find something that I wanted to take a look at." Elaine dug the slip of paper out of her jacket pocket and held it out. "This makes absolutely no sense, it's just a bunch of numbers. But why was it under the desk blotter if it's not important?"

"Let me see." Maggie smoothed the paper on the car's front fender.

7520-2085-131514525-135520-21-20151497820-96—

"See what I mean? It's just a string of random numbers. Do you recognize any part of it? A combination for the safe in your office maybe? It could be code for tracking a package. I should check with UPS."

"Wait. I have an idea; give me a few minutes." Maggie walked through the garage, stepped up into the kitchen, and returned with a notepad and pen. First, she copied the numbers and then wrote something above them. More scribbles and finally she looked up. "I've got it." She handed the notepad to Elaine.

Get the Money See U Tonight If—

"It looks like the person writing the note got stopped. The 'If' at the end would seem to indicate the person was about to offer an alternative of some sort. A condition that might make some sort of difference."

"How in the world did you figure this out so quickly?"

"Well, the 2085 combination of numbers helped. This is a standard child's code based on the alphabet and 2085 is 'the'—t is letter number 20, h is 8, and e is the fifth letter in the alphabet. There are twenty-six letters total and give each a numerical equivalent as to their place, and spell out your message. It's as simple as that, but would fool most people. Dan used to drive his sister nuts writing everything in this code."

"I'd guess that the person who wrote this note also sent the text saying he was outside the other night."

"I'm not sure we know much more than we did other than the meeting with this person involved money."

"I wish he or she had been able to finish whatever they were going to say. That 'if' is rather ominous. Maybe it was going to be a threat. If you don't show up, something will happen that seems to have a sinister meaning. This is all a little scary. I think I'm ready for a cup of coffee, and maybe a tuna sandwich. How about you?"

"Sounds perfect."

Maggie slipped the coded message into her notebook, carried both inside, and spread the slips of paper in front of her on the kitchen counter. "I just keep thinking I've missed something. But the message is certainly straightforward, nothing left to conjecture. Oh wait. I haven't been thinking straight. How could I have missed it?"

"What? What did you miss?"

"I feel rather dumb touting my code-breaking skills and then goofing up so badly."

"Maggie, tell me. You're making me crazy."

"The 'IF' isn't a part of speech, it's initials. 'IF' stands for Ian Fredericks. I'd put money on it. And you said someone with an accent called the law office for Rick. Mr. Fredericks came to the H&H office to leave an invoice for Hank while I was standing in for Sue Ellen. Seemed upset that he wasn't getting paid on time. The invoice was for twenty-five hundred. I don't know that his looking for payment has anything to do with the entire safe being empty the next morning, and Hank admitting to emptying it. Maybe Hank did need cash to pay off workers. But somehow this Ian had hooked up with Rick and they had some sort of deal in the making involving money, too. Was he just looking for his payment for work? The three thousand you found here in the couch would have covered Mr. Frederick's invoice."

"That's true. Maybe that's all it was. What made you think of this Ian Fredericks?"

"He was from the islands with that melodic cadence to his voice. Sounds like he had also contacted Rick at work, so the connection made sense."

"I think it's time I did some online tracing. I'll call Ginny and tell her I won't be back in the office today. I'll set my laptop up out here and give you your room back."

"No need. I'm going to load up and go back to Devil's Bend this afternoon and then bring the RV back up to the park in Flagler Beach. I have a driver hired for the morning. I'll follow him back and get my car worked on in Palm Coast. I'm sure the inland roads are clear and open to travel by now."

"Before you go, tell me more about Ian Fredericks—anything you can remember—what he looks like, mannerisms, your reaction to him."

"He made me so ill at ease that I brought Simon to work the next day. He was big, not fat, more all muscle. I would guess his age to be forty-something but the beard and straggly hair made him look older. Supposedly, he was an electrician and worked for Pelican Electric out of Palatka—that was the company listed on the invoice. He was handsome in a dark, shifty sort of way. And I remember thinking he probably lived on the streets. He didn't seem to have had access to a shower recently."

"I'll check out Pelican Electric for starters, along with trying to come up with a photo of the man."

Elaine topped up her coffee and added additional half-and-half before opening her laptop. Even though she had access to good identification software, Elaine often logged onto social media first to find a photo. No such luck this time. There were several Ian Fredericks but all were teens or in their early twenties. A couple were cutesy beach photos of guys with girls in bikinis. Nothing fit the description Maggie had given of a man who made her feel uneasy.

When Elaine did an in-depth search, the only Ian Frederick who was close to the suspected age, forty-eight years, had died two years before in a car accident outside Orlando. Stealing identities from the dead was not uncommon. Could this Ian be a complete imposter?

A quick search for Pelican Electric in Palatka came up with a former mom-and-pop business that had shut its doors last year. Dead ends. Who was Ian Fredericks? Why did he have an invoice, obviously bogus, for work supposedly done on Hank's schooner? And why, if the 'IF' on the note was his initials, was he demanding money from Rick? Maybe it was time to share what she had with Chief Mitchell. But this had to be done carefully. The information she had involved Dan's client and Maggie's former boyfriend. Other than the suspicious death of Rick Elliston, had there been other wrong doing?

Chapter 20

Dan drove a mile up A1A and crossed the Bridge of Lions which connected downtown St. Augustine with Anastasia Island. He had promised Hank that he'd do an assessment of the damage to the marina and see if he could find someone to give him a time estimate of when Hank could bring the *Moonstruck* back.

He was just about ready to say the city had dodged the worst of it, but that was before he saw the remains of the slowly receding water. At least, wind damage was minimal and secondary to that caused by water. From the apex of the bridge, the spires and towers on the Basilica and Flagler College were intact. The storm seemed centered around King Street downtown and involved horrific flooding that even though the water had mostly receded, there was evidence that it had stretched for blocks—something high tide had made far worse than it might have been otherwise.

He had seen the newspaper. The *St. Augustine Record* had captured the Episcopal Church's mounds of pumpkins stacked in the church yard waiting to be sold for a Halloween money-maker when some two hundred of them had taken off in the current and bobbed their way down the street to be lost or simply pilfered by those who helped themselves. The picture still made him smile and put a lighter spin on the toll exacted by the rising water.

Dan was almost afraid to go to the marina. But he parked about a block away, staying out of the way of city clean-up crews. He tried to prepare himself for what he would find. He knew the storm hadn't spared the marina—high water and boats with nowhere to go didn't mix. The walkway down to the dock was gone, at least in part. And in the distance, he could see eight boats of varying sizes had ended up on top of one another or partially capsized next to the dock. There were close to a hundred slips in all and most seemed to have withstood the fury of the storm. At least with a hurricane there was time to move boats to safer areas.

Still the wreckage was notable. Several slips needed to be reconstructed, the dock replaced or repaired in spots, in addition to the damaged boats being lifted out of the water. There wouldn't be any tours taking off from there any time soon.

It was good to know that Hank wasn't under a time constraint in removing the *Moonstruck*. It had paid off having his own boatyard. Dan hadn't heard from Hank but no news was probably good news. No doubt keeping both schooners away from St. Augustine had been the right move. And then his phone rang.

"We've got a problem." Hank Beaufort sounded like he was talking through clenched teeth.

"What's up?"

"The *Moonstruck* was torched. Burned to the waterline."

"Storm related, or arson?"

"Too soon to tell. I've done the reporting. Now, I'm trying to get someone out here to take a look. I called UL&C; they indicated you would be their choice of inspector. I imagine you'll be getting a call."

"Whether I'm assigned to take a look or not, I'm on my way down. See you in half an hour."

Dan had barely hung up when he got the call. His boss thought he was in a unique position to do the research on this one—the assignment was his to investigate the fire aboard the *Moonstruck*. And, yes, Dan was in a so-called 'unique position' in that he had access to particulars, such as the history leading up to this point; but the knowing might also get in the way.

Elaine was up-to-her-neck deep in recent Beaufort family-related ordeals. And his mother? He didn't even want to go there. This wasn't going to be an easy assignment. And, if he were being truthful, boat fires weren't his strongest area of investigative expertise. He had probably handled three in his entire professional career. And one of those had been a neighbor's bass boat that had succumbed to a forgotten, smoldering Cuban cigar.

Something told him this situation was far more complex. All boat fires were notoriously difficult in many ways simply because fires on water were so different. It took a different mindset to approach an investigation. Construction of boats led to varying means of ventilation.

Steel hulls versus wood versus fiberglass—each entirely different from the other in characteristics. And this was before addressing what might have been stored onboard in the way of fuels or other materials.

Every boat—barge, fishing trawler, tug, freighter, tanker, drilling rig, yacht or schooner—presented a challenge all its own. This was not an assignment he looked forward to. At least he wouldn't be dealing with multiple insurance carriers. It would pretty much be his show and his only. That was a definite plus.

The minute he got back to the car, he turned the radio on to get an update on storm damage. Sure enough, traffic was being diverted from A1A south out of St. Augustine because the scenic ocean-front highway had washed out in several spots. Dan took King Street across town and picked up Highway 1.

* * *

Dan parked in the lot in front of the largest of the empty warehouses. Once Hank got everything set up, this was going to be an impressive undertaking—a showroom, multiple slips for additional boats for sale, repair facilities—there was even a rumored coffee shop with lunch counter. The possibilities were probably endless.

Hank had picked up additional acreage and had shared that he saw a 'Boat Mall' eventually—a sales center on the water to rival the Auto Mall off of I-95 in Daytona. Big dreams—ones that held promise. He didn't need a hurricane to derail them.

Dan walked through the building and noticed the open two-story showroom was poised to be transformed into the

Boatarama. This had been in the works for awhile and now that Hank had closed on the property, the transformation could start. There was painters' scaffolding waiting to be put into place, boxes of new ceramic tile— It was certainly going to be grand and cost its owner a mint. Eventually there would be cubicles for ten or more sales people. Dan didn't see one thing that wasn't going to be an expensive undertaking.

He was almost to the back door when Hank joined him. "I still can't stand to see her like this. It's like losing my firstborn." Dan wasn't certain how a man could lose his wife and stepson but appear to grieve more for a boat. But no one was paying Dan to judge. He needed to keep an open mind.

"I wanted to say how shocked and saddened Elaine and I are at Rick's death. We both enjoyed working with him and having him stay with us for a brief time."

"Thank you. Ginny shared with me that Elaine came into the office to collect Rick's belongings and said you'll store them at your place until I can decide what to do with everything. I appreciate your helping me out. It's no secret that I got a little sideways with the kid, but no one should die like that—or die so young. Now, let's get this show on the road."

Hank pushed open the showroom's back door and stood to one side letting Dan walk ahead of him.

"I hope you're prepared—she ain't pretty."

Even after being warned, when Dan saw the *Moonstruck*, it was shocking. Half-submerged, a gaping, blackened stretch of deck, the hull collapsed … If he had to guess, he'd say he was looking at a total loss. Salvage wasn't going to be cheap.

"Not much to work with." Hank stood quietly shaking his head.

"True. Didn't anyone see what happened? I thought you had several men at the warehouse."

"You must mean the six guys who went drinking and then couldn't get back because of the storm. I'm pissed, can you tell? Guess I don't need to add that they're off the payroll. They'd come highly recommended, too; but I didn't have a good feeling about the group. Ron had offered to stay and give me the truck to get back to St. Augustine, but I insisted he come with me. Why would I need an extra guy down here when I had six in place? You'd think I would have learned a few things in life by this time, wouldn't you? Like trusting people you don't know to do what they're told."

"I'm assuming that you're going to bring her up?"

"Yeah, unless you got scuba gear. Sorry, I don't mean to be a smartass. I'm just not taking this very well. Puts a real crimp in my plans. I'd hoped to have the tour business up and running—more than paying for itself to the point where I could put my time in down here and give someone else a chance at chauffeuring tourists around. I was toying with putting the *Moonstruck* on the market—make her my showpiece; a boat and a business all in one deal. She would have made a great attraction for marketing Boatarama. Now this."

"I know you weren't being serious about scuba gear but it would be best to do an underwater check before bringing her completely out of the water. Is there any place in Daytona that rents a scuba set?"

"I think I can fix you up. I've got stuff in storage in St. Augustine that will work. And you'll have Ron to help you.

He can take orders, and do what you want him to. Luckily, we're not talking a lot of depth here. Approach depth is about fourteen feet and depth at dock closer to sixteen. But if we can give you forty-five minutes to an hour on air to check her out, that's probably all the time you'll need."

"Sounds right."

"I'll send Ron up to the storage unit. I'm thinking a mask, suit, compressor, ballast weights, a cutting tool, lights—can you think of anything else?"

"That should cover it. I'm going to get some pictures topside while we're waiting for Ron to get back."

The five anchors Hank had used to secure the *Moonstruck* were still holding what was left of her in place. Only a thin film of oil and fuel was forming above the wreckage. If there was evidence of tampering, cut fuel lines, explosively rigged engine, accelerant containers, he would be able to take samples. Low tide would make access easy and had kept the wreckage more or less intact. The schooner was gutted but hadn't broken apart.

The center of the deck was pretty much gone, with just a gaping hole left. Dan couldn't help but think of the sunset sail they had enjoyed just last week. A chair and music stand had floated up against an ice chest and were pressed under the railing. Always interesting what was lost in catastrophes like this and what survived. Pillows from the benches that had formed the seating for passengers floated along with life jackets gently bouncing against the dock. He was curious to know what he'd find below the waterline.

In the meantime, while he was waiting for Ron to bring back the diving equipment, he'd gotten his laptop from the car and asked Hank if he could use an office inside.

He needed to review the specs on what UL&C expected him to research and include in his report. He also needed a schematic of the schooner itself. He'd use the drawing to pinpoint where the fire started and how it had spread. This was going to be one long afternoon.

Chapter 21

Finally, Elaine had the house to herself. Maggie had taken off to meet the driver who would be bringing her RV back up to the Lazy Daze RV Park and Dan was going to be late. Working with Hank Beaufort had turned out to be time-consuming and more than a little challenging. But the quiet gave her the perfect setting to finish her searches on Hank Beaufort's possibly suspect personnel.

A quick search on Ron Carter unearthed two prison stints—both for drug trafficking—but nothing for the past seven years. It would seem he'd turned into the model citizen. The past five years chronicled jobs for several large boat builders as a journeyman woodworker specializing in teak appointments for multi-million-dollar yachts. That was an occupation that she didn't even know existed and, apparently, he was good enough to be in demand.

Most disappointing was the lack of information on the elusive Ian Fredericks. She was pretty certain that he'd borrowed an identity, which always made things more difficult. She had a couple other avenues to try but first she needed a cup of coffee.

The ringing of her phone put coffee on hold. The number wasn't familiar but it wasn't marked scam.

"Hello."

"Elaine Mahoney?"

"This is she."

"I'm sorry it's taken so long for me to get back. This is Nancy, Nancy Hunt, the Beaufort's neighbor. You had inquired about our house camera's possibly capturing something on the night Hannah died? Well, my husband has had a chance to take a look and instead of trying to describe it, he'd like you to take a look with him. He's home for the next couple days but this afternoon would be great if you're free to stop by."

She felt a rush of excitement that surprised her. She really was invested in finding closure to Hannah's death. Could this be the deciding piece to the puzzle? "I can be there in an hour if that's convenient."

"Perfect. We'll see you then."

* * *

Elaine knew that she was allowing her imagination to run away with her, but why would Nancy Hunt call if they hadn't found something? With Rick's death she didn't even have a legitimate reason to be pursuing the death of his mother. She had to be honest. This was all her own curiosity or maybe a gesture to vindicate Rick—prove his conviction of wrongdoing to be either true or false.

Nancy met her at the door and introduced David, a gangly, bespectacled, nerdy looking man with a slightly moist handshake.

"We wouldn't have anything to look at if the wind hadn't repositioned the camera on the far southwest corner of the roof. We were having such a varmint problem that I put in additional cameras last spring. You might also be interested in the second story camera that captured the Beaufort's driveway that evening. Anyway, follow me, the cameras feed into the monitors in this room off the kitchen."

Elaine followed David to what might have been meant as a pantry now fitted with a built-in desk along one wall that held a bank of six monitors, all trained on varying areas outside of the house.

"I made a copy of what I thought was pertinent. We can view it here." He rolled two desk chairs to a table holding a laptop. "I apologize for the tape's quality. The night was cloudy with very little moonlight to help get any clear shots. But I think there's enough to be of interest."

"Anything to help law enforcement understand what happened is much appreciated."

"I'll just say this now. I've been reluctant to get involved. But Nancy and I were quite fond of Hannah Beaufort. She was a dear friend and had been helpful to us in the past when my family came to visit by offering a couple bedrooms in her house for unexpected overflow. I guess I feel I owe her—even in death. And now her son is gone, too. It's sad beyond words."

"I agree. If there's been a crime committed, I'd like to

see restitution."

"Then I think you'll find this of interest." David turned on the computer and opened a file positioning the screen so that Elaine had a clear view.

This segment was obviously of the Hunt's house showing their driveway and a portion of the street in front facing north. As Elaine watched, a white pickup truck drove slowly by, quickly becoming obscured by the overgrown vegetation between the two houses.

"That's just to show you the truck and the direction it was coming from. Let me open a file from the second story camera and you'll see where it ended up."

There was more moonlight in this frame as Elaine watched the same truck pause in the street, pull forward and then back into the Beaufort driveway.

"It's a Florida plate. Let me zoom in. I think you can see a section of the tag in this frame." David paused the video. "You can't see much but it's a specialized plate— buying one helps save sea turtles. I've always liked the turtle motif there in the center. You've got the turtles and two numerals that look like a two and a five. I can't make out the rest of it."

"Is that Hank's pick up?"

"I don't think so. At least it's not the truck I'm used to seeing Hank drive. Hank's truck is dark … black, maybe. I'm not familiar with this vehicle. Plus, this is a Chevy and Hank owns a Ford."

"What time was this captured?"

"Earlier in the evening but after sunset. I'd guess six-thirty. The moon was just coming up. I'll check the time stamp on the original tape."

There didn't seem to be anything else to see. Elaine

waited while David closed the file and opened another. "Here's the segment that I think you'll be interested in." He sat back, giving her a clear view.

This time Elaine knew exactly where she was—on the widow's walk. The entire structure was bathed in shadows. She leaned forward; there was movement but low to the floor. Then a flash of light at the back of the frame coming from the opening and closing of the elevator door and she watched as Hannah Beaufort partially came into view. The actual elevator door was out of the camera's range but as Hannah moved forward, she reached behind her to the wall on her left before taking a couple more steps, leaning forward looking up at what Elaine knew were the strings of lights along the outside edge of the railed rooftop platform. It was obvious. The lights hadn't come on. It appeared that Hannah stepped back to try the switch two more times before walking to a center post, leaning out over the railing while looking up at the cupola and to her right.

The moon chose that particular instant to drift behind a bank of clouds cutting visibility by at least fifty percent but not before Elaine watched Hannah step up to the bottom railing and then, one foot at a time, rise to stand next to the post supporting the turret. Almost in slow-motion Hannah started to turn and swing a leg around this support, lifting her foot from the rail, when there was distinct movement behind her. The shadow of a figure suddenly rose from where it had been probably crouching on the floor directly below her to forcefully lunge, planting a hand directly in the middle of her back. Caught off balance, Hannah flew outward and quickly disappeared from the frame. The figure who had pushed her dropped from view and didn't reappear. There was a flash of light as the elevator doors opened and shut but it was impossible to see who had entered. The door was obscured by the cupola's overhang and what was by now impenetrable shadow.

"Can you replay that last part?" She leaned closer to the screen.

Once again, she was watching the murder of Hannah Beaufort. She clutched the arms of the desk chair willing herself to sit up straighter and concentrate on the screen. She swallowed hard. This was exactly what she had hoped to find. It was proof of a murder. Heart wrenching, but there was not really a lot to see. It appeared to be a male wearing gloves, a dark shirt or jacket with long sleeves, and a ball cap turned backwards. The cap's insignia could be a Yankee's logo but it was difficult to tell. The person seemed to be somewhat slightly built but even that could be misleading because of the shadows and next to non-existent lighting. Only a portion of the figure had been captured by the camera. The only thing that was proved beyond a doubt was that it was a murder. Hannah had been pushed to her death. Rick had been right.

Elaine sat back in her chair as David closed the laptop. "I'm sure you know how to handle this but I'd guess the police will be very interested. Here's your copy." He handed Elaine a flash drive. "I've made a duplicate and the original video is in my office safe."

"Nancy and I are shocked. We had no idea. Hannah was a wonderful friend; we both wish you well in finding the person who did this."

* * *

Elaine drove back to the townhouse. With a cup of coffee in hand, she took the flash drive to the office. She was going to try and figure out how long the truck had remained in the Beaufort's driveway on the night of Hannah's death. Was that the murderer? The person who would sneak up four stories and hide on the widow's walk, even dismantling the lights so as to lure Hannah to her death?

The pickup's driver's side was obscured in shadow and opposite the camera. The lights in the cab coming on and then quickly blinking off indicated that someone had exited the truck. According to the time stamp on the tape, the entire segment lasted fourteen minutes before the lights in the cab came on and off once again activated by the opening and closing of the truck's door. Time enough to commit murder? Probably. And the coroner hadn't been able to pinpoint the time exactly but Hannah had fallen to her death between six and seven p.m.

The shot of the truck going back down the driveway and turning north was totally shrouded in darkness. Even watching it two more times, there was just no way that she could make out the driver. At least it looked fairly certain that the individual had been alone. There was no indication of anyone riding shotgun.

So, what did she really know? On one hand the tapes were conclusive—at least of wrongdoing; on the other hand, they only added to the mystery. She sat back, sipping her coffee. She needed to call Chief Mitchell and stood up to retrieve her cell phone from the couch. Someone, probably Dan, had moved the three boxes of Rick's belongings into the office, placing them on the floor just inside the door. It took her a minute to realize that she was staring at the box of Rick's clothing from Stanley and Stanley. Right on top was a baseball cap with a Yankees logo.

Coincidence. Plain and simple. There had to be thousands of baseball caps with that team's insignia, more like millions. It was not unusual for Rick to own one. Yet, what looked to be a similar cap was captured on a figure pushing his mother off of a railing four stories above the ground. She lifted the cap and then simply stared at the pair of black gym gloves underneath. Lifter's gloves with the fingers cut out. Was the hand on Hannah's back wearing this type of glove? Could she even tell?

If the video was inconclusive, maybe there was more conclusive evidence, and right in front of her, at that. She walked to the kitchen and took two plastic bags out of the drawer next to the fridge and returned to the living room. With her hand shielded by a bag, she gingerly picked up the baseball cap. She turned it over, checked inside and out. It looked new, no creases, no sweat stains. But then the tiniest bit of matter caught her eye—a hair inside the band on one side. She carefully placed the cap in one of the bags and moved on to the gloves. There was nothing to see but maybe DNA would be more enlightening. Again, very carefully she deposited the two gloves in the second plastic bag.

And then she had a moment of feeling foolish. Was she starting to overreact? Treating everything like some discarded segment of *NCIS*? Everything even remotely related to Hannah's death was taking on special meaning and she had to stop this suspicious overthinking. Baseball caps and gym gloves? She had to remind herself that Rick was Hannah's son; there was simply no way that he could also be her murderer.

It was probably time to just turn over what she had to the police and back away. But she would request that they do a DNA test in their lab on the cap and gloves because some little voice inside her was whispering, 'you never know'. But she was smart enough to know she needed distance. It was time for someone else not so invested in personalities to take over.

However, she did grab another bag and walk back to the box holding the mishmash of items from Rick's desk drawer and retrieved the phone. It was in two pieces and she hadn't paid any attention to it before, but it might be important. That was it. She couldn't think of one more thing of possible interest.

She picked up her phone, made a call to the chief's office, and she had an appointment for ten in the morning.

Chapter 22

Dan would be the first to admit that pulling on a wetsuit and jumping into murky, cold water was not his thing—a part of the job that he was seldom called upon to do, thank God. Whenever possible, a hands-on inspection before a damaged boat is taken out of the water is much preferred especially if, as in this case, the fire's cause was unknown.

It might be overkill, but Dan took pictures of everything that might possibly be linked to a lightning strike or a plant of explosive material. The engine was pretty much obliterated. The door to the head was gone and the ladder from the deck to the area below was in splinters. The middle of the schooner was folded almost in half; the fore and aft sections facing each other. The steel hull looked to be in pretty fair shape and possibly salvageable.

Below what had been the upper deck, one weird detail was the thirty or more thin blue strips of paper, some connected at the ends to form a small circle, caught on various pieces of decking or floating against the partially collapsed ceiling—exactly like the thin, blue paper band holding the packet of money he'd found in the couch at the townhouse.

Using his underwater flashlight, Dan looked for bills that might have floated loose. But there were none, only the bands eerily bouncing around in the wake and the smallish, square door with a hole in the center to what certainly appeared to have been a safe lying on what was left of the floorboards.

Fifty-five minutes later, Hank helped him back up onto the dock.

"Get everything you need?"

"Pretty sure I won't have to go back in again."

"Well, I'll leave the suit in the office, just in case. Looks like the *Moonstruck* will be here for another week; so, if something comes up, you'll have access. As you can imagine, salvage crews are backed up after the storm. This is a bit of a setback on completing this part of the dock, and I'm going to have to decide if I want to stay in the tourist business and not sell the *Moonstruck* after all. If I thought she could be rebuilt, I guess I'd be tempted. She meant a lot to me but as I'd mentioned, I had decided to put my eggs in one basket and expend energy getting Boatarama off the ground. We'll see. I still have the *Nomad*. At least, it weathered the storm in good shape. Ron will be bringing it up to St. Augustine in a couple days."

"Any chance I could use your office for the afternoon?

I need to download these pictures and tag the samples. I'll get my preliminary report in to UL&C, hopefully within forty-eight hours, and a copy to you. If I find anything suspect I may overnight it and have the company lab do the analysis."

"Be my guest; the office is yours. I'll be around if you have questions."

Dan changed into street clothes and carried the camera and bag of samples back to the Boatarama's showroom. It wasn't 'if' he'd found something suspect, it was *knowing* that he had.

The engine had been sabotaged. He was pretty certain that he'd found a piece of an incendiary device, a part of a timer. There was nothing sophisticated about the device. It was basic bomb-making 101. Which, in itself, would make it harder to find the maker. And it opened a whole avenue of questions. For example, who would want to obliterate the *Moonstruck*? Who stood to benefit? The obvious answer was, of course, Hank Beaufort.

But could he completely trash what he purported to love? Dan had been impressed by the man's feelings for a boat and the way of life it had given him. In comparison, though, Boatarama stood to make its investors rich. Very rich.

Still, it didn't make sense. If you were opening up a business to buy, sell, and trade boats, wouldn't you want to find a good home for your own? Wouldn't you have things set up to make that easy? Even Hank had mentioned offering the schooner as part of an already profitable business. Surely that would be of interest to someone hoping to retire in a warmer climate. He was missing something, some big piece that would make everything come together, but for the life of him, he had no idea even what to look for.

Unless ... he reached for the plastic bag of narrow, blue strips. These would seem to indicate that at some point there had been a lot of money aboard the *Moonstruck*. His gut said this was somehow involved in why the schooner was scuttled. He still didn't really have answers, in fact, not even well-grounded suspicions. Where had the money come from? Where was it going? Why was it aboard the *Moonstruck*?

He made a copy of the schooner's schematic and penciled in what was found, and where, along with what was left, adding pictures as proof. He wouldn't be making the final decisions but there was a possibility that it might be more cost effective to total the schooner. He would get follow-up pictures when she was out of the water if UL&C requested them.

The sun was setting before he finished but he'd completed the preliminary report for the company. He emailed as much of the paperwork as he could and would follow up with hard copies dropped in the mail in the morning. Finally, he was finished, at least for today.

* * *

It felt good to just relax for an entire evening. No interruptions! His mother was on her way back to the RV campground on Flagler Beach and would call when she got settled. Elaine had opted to cook at home and had mixed a mean pitcher of margaritas for starters. With glass in hand, she asked him to follow her to the office.

"I really value your opinion." She quickly filled him

in on the Hunt's video captured by their house cameras. "I'd like you to watch this and share your thoughts." She slipped the flash drive in place and sat back. "The first file is just a capture of the front—the street the two houses face. It's the second file that's interesting. I guess I'd go so far as to say shocking."

Dan leaned in, watched the first video of the truck backing into the drive and then opened the second file. "You know who that looks like?" Dan had finished watching the video of Hannah's murder and then replayed it twice.

"Please don't say Rick."

"Come on, Elaine, be objective here. Slightly built, baseball cap with Yankees logo ... the one person who would know the routine of lighting the so-called welcoming beacon of lights on top of the widow's walk. A lot of facts point to him. I think you have to work this from the angle of ruling him out, not proving he did it."

"I'm really beginning to question whether I'm going to like this job. Staying objective isn't easy. I really hate the fact that I got personally involved. It's made unbiased thinking almost impossible."

"This is a good test. It won't be the first time that your feelings will be challenged. There's a lot to be learned here."

"Ah, the voice of reason. Why do I wish I didn't have to listen?" Elaine smiled. "You're right. I know this is probably good for me."

"What's the plan?"

"Take everything I have to Chief Mitchell. I have an appointment in the morning. I'm going in early; I need to give the company some of my time before they decide to replace me."

"Hmmmm, sounds like you're stuck with me for an entire evening. I think that calls for another margarita."

Chapter 23

Elaine left before Dan in the morning. She sounded depraved, even to herself, but they hadn't wasted the first evening alone in some time. She realized she missed their solitary life—go to bed when they wanted, make love when they wanted. She was spoiled.

And, if anything, her new career had really brought them closer—gave them common ground. She couldn't ask for a more supportive partner. It was fun to work in the same profession. Dan understood how anxious she was to share the videos with the chief. They would make a big difference in the man's investigation—make him revisit some avenues he'd already closed. But would he also suspect Rick?

She was still having difficulty with Dan's assessment.

She simply could not allow her mind to go there. There were other answers; she just had to find them. What was it Dan had said? She should work at ruling Rick out, not proving he did it. That was easier said than done, with so many bits of evidence pointing his way. Pulling into the lot behind the office, she waved to Andy who was backing the company pickup into a parking space next to the back door and waited for him to exit the cab.

"Andy, I didn't expect to see anyone here this early. I'm glad to see you survived the storm."

"You guys come through it ok?"

"Some water but the sandbags did their job, very little got into the garage."

Andy walked to the back of the truck and took a chain saw from the bed. "I need to clear the back of this lot before I do anything else. Thought I'd get started before the lot fills up. That storm was wicked. Have you seen downtown?"

"The streets closer to A1A looked pretty good coming in, but I guess King Street didn't fair too well."

"At least it's safe. The crews have been out since the middle of the night taking care of downed power lines. Our tax dollars at work."

Elaine walked around the truck glancing back before she unlocked the door. And then she froze. The turtle on the license plate fairly jumped out at her. That and the number two followed by a five. And, of course, the truck was a Chevy. That was the pickup parked in the Beaufort's drive at the time of Hannah's death.

Well, maybe this was a good thing. She could question Leon about the whereabouts of the truck on the night of Hannah's death. Had someone borrowed it? That would give new focus to the inquiry. She found herself silently praying that it would have nothing to do with Rick.

But, it did. Leon called Andy in to double check but he recalled letting Rick borrow the truck to pick up a rowing machine from the Beaufort's. Hank had made it clear that he needed to get all his stuff out of his mother's house, pronto. Rick had come to him asking for a loan of the Chevy for the evening. Leon admitted that he had never put two and two together—that the evening in question was the evening of his mother's death.

"Is this important?" Leon seemed to suddenly realize that he was placing Rick at a murder scene and maybe implicating him.

"Probably not. Someone in the neighborhood saw the truck in the area." Elaine downplayed any importance. She wasn't about to go into the videos and field questions that she had no answers for … yet.

Andy followed her to the back, but instead of going into the parking lot, he stopped at the door to her office.

"Gotta minute?"

"Sure, Andy, come in."

She noticed he looked around before stepping through the door and then quietly closed it behind him.

"Ms. Linden, I think the old man is slipping a little. I don't want anyone knowing I contradicted him, but Rick didn't have the pickup that night, the bread man took it home or at least I think he did."

"Leon? How do you know?"

"It was August fifth. I'd been using the truck for a couple days while my car was in the shop. It was supposed to be done that morning but when I got to the shop, they weren't finished. So, I kept the truck. When I got here,

Ginny apologized but said that Leon needed the truck that evening and she offered to give me a ride home after work."

"Was that usual for him to borrow the company truck?"

"He never had before, at least not that I knew of and I've been working here for three years. That Lexus out there is his baby—comfort all the way. He's not going to bounce around in a pickup unless he has a good reason."

"So, you don't think he took the truck to Rick, or had him pick it up here?"

"I don't know about that. I just know he didn't loan it to Rick in order for him to get his stuff. Leon was right about one thing; Rick had been kicked out of the Beaufort house. But he called me about lunchtime and asked if I could help him move some things after I got off work. He needed a pickup, and I already had the truck checked out; so, I met Rick at the Beaufort's about four. We got the rowing machine and a couple boxes of books plus his clothes. I offered to hang onto his things until he could find an apartment. After we finished loading, Rick followed me in his car back to my place to unload, and I brought the pickup to the office. I left it parked out back. Ginny was as good as her word; she gave me a ride home and we stopped at the diner. My treat." A sheepish smile, "That's probably why I remember it so well."

"I really appreciate you telling me this. And I won't say where I heard it."

"Thanks." Andy gave her a wave and was out the door.

Did this new information change anything? Probably not. It didn't rule out Rick having the truck that evening. He must have lied about why he needed it. Leon wouldn't have known the difference. Rick still had his convertible back then, but that wasn't a vehicle that would hold much—certainly not a rowing machine; so, Leon wouldn't have questioned the request. But the person on the video wasn't moving a rowing machine, at least not putting one in the back of the pickup and according to Andy, all of Rick's things were already gone from the house anyway.

So, if Rick did borrow the truck, why did he need it? It made the most sense that Rick would have picked up the truck at the office. There wouldn't have been any reason for Leon to have taken the truck home only to have Rick pick it up later. But she was back where she started—why did Rick need the truck if he'd already moved all his belongings? Back to more unknowns.

Then, she had a bright idea—why not check the firm's parking lot cameras on that evening? That would tell her if Rick had left his car and picked up the truck. She crossed her fingers that the tapes from a few weeks back hadn't been discarded or erased. Andy would be able to check, and she thought she could trust him to be discreet. She asked him to save the video and email or text the file to her cell phone.

A couple hours on the computer for company business and then she was off to see Chief Mitchell. King Street was fairly clear of debris, but evidence of high water was everywhere, from standing water in flooded yards to water marks six to ten inches above the ground on the fronts of buildings. The storm hadn't been kind. Mud brown was the new color for streets and sidewalks.

Compared to the last time she was there, the police station seemed almost empty. No one was waiting in the foyer, the hallway was clear, and several offices had their doors shut and blinds drawn over windows. It would appear that the force was working in the field. There was probably more than one part of town that needed to be patrolled.

"Elaine Mahoney, good to see you again—and good to see you survived the storm." At exactly ten, the chief opened his door and motioned for her to come in. "I have to admit I'm curious about this new information you mentioned when you called."

"It's all right here." Elaine handed him the flash drive. "I finally heard from one of the Beaufort's neighbors. Their cameras caught some interesting images the night Hannah Beaufort died." She took a chair in front of his desk and waited while he opened his laptop and inserted the flash drive. Viewing time was under four minutes and she could tell he watched the segment on the widow's walk twice. Finally, he sat back in his chair.

"Wow. I think we've got ourselves a new ballgame. I'm assuming you're submitting this as evidence?" He had slipped the drive into an envelope.

"Yes."

"Let me hear your thoughts. Anything you want to add?"

"I'd like a lab to test this cap and gloves for DNA. The phone may be a dead end but it's best to check." Elaine handed him the three plastic bags of articles and filled him in on finding the baseball cap and gloves among Rick's belongings, as well as his possibly having borrowed the pickup that evening, but ended by saying she was simply not able to even imagine Rick hurting his mother.

"I have a tendency to agree. I'd rather think someone was setting him up, but who would have guessed that cameras would capture the event? Why would someone even think he needed to 'stage' his actions?"

Elaine nodded. "My thoughts exactly. And, of course, Rick can't be questioned now."

"That's beginning to seem convenient. I've got a detective on Rick's death. Between you and me, seems Rick was a money-mule, at least that's the word on the street."

"A money-mule?"

"A courier on a bigger scale. Any sums that needed to be transferred, change hands maybe from one gang to another or from one scammer to someone legit, would be turned over to a person everyone trusted. A group living on the streets can have one or two such people. It usually involves drugs and large sums of money, but often a mule moves money obtained from victims of fraud. And, as a job, becoming a mule is a lot more prevalent than one might think—students, retirees, small business owners, anyone needing a second income or to pad the one they have can fall victim to what might appear as an innocent, and legal, handling of assets. You know those 'work from home ads' on social media? Some of those are set up to lure in the unsuspecting. What could be more innocent than 'Here take this money, put it in your account and then be ready to turn it over or move it to another account when we tell you.' A lot is done electronically. 'And oh, by the way, here's two or three thousand or maybe even five for your trouble.'"

"I had no idea, but Rick certainly fits the picture of someone needing money before Leon Stanley hired him."

"Exactly. I don't think Rick kept his hands clean, and he may have been coerced. I think we have to keep in mind what his mindset was after the violent death of his mother."

"He was probably ripe for someone giving him attention, trusting him, helping him out when he was thrown out."

"That's what I'm thinking. I'm going to ask you not to share any of this information with anyone. I may stop by and thank the Hunts but also ask that they don't share what they know. There's always the possibility of putting the innocent bystander in danger just for doing a good deed. I'd like the man who pushed Hannah to feel safe—at least undetected. And I don't want my man who's investigating Rick's life on the streets to have his time wasted. I'm sending the videos to our lab. You'd be surprised what they can see with equipment to enlarge and separate areas of interest. We'll be in touch. And, Elaine? Good work. I think you're in the right business. I'll let you know the minute we hear anything."

Elaine walked back to her car. That had taken less than half an hour but she felt good about turning over her findings to the chief. And she felt pretty good about there being no loose ends. She could take a deep breath and just wait. She felt slightly remiss at having spent so much company time on Hannah's death, but it was the firm that had brought her the case to begin with. And certainly no one had said anything.

* * *

The note on her office door was from Ginny. "Let me know when you get back." Elaine hung her jacket on the back of her desk chair, dropped her purse, and headed back out into the hallway.

She'd promised Ginny an afternoon to go over files.

She knew Leon had earmarked several for her attention. Her next priority would be a court case coming up. A slip-and-fall with reluctant witnesses that Leon suspected had been paid to report negligence on the part of the company—real or imagined. He hoped that she might be able to find someone who would talk and give an honest report as to what happened.

"This is great. I've cleared my schedule. We'll have some uninterrupted time to catch up. The storm has caused so many appointments to cancel that the office is quiet for a change. I want to thank you again for taking care of Rick's things, clearing the office. I really appreciate that."

"Not a problem, but I did get yelled at by my boss."

"Leon? What happened?"

Elaine shared his being obviously upset by finding her gathering Rick's belongings but then apologized profusely before leaving her to finish.

"Oh, I hope you weren't too upset. He just hasn't been himself. Can you keep a secret?"

"Of course."

"Well, it's just my opinion, but he really took Hannah Beaufort's death hard."

"He's said that she was a good friend of both him and his wife."

"True, but it was a bit more than that. Earlier in the summer I came back into the office in the evening and found them. You know, doing stuff … in his office."

"Leon and Hannah? Doing *stuff*?"

A solemn nod. "Sex." This last word was whispered and Elaine wasn't certain that she'd heard correctly. "I'd walked into his office without knocking—but at eight in the evening with the lights off, why would I even suspect anyone was there. There hadn't been any cars in the parking lot. Of course, they were mortified. Poor Leon had lost his wife a year ago June, but Hannah was married. Saying the situation was awkward doesn't do it justice. At least, Leon still had his underwear on, and Hannah grabbed a sweater to wrap around herself; but they weren't just playing doctor."

"How embarrassing for you. What did Leon say?"

"Not a word—acted like it had never happened. I'm sure he knew that I wouldn't say anything. I'm only mentioning it now because ever since Hannah died, he just hasn't been himself. Yelling was becoming a norm, and I don't want you to feel badly. It wasn't personal. I have reason to believe the anger was simply misdirected. I think that they'd broken up before her death."

"Why do you say that?"

"He'd ask me to call her and have her meet him someplace for a drink or dinner and she'd blow him off. She stopped calling here or coming by all together. I firmly believe that he loved her and was heartbroken when she decided to end their relationship. Plus, and totally irrationally, I swear I think he was pissed that her accident ruined a chance at reconciliation. He just didn't handle it well. I think his wanting to help Rick is some part of his guilt, an overcompensation for an inappropriate affair with his mother."

"Was the affair something unusual for Leon?"

"Absolutely. He was very married, if you know what I mean, and devastated when he lost his wife. Hannah, on the other hand, had somewhat of a reputation. This is a small town, Elaine, gossip is a staple. She and Hank seemed to have a workable 'open' marriage. And she was so beautiful. Even in her fifties, she could turn heads."

"I think you're right; guilt might be the underlying emotion here. That probably does explain the scooter, the job—even the promised apartment."

"You're not still working on the case, are you? I mean with Rick gone I'm sure it's been closed. I was kinda surprised when Leon set you up with Rick in the first place. Again, more to appease a very upset young man than seek justice. I wholeheartedly believe that poor Hannah most likely just slipped. I can't buy the suicide theory. She just had too much to live for. And, I felt badly that you didn't get paid—that is, I never saw an invoice."

"Oh, don't worry about that. I was glad to be helpful." Elaine purposely didn't react to Ginny's assuming she was no longer involved with Hannah's death. Or that Hannah's death was an accident. Chief Mitchell was right—the fewer people who knew the content of the videos, the better.

"I meant to ask if you'd heard of a service planned for Rick."

Ginny sighed, "It's been impossible to get Hank's attention—just too much going on after the storm. Originally, Leon had mentioned a celebration of life, maybe something at the church where they honored Hannah, but I don't think anything has been done. I'm sure we're a month away from Hank being able to get this organized. The autopsy is slowing things down, too. The police are calling it a possible suspicious death, so the coroner will take his time."

"Let me know if you hear differently. I'll be working from my office the rest of the week."

"Oh, good. I've been meaning to hand these off. Here you go, homework."

Ginny handed her four more case folders that Leon had requested Elaine take a look at before meeting with him in the morning—a worker's comp case, a very high-profile divorce, a land swindle, and lastly, a medical malpractice. That was going to keep her busy.

It was just after four when Andy knocked on her door. "Come in." She got up and moved to the couch and offered him coffee or a soft drink.

"Too close to going home, but thanks. I texted the file but thought I'd just tell you what was on the parking lot tapes. Basically, a whole lot of nothing unless one raccoon, four feral cats, and a bunch of wharf rats would interest you."

"Probably not." Florida had more than its share of wildlife, even in the city.

"Well then, you're gonna see Leon leave via the back door here at around five forty-five. He puts his briefcase in the backseat of the Lexus and gets into the pickup and takes off. The Lexus is here for the next two and a half hours, and then Leon returns around eight-fifteen, parks the pickup next to the back door, gets into the Lexus and leaves."

"No Rick?"

"No Rick—not the person, not his car."

"But you're positive the truck was here all night?"

"I spot checked the camera captures until people started coming into work the next morning. Leon drove in at eight fifteen a.m. in the Lexus. The truck never moved after eight something in the evening. Yep, it was here all night. You've got a copy of the video."

Interesting. Hannah died sometime before seven. According to the charts, moonrise had been six-fifteen p.m. that evening with dense cloud cover until after ten. There was taped camera capture of the company pickup sitting in the driveway of the Beaufort house for fourteen minutes and during that time someone pushed Hannah Beaufort to her death.

Elaine took a deep breath. The question was, where did she go from here? Had she even zeroed in on the right pickup? Was it possible to do a check on white Chevy pickups with personalized turtle plates? But the numbers two and five were conclusive, weren't they? She had the right pickup. Maybe she was just reluctant to name her boss as a suspect.

Or was the more apt question, would a man trying to reconcile with his girlfriend or lover kill her? Could she really believe that Leon Stanley was the man on the widow's walk? Other than the timing and the whereabouts of the company pickup, could she really say that the footage from the Hunt's outside camera proved beyond doubt that the hand on Hannah Beaufort's back belonged to her former boyfriend? Just like she couldn't say decisively that the baseball cap and gym gloves that presumably belonged to Rick were the ones in the video either.

Instead of one, she had two equally unlikely suspects—a young man she'd come to really care about, and her boss. Did she go back to Chief Mitchell with this new information?

Chapter 24

Another half day at the Boatarama. Dan didn't mind driving down to Palm Coast; it was a short twenty-five miles from the townhouse. Still, he'd rather do a number of things instead of having to break the grisly news that the *Moonstruck* had been sabotaged. Hank had requested that he meet him at the dock of the warehouse and make use of his office if he needed to.

Dan hadn't heard from the lab but Hank was beside himself, wanting answers about the fire on his schooner. Dan had sent the samples on, but he had photos of each. It was probably time to just tell Hank, at least from the evidence he'd collected, exactly what had taken place. With what he was looking at in front of him, the lab's consensus wasn't needed to confirm that someone had purposely blown up the *Moonstruck*.

Sharing that with Hank wasn't going to be pleasant. And he had a feeling that even if Hank knew the motive, he wasn't about to share it. And the money wrappers— those blue bands tantalizingly floating around the cabin? Would Hank be able to explain those?

Dan spread the photos out over the desk in Hank's office and rearranged them in upper to lower deck sequence, then waited for Hank to join him. Hank was on the dock, giving instructions to a salvage crew. It was a miracle that he'd found a company only two days after the storm. Probably meant that he paid more to have the job done so quickly.

Dan assumed that Hank had alerted the Coast Guard as to the fire onboard and resulting damage. In that way it wasn't much different than having an auto accident— authorities needed to be notified along with the insurance company in a timely manner.

"Take a look." Hank had just walked into the office, and Dan motioned to the top of the desk.

"And I'm supposed to be looking at?"

"Remote controlled incendiary device. Look at photos numbered three and six." Dan didn't say anything as Hank took a pair of readers out of his pocket before picking up the two photos.

"Doesn't look like an accident, does it?" Hank continued to look at the photos after dragging a chair up to the front of the desk.

"That piece of a timer is a pretty big clue."

"None of this answers the question 'why'." Hank put the photos back on the desk and sat back.

"No ideas? No one you can think of who might have

wanted you out of the business?"

"Nope. It's not the easiest way to make money. In fifteen years I've had maybe three offers to buy me out."

"Speaking of money, maybe you can explain these bands. Looks to me like they might have come off of packets of bills." Dan handed him a photo of the twenty-five plus strips of blue paper. Hank barely glanced at the photo before placing it back on the desk. He then stood up, walked to the window, and looked out at the empty showroom for a few seconds before turning back.

"The truth? I was f-ing robbed. There was fifty-five thousand in cash in the safe. Now, why the person or persons had to set fire to the schooner, too, is beyond me. They didn't need to cover their tracks in the middle of a hurricane. I had taken the money out of the office safe the night before and had it with me when I moved the *Moonstruck*. What could have been safer than stashing the cash aboard her? I needed to pay off workers here and pay for the slip and some minor repairs at the marina where I took the *Nomad*. What was left over was my running money for the next two weeks."

"Who knew the money was here?"

"A lot of people knew I had the money on me—including your mother."

"My mother?"

"Don't get me wrong. I'm just trying to say that too many knew. I know it's stupid but I often carry cash, just usually not that much. Itinerant laborers, some repair shops on the water, privately owned docks—most operate on a cash basis. A few miles out on the ocean and something goes wrong, you don't have the luxury of running to the bank. Electronic banking has changed that to some degree, but guess I'm just old fashioned. Hindsight says I should have made it to the bank, but the storm put the kibosh on that. There had been a sales dinner in Orlando to entice interested investors to make a monetary commitment to our project—secure a ground floor spot in our projected future of Boatarama. The money wasn't exactly mine and needed to be kept separately. With the storm coming on, I knew I'd be facing a possible need for cash, so I kept it."

"Have you reported the incident as a robbery?"

"No, not in so many words."

"Which means there might not be a paper trail?"

"Not one that I want exposed. The Orlando dinner wasn't the first; we're in the middle of privately selling shares in the Boatarama. This is a little bit under the table; we won't go public for a few months. But we are letting people get in on the ground floor—a truly fantastic opportunity. We've portrayed it as a safe, quick ROI. Pictures of a scuttled schooner and news of a robbery aren't going to instill confidence. I have fifteen vessels for resale under contract, with more being considered. Someone putting a few hundred thousand dollars' worth of vessel with us on consignment has to know it's safe. Out of necessity, I'd like to keep this under wraps, as they say."

"So, what is the story?"

"I have a bulletin going out to investors, as well as customers discussing the storm and its impact on the area, not just our marina. I've put out the word that we're building in several safeguards—bomb proofing the docks with stronger pilings, overall reinforcing the entire wharf area as a result. We've planned an open house first week in January. I want visitors to have a selection of boats to view in comfortable surroundings, and know that we can deliver on what we've promised."

"Will you be ready by then?"

"We'll make it. The showroom will be finished. We're adding an oyster bar and a viewing room for prospective buyers to take a look at our inventory. I'm waiting on three top salespeople to join us and the delivery of five new 18-wheelers modified to haul boats. I'd like your mother to step in and oversee the renovation here and stay on as a project manager."

"Have you asked her yet?"

"No, you make it sound like she might not accept. I feel badly that without the *Moonstruck*, she doesn't have a job in the information booth at the marina, or one as a hostess on the schooner. She'd be great down here."

"Believe me, I wouldn't dare speak for her, but I think it would be a good fit. Ask her."

"Top of my to-do list."

"I'm going to stick around and wait to get additional photos once the salvage crew has her out of the water. I should be able to finish my report after that."

"Hey, take your time, this space is yours. I'm having lunch brought in for the crew around eleven. Help yourself. Text me if you have any questions. I'm going to run back up to the city but I'm reachable."

Chapter 25

Elaine was feeling virtuous. Early afternoon and she'd already found a possible witness to the slip-and-fall who was willing to meet with her. The pharmacy of the store in question had a delivery person who had called the office with information. Likewise, research had turned up a criminal record for the broker of the real estate firm involved in a possible bogus land deal, and the malpractice medical claim brought to light a physician on probation from India for literally cutting off a man's leg—the wrong one. How did those things happen?

She was pleased with the results of her research. Not bad for a half day's work. She owed Leon results. She didn't want him to regret hiring her. She was thinking of taking a break when Andy knocked on her door.

"Ms. Linden, think I could get you to let me pick up the scooter this afternoon? And Mr. Beaufort also asked me to pick up any of Rick's belongings that you might have."

"Not a problem. It's one-thirty; I can go now and call it a lunch break."

"That'll work."

* * *

It didn't take long for Andy to load the scooter into the pickup bed and tie it down. He'd even thought to bring a ramp. Elaine carried out the box containing the items from Rick's desk and the two boxes, one of clothing and the other of books, and gave them to Andy to put into the truck's cab. He passed on a sandwich and headed back to the office in half an hour. It was only after he'd left that Elaine remembered the two manilla envelopes of items that Maggie had taken out of the scooter's saddlebags. She couldn't imagine anything too important. She'd look through them later.

She started a pot of coffee and then smiled. Who was she kidding? She wasn't going to wait until later to look at those envelopes; she was going to take a look now. Maggie had left them on the desk in the guest room and Elaine brought them out to the kitchen.

The first envelope was full of the syllabi from several classes, a fifteen-page paper entitled, *Vegan Revisited*, and several parking tickets from an on-campus lot marked paid. Nothing of interest.

The second envelope was bulkier and contained what looked to be personal information such as recent screenshots of a bank account—the top sheet being less than a week old, with others dating back some three months. What immediately caught her eye were the amounts—all two to five thousand dollars and all paid to Rick Elliston by H&H Enterprises.

She quickly looked through the other pages. Some weeks there had been two deposits. And it all added up to a lot of money, close to forty thousand. He was still getting thousands, even after Hank had supposedly kicked him out and had his car repossessed. It was evident that he didn't have to live on the streets. So, why had he?

And didn't Hank have to know that Rick didn't have to be homeless? That he had money deposited by H&H Enterprises? It wouldn't seem so. But even more unusual was the fact that there had been no withdrawals. Rick had not used any of the money that had been deposited.

That still left the question, where was the money coming from? Was this proof that Rick had been a money mule? If so, then what was of most interest was that his stepfather was the one needing money moved; that is, if H&H Enterprises was the Henry and Hannah corporation of record. But why wouldn't that be disguised? That was like a huge red flag—as if someone was wanting to set up Hank. But for what? Misuse of publicly received funds? Maybe, drug trafficking? But how did she prove any of that?

Wasn't she letting her imagination run wild? This was crazy-making. She needed to get back to work. She gathered up all the papers and, stuffing them into the envelope, she walked out to her car. She had to give Stanley and Stanley some quality time. Had being a P.I. become a job or an obsession?

* * *

But an hour back at the office working on the slip-and-fall file, she couldn't keep her mind from wandering. Murders, money-laundering, sabotaged schooners; it wasn't a simple puzzle. She was wrestling with whether she should share Leon Stanley's possession of the company pickup on the night of Hannah's death when Ginny buzzed her to say she had a call on line one.

"Elaine? Rob Mitchell here, gotta minute?"

"Of course, Chief. I was just thinking about giving you a call."

"I'd like to meet with you tomorrow at your convenience, but I'd prefer first thing after lunch if that's good for you. I've put together some photos to see if you recognize anyone. It's a combination of people who have worked at the marina and on the *Moonstruck*, as well as some who live on the streets. I'll admit that my crew is having difficulty putting names and faces together, and you might be able to help."

"Of course, I'll give it a try. You know who might be better at viewing a lineup is Maggie Mahoney, Dan's mother. She's been doing some work for Hank Beaufort."

"Sure, bring her along. See you at one."

* * *

Maggie had been ecstatic to help and picked up Elaine at Stanley and Stanley's just before one the next day. Elaine promised lunch after they finished at the police station if there was time. She was still modeling good behavior at the office and making certain that lunch hours didn't stretch past an allotted hour or so. She was looking forward to the meeting.

Elaine knew it was too much to hope for but just maybe the chief could help them identify Ian Fredericks. He appeared to have played a part in Rick's venturing out in the middle of the storm, and he needed to be on the chief's radar if he wasn't already. The station was quiet and they didn't have to wait for the chief to see them.

Mitchell met them at the front desk and led the way back to his office. "I'm glad you could join us, Mrs. Mahoney."

"Maggie, please—less confusing now that there's another Mrs. Mahoney."

"Good point. Maggie and Elaine, it is." He gestured to two chairs, side by side, in front of a table with twelve photos laid out in three rows of four. "I arranged the photos in a spread thinking that maybe you might recognize any teams—two or more men appearing together. Take your time, but please share anything that comes to mind. For example, if you've seen that individual at the marina, or on the streets—maybe at the soup kitchen—I'd like to know. I don't expect you to come up with names—more like situations, or even a place."

Elaine sat down and then realized that Maggie was still standing, leaning with the palms of both hands on the table's edge scrutinizing each photo.

"Oh My God, that's him." Maggie pointed to the picture on the end of the second row. "That's Ian Fredericks."

"And you know him how?" The chief picked up the photo, looked at the back, then placed it by itself on the table in front of the others.

Maggie reiterated what had taken place at their first meeting in Hank's downtown office, emphasizing that the Pelican Electric invoice turned out to be a fake. Then added that the 'IF' initials on the coded note found in Rick's belongings at Stanley and Stanley as possibly indicating the message about money was from Ian.

Elaine had brought the bank statement pages belonging to Rick and handed them to the chief. "The amounts seem to be consistent with what you had mentioned is often offered to money mules. I find it interesting that the money was apparently paid to Rick by his stepfather. And because Ian Fredericks showed up at Hank Beaufort's office with a fake invoice for a like amount, H&H Enterprises would appear to be paying him, too— for something other than electrical work maybe."

"I'm not familiar with the name Ian Fredericks, but I think you both will find it interesting that the photo Maggie picked out is of a Ron Carter. Ron is from the islands and has a history of being a drug runner. He's done time but has kept his nose clean the last few years. At least, he hasn't come to our attention for any wrong doing. He's also a skilled sailor. Hank Beaufort has hired him as a second mate on his schooners and as far as we know, he's maintained legit employment. But what you've shared would seem to indicate differently."

"I know it's too soon for the labs to get back with information on the DNA found on the articles of clothing belonging to Rick, but I'm curious."

"I put a rush on it. I'm hoping to know something by tomorrow."

"But I'm not sure what it will tell us. In so many ways, it's just one more piece of circumstantial evidence. We have videos that are too fuzzy to be conclusive, trucks parked in driveways at the time of a murder with an unidentified driver, money changing hands but no apparent crime." Elaine shook her head, "It's maddening. Where are the eye witnesses? Or people who have lost money?"

"Welcome to my world, but trust me on this—sooner or later the pieces fall into place."

* * *

Maggie dropped Elaine off back at the office saying she had a job interview at two-thirty.

"That sounds exciting. It's such a shame the *Moonstruck* is no longer. Anything you want to share about this new opportunity?"

"It's not a secret. Hank would like me to organize the office at Boatarama. I have no idea if it's temporary or permanent."

"Good luck. That could be fun. Say hello to Dan."

Chapter 26

The afternoon got busy. The Boatarama was crawling with people. Dan found himself trying to stay out of the way of the men delivering the five transport trucks, the salvage crew attempting to raise the *Moonstruck*, several off-the-street job applicants, the construction workers putting up scaffolding in the main entrance, random deliveries of materials to rebuild the dock area … and in the midst of it all, his mother walked in the front entrance with Hank by her side.

"I'd like you to meet my new administrative assistant." Hank was beaming like he'd just scored the coup of the year.

And maybe he had, Dan mused. There was little his mother couldn't do when it came to organizing. It was obvious that she was needed.

"You have my vote of confidence. You won't recognize this place in a couple weeks."

"Thank you, son. Always good to know I have your support." Maggie winked and then turned toward Hank. "Now, where do you want me to start? What needs to get done first?"

"Give me a couple minutes to get Maggie situated and then let's the two of us see how the salvage team is doing."

"Meet you out back."

Dan wasn't just being complimentary. He trusted his mother to bring some order to the chaos forming in the main entry. Already she had opened a utility room and with help was carrying out folding chairs to set up across from what would eventually be an information desk. Right now there was an open logbook on the desk and people were lining up to sign in. Finally, Hank said something to Maggie, gave her a squeeze with his arm around her shoulder and walked toward Dan.

"First time I've been able to take a deep breath all morning. Maggie's going to set up interviews on the half hour. Looks like I have some top-notch folks applying— carpenters, three truck drivers, and about half a dozen laborers for starters. I've got thirty minutes to check out the salvage crew."

There wasn't that much to see, at least, not of the *Moonstruck* herself. The dock was full of lift bags, pumps, two divers, a floating crane, the operator, and the crew in charge of it all. Expensive. Dan knew he was looking at ten to twenty thousand dollars plus. As if he'd read his mind, Hank pointed to the crane, "I could have run that thing myself, but I opted out for all the know-how that goes with renting an entire team. I know they'll do it right. I just hate to think of the money I'll be spending."

"Money probably isn't as important as know-how. The wisest thing to do was hire a crew."

"I'm not going to be able to stay for too long. Let me know how it goes. I need to find garage space for those boat haulers. I've got several boats that need to find their way down here in the next couple weeks. Once we get the *Moonstruck* out of here, I can bring the *Nomad* back and start filling up the slips with boats for sale."

"It's shaping up."

"Yeah, we didn't need a hurricane, but we'll get everything back together." Hank talked to the crane operator and said something to the dive-team before walking back toward the administration building.

Dan stayed out of the crew's way but photographed each step as the schooner emerged from the water. Two hours later the *Moonstruck* was out and on land. It was mid-afternoon when Dan stepped into some overalls to board the broken ship and do a final investigation. As far as salvaging parts, the steel hull would be moved to one of the repair garages, maybe some planking could be saved, but the engine was a loss. At least the top rigging had been removed and stored before the storm. The claim was going to be upwards of a few hundred thousand dollars.

"Mr. Beaufort?" A man who appeared to be the salvage crew foreman walked toward him.

"Mr. Beaufort is in the office." Dan pointed to the administration building. "Can I help you? I'm handling the investigation for UL&C insurance."

"I just need to let someone know that I'm clocking out now. I'll be back in the morning to dismantle her. I should be able to get here before nine. We'll need access to the storage areas, and I will need his ok before I remove any part of the schooner from the premises. Don't think we're going to have a lot to save but that will be the owner's call."

"I'll let him know." He watched as the man and three others walked around the main building before disappearing into the parking lot.

It took the salvage crew of four other men on the wharf three-quarters of an hour to load up, back the crane away from the dock and head up the intracoastal waterway. The scene was all his. He was going to do a stem-to-stern inspection, looking for anything he might have missed on the dive. Things always looked different underwater. At least this time he didn't need to confirm the cause of the fire, but he did need more detailed photos of the damage to the upper deck. At least most of it had remained out of water.

The teak and mahogany trim pieces showed some promise of being reusable. Teak's oily texture and closed pores made it water resistant and though some pieces were charred, other strips had proved durable and had survived intact. As an exotic hardwood, it was expensive but preferred for use in watercraft. Dan doubted if many million-dollar yachts were without teak appointments. There were even wood-workers whose specialty was teak and mahogany.

Movement was slow. Footing was anything but firm, and deceiving at best. Two different times Dan had stepped on what looked to be a solid surface only to have it sharply break. The second time it happened, Dan realized that he'd uncovered a portion of double-decking—he'd literally stepped into a box. Ten inches deep and roughly forty-two inches in length, plank crates lined up side by side had once filled the front of the schooner, their lids forming the planking that made up the top deck. Undiscernible before, now the containers were laid wide-open.

Dan grabbed his camera and dropped to all fours. Not all the built-in crates were completely open. He took the claw hammer from his belt and forced the lids from the two containers closest to him. Was this a leftover from some kind of gunrunning days? It was perfect for hidden cargo. Dan reached forward and swept his hand under the splintered lid to the box's back wall only to realize something was stuck at the very end.

He withdrew his hand, took off the cumbersome rubber glove, and leaned forward, thrusting his hand as far back as it would go, bringing out the plastic-wrapped rectangle. What looked to be compressed white powder. Cocaine. He'd bet his job on it. He was holding a brick weighing maybe two pounds with a card underneath the wrapping showing an Eye of Horus, a gang signature? It must be the insignia of some group. It appeared to have been stamped onto the card.

He placed the brick back into the box. For one thing, it needed to be found where he had discovered it. He slipped the rubber gloves back on, knelt on a solid area of planking and pushed the parcel back into its original hiding place. How long had it been there? Was there a way to determine if the brick was part of a recent, much larger stash? He doubted it.

The *Moonstruck* was moored at the marina in St. Augustine. To the best of his knowledge, it was moved only to take tourists on short tours of the surrounding waterways. It didn't make sense that there would be drugs aboard, possibly in a large quantity. But what a great hiding place if someone just needed somewhere to stockpile something illegal.

And weren't tourist towns great places for drug sales? Elaine had shared the chief's suspicion that Rick had been a money mule. Deposits to Rick's bank account came from H&H Enterprises—Hank's corporation. That would seem to be damaging proof that Hank knew how his ship was being used.

But what did he do now? The rules were murky. Basically, Dan only needed to alert the schooner's owner. It was not his duty to call authorities. Reporting it to UL&C came with another set of constraints. He could not remove the suspected package—that would be left to any police investigation that might follow. He'd made sure of that; the brick was back in place. The owner of the property where the possible contraband was discovered was presumed innocent until proven guilty of possession of prior knowledge of said find.

In short, the answer to 'was Hank running drugs' was not his to find out. How would authorities even be able to prove Hank's involvement or lack of it? Would the deposits made to Rick be enough?

Dan took his time checking the other rows of built-in, under-deck crates. He opened every one. All were clean. The one packet he'd found was obviously an oversight, somehow it must have been separated from what was most likely a bigger stash. His investigation of the schooner was taking another direction. He was no longer just looking for damage to the vessel; he was looking for her secrets. Was there other evidence? Other contraband?

And what did this have to say about why the ship was

destroyed? Was the bombing of the *Moonstruck* the work of some rival gang? Somebody needing to put the *Moonstruck* out of business? Maybe just anger—a fight over territory. Was the money stolen from the safe below deck tied to the cocaine and not part of initial offerings for shares in the Boatarama as Hank had said?

Hank had admitted to losing thousands of dollars. Was the money simply payment for the schooner's illegal cargo? Maybe Hank had never meant to put the money in a bank—storm or not. Maybe it hadn't been meant to meet a crew's payroll or pay rental costs for leaving the *Nomad* docked somewhere? Dan really wished he could unequivocally believe Hank Beaufort.

It was getting late and he'd love to put off reporting his find to Hank. But it had to be done. His mother was still there. He'd give Elaine a call and suggest the three of them have dinner somewhere. Someplace with a bar. He knew he'd need a drink after his chat with Hank.

Chapter 27

Oh, Dan, I'd love to have dinner with Maggie. I just have no idea when I'll be heading home. Remember the slip-and-fall case I've been working on? Well, a person who works in the pharmacy of the drug store where the fall happened called Stanley and Stanley with information. Problem is that person doesn't get off work until six and has asked that I meet him then to talk."

"Bummer. It's after five now. I'll text when we leave here and decide where we're going to eat. Maybe you could join us later."

"That's a possibility. I can't imagine talking with this guy will take long. I'll take a few notes and record our conversation. Have you two chosen a restaurant yet?"

"Not yet, I'll text when I know."

* * *

Maggie voted for the Funky Pelican, intersection of SR100 and A1A. It would be an easy drive for Elaine, and Maggie wanted to sit on the deck that had a great ocean view. For now, Maggie was helping with the interviews, and there were two applicants left to go. This was probably a good time to have his chat with Hank.

Dan stuck his head in Hank's office. "Is this a good time to talk?"

"Probably as good as any."

"Then let's take a walk down to the dock. We'll need a little privacy."

"That sounds ominous. Any reason you're being a little melodramatic?"

Dan shrugged. "Maybe."

There were benches along the wharf. Dan pointed to the farthest one, "This Ok?"

"Fine by me. This better be good."

Dan took out his phone and opened the file of pictures he'd recently taken then handed the phone to Hank. "Don't let me forget UL&C has a form that I'll need you to sign. It simply states that I've reported what appears to be contraband and where it was stored on the vessel under inspection. It also points out that I've reported this find directly to you and it will be your responsibility to report said possible illegal substance to authorities."

"What the ... ?" Hank scrolled through the photos before looking up. "I can't believe it. This could F-up everything—everything I've worked for. It would take Boatarama away from me for sure."

Dan watched the red creep up Hank's neck until the

flush colored his entire face a bright, beet hue. Was he going to have a stroke? He suddenly sat forward, elbows balanced against his knees, and put his face in his hands.

"You give a guy a chance, and he craps on you." He looked up, "I had no idea. Do you believe me? I had no idea." His arm swept in a half circle to take in the administration building, as well as the wharf. "This is the best thing that's ever happened to me. You think I'm going to throw it all away?"

"No, I don't think you would." Dan believed him. This was not an act. He was convinced that Hank had been taken by surprise and had been totally oblivious to someone using the schooner to store illegal substances. Wow, this guy didn't need to lift a finger to invite trouble.

"I'll make more money being legit than I ever could pushing this death powder. That may be a little inflated, but I'm onto something here. I'll be offering a service that there's a real need for. I don't have any reason to be messing with this stuff, taking a chance of getting prison time." He handed Dan's phone back. "But it does make sense as to who might want to bomb the *Moonstruck*. And it explains why the building materials never reached the Hilton in the Bahamas."

"You didn't make the trip to the Bahamas?"

"No. I had a meeting two days before the storm hit with an investment banker and the real estate broker who had this property listed. We met here in my office and closed the deal that afternoon. It had to be hush-hush. The deal could have been yanked out from under me; it couldn't be publicized. If you remember, I didn't know until the last minute whether I'd have a place to moor the *Moonstruck* without taking her a few miles down the coast. After the closing, I went back to St. Augustine, got money out of the safe in my office there, and put it on the *Moonstruck* for safekeeping. Between the closing here and the storm, I ran out of time. Something had to give; so, Ron took over. I left the navigation of the *Nomad* in the hands of competent sailors—famous last words."

"So, you know who was taking advantage of you?"

"Yeah."

"Care to share?"

"Let me handle this. I gotta do it my way. Allow me that. Can you put off getting your report in until the morning?"

"I suppose I could. Let's go back up to the office and make a copy of the disclaimer that I mentioned. I'll work on my report tonight and run it by you tomorrow."

"Thanks, I appreciate that. I mean it. I know you're doing me a big favor. But first I need to get the evidence off of the *Moonstruck*. Look around you. There were enough people out here working earlier that somebody's got to have seen you discover the cocaine. It's not safe where it's at. Where it was found will be in your report, right? And the brick will be in the office safe."

* * *

Elaine was excited. This would be her first field work that truly might pay off for Stanley and Stanley. She was still feeling just a wee bit guilty about all the time she'd devoted to solving Hannah Beaufort's death. And this lead had just dropped in her lap. Of course, it was premature to get her hopes up but the slip-and-fall case involved a suit for over one million and promised to go higher. The story was nothing new. A woman in her fifties had fallen inside the store of a well-known drugstore chain. She cited negligence on the store's part to maintain a safe environment for shoppers.

The settlement she sought included medical bills—the woman currently had to use a wheelchair, resulting in lost wages, and a renovation of her home to meet her needs. But most damaging, the woman now suffered seizures from the concussion due to the fall. It was not known if she would ever be able to return to work. She was the sole support of her seven-year-old grandson and her being incapacitated had impacted her ability to care for a minor. They had been evicted from their apartment and forced to rely on charity for food and everyday necessities. A compelling case—one that would tug on the heartstrings of jurors if it went to trial. There was little doubt that a jury would be swayed—if her condition could be proved.

It was a little after five when Elaine put a notebook, recorder, and camera in a tote and started out. She had to get across town during the busiest time of the day. The drugstore was on Route 1, and she wanted to get there early enough to check out the store and get some photos. She was most interested in how clean the store was now. Was the parking lot well-lighted, free of debris even after the storm?

She pulled the rental sedan into a parking space toward the back of the lot. Once again, she reminded herself that there was no excuse for not buying a car. She really had to do something now that she was gainfully employed, and it looked like the two of them would be in the St. Augustine area for a while.

The store was well-lighted and its surroundings appeared clean. She took a couple photos and walked to the back of the parking lot. Even the dumpsters were free of any spill-over. There were several cars in back, the one closest to her was an SUV with darkened windows that wouldn't have met code, a newer sedan, and a couple older model Toyotas. The area must be reserved for employee parking.

She walked back around to the front and into the store through the automatic doors at the entrance. She had been in this chain's stores thousands of times. For the most part, products were easy to find and wide aisles made getting around a breeze. It was a quarter of six and she might as well let the young man she was meeting know that she was there.

The pharmacy was the busiest corner of the store. She hadn't seen it but there must be a drive-through on the east side of the building. Two pharmacists in lab coats were dividing time working at a counter and delivering sacks to be handed out through a side window. She didn't see anyone that fit the description of her informer until a door at the back opened and a young man walked behind the counter carrying a stack of boxes. It looked like he was going to be replenishing shelves in the area. One box was marked labels, another appeared to be packets of ibuprofen, and a third was filled with syringes. People were probably already lining up for flu shots; it certainly was the season.

She walked up to the 'drop off' window and caught the attention of the young man who had just entered the area.

"I'm looking for Jonathan Ward. I'm Elaine Linden from Stanley and Stanley."

"I'm Jonathan Ward."

"I'm early but just wanted to let you know I'm here. I need to pick up some things. Shall I meet you back here in fifteen minutes?"

"That'd be perfect. I should get all this stuff put away by then."

He was a cute kid with an engaging smile and probably no older than eighteen or nineteen, Elaine decided. He had to be commended for stepping forward with information about the lawsuit. It would appear that his motive was one of wanting to do the right thing, and not something he was being paid to do. But she didn't really know that.

She had just found the aisle of paper goods when her cell rang. Caller ID indicated the office.

"Ginny?"

"Oh, Elaine, I'm glad I found you. Did you forget that you had an appointment at five?"

"I don't think I overlooked an appointment. Nothing was on my calendar for late today."

"This guy was running late. He talked briefly with Archer or Leon, I don't know which, then walked down the hall to my desk looking for you. He indicated that he had an appointment."

"What was the name?"

"He wouldn't give it. He acted pissed and said it wasn't important, he'd catch up with you later."

"This just isn't ringing any bells. I've been concentrating on the slip-and-fall case and haven't even talked with anyone not involved with the S&F."

"I know. You always let me know if you've made any appointments that I don't know about so that I can keep a pretty comprehensive schedule for everyone up front at my desk. Sorry to bother you but I wanted to check just in case Leon or someone asks."

"Glad you did. If he comes by again, you can give him

my cell number." Just to double check, she brought up the calendar on her phone after Ginny hung up. Even looking two weeks out, there were no office appointments with individual men, or with groups for that matter. She'd check with Leon when she got in tomorrow morning.

She picked up a package of paper towels and a container of toilet bowl cleaner, paid for them, and carried her package out to the car. She closed the trunk and pressed the fob to lock the car when movement at the side of the building caught her attention.

A man had just lit a cigarette and was leaning against the SUV with blackened windows. Torn jeans, dirty-gray sweatshirt, a bandana tied around his head … was he a street person? It was hard to tell, but maybe, giving this guy the benefit of the doubt, he owned the car. Loitering was such a problem in St. Augustine but this guy could just be waiting for someone to get off work. She dropped the key-fob into her purse and went back into the store. Jonathan was as good as his word and came out of the pharmacy right at six.

"I hope I didn't rush you? Did you finish putting everything away?"

"All done and then some. I even got a head start on stocking for tomorrow, but I did promise to work late tonight. This can be one busy place."

"I can see that."

"For starters, let's walk over there. I want to show you this aisle because it's the one I'll be talking about."

Elaine followed him to the aisle two over from the pharmacy containing infant care—diapers, formula, wipes, tear-less soaps and shampoos, rubber-coated safety pins, teething rings, antiseptic for sore gums—anything and everything one could want for an infant or toddler.

"I'd like to double-check your contact information and have you sign this disclaimer stating that you are sharing information of your own free will and are not being coerced or in any way threatened or bribed to give an account of an event other than what you personally witnessed."

"You have my word." Elaine produced the disclaimer and watched Jonathan sign it, adding her initials as witness. He added a second phone number to her contact list, his personal cell, and changed the apartment number of his residence. "Everything's correct now."

"Thanks. Shall we get started?" Elaine took out the recorder and got his okay to use it, but she'd also rely on taking notes, too.

"Just for the record, if there's a reason for my coming forward and sharing this information, it's because I'm tired of people taking advantage of others. Yeah, I know the store is big, a nationwide franchise, but that's no excuse for trying to bilk it out of millions. Frankly, it makes me mad."

"I appreciate that."

"I should tell you that I cleared talking to you with my boss. I just thought you should know."

"Good. That was my first question. I'd like to set the recorder on the shelf here between us. Is that Ok?" She got a nod, and turned it on. "Now, the date of the incident?"

"August 5. That was a Sunday. I don't usually work weekends but had been called in to make several deliveries. We offer free delivery of prescriptions to shut-ins and nursing homes in the area."

"Do you remember the time?"

"A little after one. I was just getting ready to mop the back entryway when my girlfriend called. I stepped away from the pharmacy and took the call there—at the end of this aisle." He pointed to a huge mesh bin with a sign that offered a deal on diapers. "I wasn't hiding, but I was pretty much hidden by the specials bin. While I was talking, an older woman and a young boy came down the aisle from the opposite direction. They stood in front of the baby soap section for a few minutes. She was talking to the little boy, but, then abruptly, she walked on by herself. The next thing I knew, the kid had taken the cap off of a bottle of shampoo and was pouring it over the floor. At that point I started to video what was happening."

"Did the woman see this—what the child had done?"

"I don't know, but she hadn't gone far. When he finished, he tossed the bottle aside and called to her. She immediately came down the aisle from the opposite direction. But when she got to the edge of the soap mess that the kid had made, she sort of kicked out her foot but then completely lost her balance coming down hard on her backside, and striking her head on the lower shelf."

"Intentional?"

"That's what it looked like—a prat fall gone wrong. Now, I don't doubt that she really hurt herself; I just don't think she planned to fall that hard. I think this was going to be quick money, a lot of it, not incapacitation for life."

"How much of this do you have on video?"

"Pretty much all of it. With halfway decent cameras on phones today, it's tough to get by with something and not be recorded. I showed it to my boss but he discouraged doing anything with it—that is, until she went after a few million or so. That's when the corporation hired a local firm to support their big guns and Mr. Stanley sent you over."

"My office email address is on my card. Send me a copy of the video. In the meantime, I'll rework my notes, watch the video, and have you read my report and sign to its accuracy. I'll call first but I should be able to run by tomorrow afternoon. Thanks for your help."

Elaine switched off the recorder and dropped it in the tote along with her notebook as Jonathan walked back to the pharmacy. It was six thirty-five. Funky Pelican was a good half hour drive from there but a late dinner with her two favorite people was worth twice that distance.

As she walked out the door, she noticed that someone had moved the SUV with the heavily tinted windows and parked it next to her sedan. In fact, it was so close there was no way she could even open her driver's side door. Had someone scraped the side of her car to park so close? And why? Was this a joke? She didn't see the man who had been leaning against the SUV earlier. In fact, there wasn't anyone around. It was now dusk, and wasn't it strange that the lights in the parking lot hadn't come on?

The interior lights in the SUV flickered, heavily muted by that dark tint, but the back door suddenly opened and two men jumped out, rushing her and knocking her to the ground. Tape went around her mouth and a cloth was quickly and tightly tied over her eyes. She struck out with a fist only to have her arms grabbed and both hands forced behind her back to be taped at the wrist.

Kicking made one man curse before binding her ankles. The other man hoisted her over his shoulder and literally threw her into the back of the SUV. He covered her with some kind of light piece of canvas and slammed the door shut.

The blindfold was too tight, the tape pulled her skin,

but she was alive. Ruling out some macabre change of intent, she probably wasn't going to be killed—at least, not right away. This was an abduction. Was she going to be offered to the highest bidder? But why? What did she know or what had she done to make her some sort of valuable pawn? What if it was mistaken identity? What would her captors do when they discovered they had the wrong person?

She had to shut down this way of thinking and concentrate on where she was and how she was going to escape. No more stopping and starting would seem to indicate that they had left St. Augustine and were on I-95. She recognized the sound and buffeted feel of large trucks as they passed by. If she had to guess, she'd say they were heading south and fairly quickly.

Luckily, Dan was expecting her to join them at the Funky Pelican restaurant about now. He would text or call and be worried when she didn't answer. Her purse, tote, and phone were all scattered on the drugstore's asphalt parking lot. She just hoped someone would find them and turn them in, not steal them.

But how long was it going to take Dan to figure out something was wrong? And then, what would he do? What *could* he do? She didn't expect him to know any more about why she was trussed up in the back of an SUV barreling down the interstate than she did.

Chapter 28

The Funky Pelican was a tourist spot with great outdoor seating, offering an uninterrupted view of the Atlantic. Preferred seating if you didn't mind fighting off various birds who seemed to think all French fries were up for grabs. There was just enough breeze outside to make Maggie vote for a booth inside because, even with lights on the neighboring pier, it was dark. It was already a little after seven but two margaritas and an appetizer would keep them busy until Elaine joined them. She should be there any minute.

"I was sure she'd call or text when she left the drugstore." The appetizer was gone and he'd just turned down another marg. Dan checked his watch, a quarter to eight. "I'm going to text. I don't want to interrupt anything with a phone call if she's still in a meeting. I know she'll join us as soon as she can. Let's go ahead and get our orders in."

Fish tacos and shrimp and grits arrived but still no Elaine. It was now an hour past any reasonable time that they could have expected her. Had there been an accident? Dan quickly checked the local online news. Nothing reported. She wasn't answering texts; he'd call. No reason he needed to be worried about interrupting her now, she couldn't still be working.

"Hello." He got an answer on the first ring. But it wasn't Elaine. The voice was male and young. What was going on?

"My name is Dan Mahoney. I just called my wife's phone. Who are you?"

"Oh, Mr. Mahoney, I don't know what happened. I work at CVS on Rt. 1 just south of St. Augustine, a block north of the Shores complex. I was meeting with your wife but she left over an hour and a half ago. I ended up working late and just walked out to go home when I found all her stuff in the parking lot, like she'd just dumped it— her purse, phone, recorder. And I think her car is still here."

"I can get there in twenty minutes. Can you wait for me?"

"Sure. Just ask for Jonathan; I'll be inside."

Dan hung up and was already out of the booth. He quickly shared what Jonathan had said and suggested Maggie at least go ahead and eat.

"You're kidding, of course. I'll get these orders boxed to go and meet you at the drugstore."

* * *

Elaine was forcing herself to take deep breaths and expel the air back out through her nose. The tape over her mouth was more than annoying. They had to have been traveling for at least an hour—and still on the interstate. What was the destination? She had to keep her wits about her.

Before she was blindfolded, what did her captors look like? Age? Ethnicity? Tattoos or other marks? It was difficult to come up with details. One wore a stocking cap pulled low over his forehead and he had a gold stud through the edge of one eyebrow. The other man, the one who picked her up, was all muscle and taller than the first guy. But wasn't there a third man? Someone who had slipped behind the steering wheel and left the actual 'grab' to the other two. The one who started the SUV and rolled back for the others to jump in. She hadn't seen him clearly at all. But why in the world were three men lying in wait for her to come out of a drugstore at six forty-five in the evening?

She wracked her brain. What did she know about anything that made this kind of abduction necessary? It wasn't a robbery. Her purse had been yanked off of her arm but thrown aside. She'd had fifty dollars in her billfold; surely that should have been of interest. No one even checked. Money hadn't been the motive.

Finally, the SUV must have taken an exit off of the interstate. At least, there was a fair amount of stop and go movement indicating traffic lights. They must be going across a town, now and then the honking of horns, squealing of tires, and even the siren of an emergency vehicle bombarded her consciousness. Then it all stopped. They rode for probably ten minutes in absolute silence aside from the SUV's sounds of gears changing, and tires crunching on what must be gravel.

When they stopped and the back door was opened, she heard water. That telltale lapping sound of little waves rolling up against something stationary. A dock? It must be. But she didn't have time to figure it out before being wrapped in the canvas sheet that was covering her and being pulled out of the SUV.

Once again, she was hoisted over the shoulder of the larger of the three men. He didn't waste time in sprinting down what must be some kind of gangplank and onto a boat. The gentle rocking and occasional splash would suggest a marina of some sort. At least the boat seemed securely moored.

Doors thudded open and this time she was carried down a flight of stairs. She must be below deck on a bigger than average vessel. One more door crashed open and she was carried into an area that seemed to contain a bed. Her captor tossed her on a mattress, unrolled the canvas, and pulled it out from under her.

"Ms. Mahoney, welcome. May I suggest that you pray your boyfriend cares enough to save you?"

Then he left. She could hear footsteps above her before they receded into nothing. She had been abandoned in what was probably a large boat, at night, maybe an hour and a half from St. Augustine and her boyfriend was supposed to save her? Boyfriend? What the hell was going on? But didn't that melodious cadence to his voice suggest where her captor was from?

* * *

Of course, no one had seen anything. Dan stood with

Maggie and Jonathan in the CVS parking lot. Jonathan shared that the breaker for the lights surrounding the lot had been thrown earlier, but, again, no one had seen who had done it. The lights were now back on and Elaine's car sat by itself, still locked. The only known? Elaine was gone.

"I'm going to call Ginny; her home phone should be in here." Dan pulled up Elaine's contact list on her phone. "Maybe if we check Elaine's office there will be some clue. I just wish I knew what I was looking for."

Ginny quickly agreed to meet him at Stanley and Stanley and could be there in ten minutes. Maggie needed to go by their townhouse and feed Simon, but begged Dan to let her know the minute he knew something. She'd wait at their house until he got back just in case Elaine miraculously showed up. Dan asked her to likewise call him if it looked like Elaine had been to the house earlier.

* * *

Did he call the police now? Or did he try to run down any possible lead on his own? Law enforcement could sometimes endanger the victim by trying to piece together the circumstances leading up to what still appeared to be an abduction. And if she had been abducted, wouldn't he have received demands from the criminals holding her? And what on God's earth could they want? He couldn't think of one thing either one of them had to offer.

There were three other vehicles in the parking lot when Dan pulled in, a Lexus and a couple pickups. He knew Ginny's car was a hybrid Toyota—one of the Stanley brothers had even put in a charging station at the back of the lot. When the Toyota turned in the drive, Ginny drove to the back of the lot, hopped out, and connected the charger before joining Dan at the back door.

"Forgot to top up the battery earlier. I love the convenience of having a charging station at work. One of those perks that I wouldn't find elsewhere. This is really a great place to work." She took out her keys, "Oops, guess I won't need these. The door's open. Looks like Leon is still here." She pointed at the Lexus parked just a few feet away. "Must have a meeting, but we shouldn't be in anyone's way. Elaine's office is in the back."

Dan was feeling a little guilty that he hadn't visited Elaine's office before today. That was always the drawback to two-career families. People got busy and to some extent led separate lives—one, at home; the other, at work. The minute Ginny flipped on the overhead lights in Elaine's office, Dan had to smile. There wasn't a thing out of place. Even an extra jacket was hanging neatly from a clothes tree behind the door. On her desk, pens and pencils were in a pottery cup that Jason had brought back from the Orient. Family pictures were aligned perfectly across a credenza behind her desk. Her laptop was closed and placed to one side. Dan even doubted that there was one speck of dust anywhere.

"I want to check her conference room. It's just next door." Ginny led the way and with lights on, it was obvious that Elaine again had left everything in order.

"Can you think of anything unusual that might have happened today—or earlier this week for that matter?"

"Interesting. Now that you ask, there was something. A man who had probably been meeting with one of the partners was trying to find Ms. Mahoney. I hadn't seen him come in. I had been in the back hallway trying to fix a printer glitch. I found him just standing by my desk looking at my calendar. He didn't give his name and he wasn't on anyone's list of appointments. I keep a master schedule of everyone's comings and goings at my desk and where they'll be. He appeared to be trying to find his name on her schedule."

"And that's all he wanted?"

"Yes, the indication was that he'd had an appointment with Elaine. When I said that she was out on assignment, he left. I even called her to make certain that she hadn't overlooked a meeting but she didn't remember making any late afternoon appointments for today and was certain it was a mistake. I meant to ask Leon if he'd spoken to the man, but he's been so busy. He heads up two local charities and they have been planning the Christmas toy giveaways."

"Think he'd mind if we interrupted him now? I want to give Chief Mitchell all the information that he might need, but I feel that time is running out. I need to call the police."

"Let's go see."

They had barely turned the corner that led to the east wing of offices when the yelling stopped them. Even through Leon Stanley's closed office door, the anger was palpable. And from the couple words that Dan could understand, the argument seemed to be about money.

"Oh, my God, that sounds awful." Ginny had raised her hand to knock but just stood there frozen. "I have no idea who's with him."

"I think we should find out. Go back to your desk. I don't want you involved in something that might be dangerous. I mean it. Go."

Dan reached around Ginny and rapped twice on the door and then stepped back and watched her retreat back up the hallway. The quiet was instantaneous. There was a shuffling sound, probably of chairs being pushed back from a table, and a brief, muffled conversation, then the door opened.

"My apologies. I'm Dan Mahoney. We met at Hannah Beaufort's memorial."

"Of course. Come in." No handshake just a step back so that Dan could follow Leon into the room.

And that's when Dan saw the other person. "Hank?"

"What's up?" Hank stood and moved to stand by Leon.

"I'm missing a wife. It would appear to be an abduction, but I haven't received any demands. So, I don't know what to think." Dan quickly shared finding her abandoned car in the drugstore parking lot along with personal items. "I'm wracking my brain trying to figure out why she would be taken. I'm here because Ginny said a man was in the office earlier indicating that he had an afternoon appointment with her. She thought he might have met with you first."

Leon shook his head. "No, not with me. It was a slow afternoon."

"Ginny thought he came from this direction, maybe walked by your office, Leon?"

"I had a zoom meeting with county officials over Christmas planning, but no meeting with anyone in my office. My door was closed with a Do Not Disturb sign on the doorknob. No one knocked, but I wouldn't have seen anyone walking by either. I'm not of much help. So, you haven't received any demands?"

"None."

"No offense, but I don't see anyone holding her for ransom, that is, trying to hold you up for money," Hank offered.

Dan chose to ignore the fact that he might not be

monetarily of interest—the lack of a net worth that would be of interest to criminals. He actually agreed and thought he knew of another reason that might make Elaine a target. "I don't think it's about money. But it might be to shut her up. Whoever murdered Hannah might want to find out what Elaine knows."

"God damn it!" Hank exploded and slammed his fist on the conference table. "My wife committed suicide. How do I get you numbskulls to understand that? No one murdered her, no one pushed her to her death—she jumped. Are you listening to me? She jumped. I don't like to think about her being so despondent as to want to take her own life, but it happened. I wasn't there; I couldn't stop her. I'm beating myself up over that. I loved that woman. We had been together fifteen years. Not all good ones, but here and there some that were pretty terrific. I let her down. When she needed me, I let her down. With everything else that was going on, she was still my wife."

"So, you're willing to look at the video that was caught on a neighbor's house surveillance camera that captured Hannah Beaufort being pushed off the widow's walk on the fourth floor of your home? You're willing to meet with Chief Mitchell to see if you can identify the killer?"

"Pushed? You have proof?" Hank was gripping the edge of the conference table, his mouth hanging open. "Rick was right? She was murdered?"

Dan nodded. Hank's knees suddenly buckled and he sat down hard on a chair at the end of the table before covering his face with his hands and slumping forward, head touching the table top. The man was beside himself. Once again, Dan was honestly afraid Hank might be facing a physical issue—cardiac arrest?

Color had drained from his face and his breathing was labored. In that second Dan eliminated him as a suspect. This was not an acting job—some over-the-top, melodramatic show of emotion strictly to impress Dan. The man was in pain and disbelief. Leon walked over and placed a hand on Hank's shoulder; but he, too, looked shell-shocked.

"We all sold Rick short. No one believed him. Granted, he shouldn't have been so verbal about pointing a finger at his own stepfather, but we should have listened." Leon went to an under-counter fridge and brought a bottle of water back to Hank before sitting down next to him at the table. "Does Chief Mitchell have any leads?"

"I have no idea but Elaine might, and someone could be trying to silence her. That's the only thing that makes sense. I know she was planning on meeting again with the chief."

"No, there's something else." Hank sat up, took a long drink of water, and pushed his chair back. "I thought this was my problem and my problem only, but guess like a bunch of other things, I was wrong."

"How so?" Hank certainly had Dan's attention.

"I received this about a half hour ago." Hank handed Dan his phone. "Read the text. That will explain what happened."

If you want to see your girlfriend again, forget about the package you found on the *Moonstruck*.

"They grabbed the wrong Ms. Mahoney?" Dan was incredulous.

"Yeah, looks like it. There's no doubt that I have a soft spot for your mother and I wasn't keeping it a secret. I'm sure there were plenty of people who would have given the name Mahoney to her captors. Not everyone would have realized that there were two Mahoneys."

"So how did her captors find out about what was hidden on the *Moonstruck*?" Dan knew he had only told Hank.

"Remember when I asked you to withhold your report until morning? That I would handle it?"

Dan nodded. He'd been reluctant but overnight wasn't going to make a big difference. There wasn't a huge need to be timely—at least, he hadn't thought there was. And it was something that was going to have to be carefully handled. But it obviously wasn't. And now the stakes had been upped about a thousand percent. His mind was racing. How could he get Elaine back—safely?

"I needed time to get ahold of Ron Carter. Ron's my right hand. I've put my trust in his honesty and his ability. Apparently, I've been wrong. He's already done time on drug trafficking charges years ago. I guess it was easy to get in touch with his old contacts. And what a sweet setup a couple schooners proved to be. He never loaded the *Nomad* with supplies to be delivered to the Bahamas. Instead, he delivered a cache of cocaine. Bricks of the stuff that he'd stashed aboard the *Moonstruck* until he could move them to the *Nomad*. I should have been on top of this. But I was too busy inking the bottom line, making the Boatarama mine. I never suspected a thing; and, God knows there were plenty of places around the marina, even on the two schooners, to keep the drugs out of sight."

"What do you propose we do?" Dan was more than curious; he wanted answers. Elaine's life was in his hands. Could Hank look the other way? Let the drug deal involving his schooners go unreported? That might be the only way he could ensure Elaine's safety. But would Ron Carter and his thugs trust Hank? Believe that he could just look the other way? This would be a real test of Hank and Ron's friendship.

"Let me bargain with him. I'll offer him the *Nomad*— free, no strings attached for Elaine's quick and safe return. I think that will have real appeal. He could take off for the Bahamas and get lost in the islands. I think he's going to see it as a positive. The schooner and my word not to turn him in. He'd be a fool not to jump at a chance to own his own business. I know the man. I don't think he'd harm Elaine unless he felt cornered, betrayed; and then, I wouldn't put anything past him. He can be one mean SOB."

"I can't imagine him turning down your offer. Once he finds out his mistake—that he has the wrong Ms. Mahoney, I think he'll be willing to bargain."

"I hope so. Follow me back down to the Boatarama. I have all the papers for the *Nomad* in the office there. I'll sign her over to Ron and he can bring us Elaine and I'll make the transfer of the *Nomad* official. I'm texting him now with the deal. I'll ask him to meet us at the Boatarama. He was supposed to have been bringing the *Nomad* back there tonight. He may have docked already."

"Thank you."

"I'm so sorry about all this. But Ron knows I mean what I say. I won't get him in trouble."

Leon walked with both men to the back door, wished them luck, and watched as Hank pulled his pickup out of the parking lot first, closely followed by Dan's Land Rover. Then he reached into his shirt pocket and drew out his cell phone. He didn't hesitate before dialing.

"U.S. Coast Guard? I have a maritime infraction to report … an abduction and possible contraband."

Chapter 29

The boat was moving. Elaine was smart enough to realize that it must be under sail because there was literally no sound. At least not from engines. Footsteps crossed and crisscrossed the deck above her. They must have put up the sails. She couldn't tell how many people were on board but she guessed at least four.

The big question was, where were they going? Had they contacted Dan? Or whoever her boyfriend was supposed to be? Was there some predetermined destination? Maybe someplace where they would let her off? No, that was probably stretching it. She was a bargaining chip of sorts; something to trade—but to whom? And for what?

Suddenly the boat shuddered and the sound of engines drowned out even her thoughts. Were they turning around?

They had certainly picked up speed.

She heard someone turn the door handle and walk into her room. She was still lying on her side on the mattress where she'd been tossed after first coming aboard. She couldn't scream; she couldn't see; she couldn't move. Suddenly she was grabbed by the shoulders and dragged upright, then not so gently pushed into a chair. The blindfold came off and the man cut the tape binding first her hands and then her ankles.

"You need bathroom?" Elaine nodded. "I help. You come with me." This time the man steadied her as he lifted her up. She leaned against him until she felt the cramps in her legs subside and she was able to stand on her own. "You OK now?" Again, she nodded. "Then you follow." He opened the door to a narrow hallway and pushed her in front of him. He pointed to a door at the end. "That head. No take off tape." He pointed to her mouth. "I wait here. You pump ten times when you finish."

Elaine entered the closet-sized bathroom. The toilet itself looked normal, just small and squeezed up against a small sink on one side with the wall on the other. The pump was on the right side of the toilet and had a lever that worked as a plunger. She guessed she could figure it all out. She was relieved to find a roll of toilet paper sitting on the edge of the sink.

Her captor was as good as his word and was still standing in the hallway when she opened the door. Only this wasn't the same man that had brought her to the bathroom. This was a man who looked exactly like his mug shot. Ian Fredericks or Ron Carter, whatever his real name was, stood directly in front of her.

With a slight bow, he extended his hand. "Please accept my apologies. I am to understand that I have the wrong Ms.

Mahoney? You are not the girlfriend of Hank Beaufort? Here, let me get that tape off." He stepped forward and in one swift move, ripped the tape from over her mouth. "Much better, no?"

"Thank you." Elaine flexed her jaw and rubbed at the residue left on her cheeks as the stinging subsided. "Dan Mahoney is my husband. I believe Mr. Beaufort has dated his mother."

"Yes, I understand now. The joke is on me. But I can see why Hank would have been very interested in you." Elaine didn't feel the least bit flattered as his eyes roamed over her body. She wanted to wipe that smirky, half-smile off his face. This was a man used to women fawning over him. Well, not her. She admitted that she could enjoy listening to the melodic cadence of his voice, but only if she didn't have to look at him.

"Could I get a drink of water?"

"But, of course." He banged on the wall next to him and almost immediately the door behind him opened. He said a few words and the man disappeared only to reappear quickly with a bottle of water. He opened it and handed it to her. "It is a shame I have no champagne on board. This is cause for a celebration, wouldn't you agree?"

"Would we be celebrating my release?"

He nodded, "And the absence of any criminal charges against yours truly. You should be happily back with Mr. Mahoney within the hour."

"Where are we?"

"Fifteen minutes from docking at the Boatarama. You are very valuable cargo. I am going to trade you in on a schooner. This one to be exact. You are the price for the *Nomad*."

"Did Hank say that?"

"Hank *promised* that. Your safe return and she is mine. And a little indiscretion … what shall I call it? A sales trip marketing some very expensive, but illegal cargo will be forgotten … overlooked out of the kindness of his heart." A forced laugh. "I never thought I would be commenting on Hank Beaufort's kind heart. I would have said it was mostly black."

Elaine wasn't sure she was following—sales trips and marketing something illegal? That wasn't making sense, but the realization that freedom was literally moments away gave way to elation. She was unharmed and going home.

"Let's go up on deck. I need to bring her into the dock where, I believe, you'll find your welcoming committee." He held the door open, then went up the ladder first, turning to give Elaine his hand, steadying her as she stepped onto the upper deck.

The evening was serene, the beauty of her surroundings mesmerizing. The men working behind her weren't an intrusion; she hardly noticed them. Elaine leaned against the railing watching the wake spread out behind the *Nomad* as the schooner hurried toward the Boatarama. The moon was almost full and hung suspended in a cloudless sky. There was a certain peacefulness of water and sky together meeting at a limitless horizon. She could understand the love of tall ships and the centuries of men who explored the world in them.

As the schooner docked, she waved to Dan who was running down the walkway with Hank close behind. Dan didn't wait for the schooner to be tied down but once she was close, he vaulted over the side and grabbed Elaine in a smothering bear hug.

"I was scared to death. Are you OK?"

"Not a scratch. But as evening sails go, I'd rather have spent the time on deck."

The kiss was lingering and both whispered "I love you" at the same time, then laughed. It felt so good to be safe. Elaine took Dan's hand as they waited for the crew to secure the schooner before debarking and heading up the walkway.

"Did Ron tell you he's the new owner of the *Nomad*?" Hank and Ron caught up with them and they all paused to look back at what was now Ron's ship. "Can you promise me you'll do right by her?" Hank got a nod and the offer of a handshake.

Elaine knew there was some kind of barely veiled message that passed between them, but she didn't have a clue as to what exactly it was. She was just so thankful that Ron had done the right thing and kept her safe. Then the idyllic scene was shattered by a yell of "Starboard," and everyone turned to look over the bow of the *Nomad* to the right. Charging toward them at a high rate of speed was a Coast Guard cutter, blue lights flashing.

Still some seventy-five feet from the dock, a bullhorn wielded by a uniformed officer at the helm ordered all of them to stand with their hands behind their heads. As the boat bounced against the dock before being steadied, three officers jumped out and jogged toward them.

"No one move. Now, who's carrying?" Ron and Hank answered in the affirmative and two guardsmen retrieved a boot gun from Ron and a Glock that was tucked into the back waistband of Hank's jeans.

"It's been reported that this schooner, the *Nomad*, has been involved in transporting illegal substances for sale in the Bahamas and has taken a Ms. Elaine Mahoney as hostage, endangering her life."

Elaine heard Ron hiss the word "bastard" as he looked at Hank. He must be thinking that Hank had turned him in. Elaine cleared her throat and stepped forward. "I think I can explain some things. I'm Elaine Mahoney. I was meeting my husband here and was given a chance to share a trial run of the *Nomad*. Mr. Carter has purchased the schooner and offered me a chance to join him for a short sail down the Intracoastal while we waited to be joined by Mr. Beaufort and my husband. It was just a brief onboard check of equipment before returning to the marina. I assure you I was not kidnapped."

"I need to see identification from each of you. Thank you, Ms. Mahoney. Your explanation certainly differs from the report I was given. But I'd be the first to say we are often given misinformation. Are the offices open?" He pointed at the administration building.

"Yes, the building is in the midst of a renovation, but open," Hank answered.

"Then I'll ask that you meet me there." He looked at the driver's licenses that each had handed him. "Mr. Carter, I'd like you to accompany me onboard the *Nomad*. I need to take a look at your logs and make certain the vessel is not carrying contraband."

Ron, the lead officer, and the two guardsmen turned to walk back to the *Nomad* and Hank, Dan, and Elaine continued to walk toward the Boatarama office.

"Is she clean?" Dan asked.

"Fingers crossed," Hank answered. "We'll know soon enough."

Chapter 30

"You know who sicced the cops, so to speak, on Ron, don't you?" Dan was sitting at the conference table in the foyer. "Only one person had the information besides the two of us."

"Yeah, but why?" Hank stood by the floor-to-ceiling glass windows overlooking the dock. Lights from the Coast Guard cutter illuminated the *Nomad*. He could see the men walking back and forth, then the two disappeared below deck. So far, in thirty minutes' time, it didn't look like anything out of the ordinary had been found.

"Don't leave me out of the loop. Who are you talking about?" Elaine had made coffee and had just set a pot and three cups on the table.

"Your boss. I interrupted Hank and Leon at the law

office when I was trying to find you. Hank shared that he'd gotten a text from Ron saying he had you, that is, he had Ms. Mahoney who he thought was Hank's girlfriend. Ron didn't want the report I was preparing to be submitted. You were leverage to keep Hank from reporting that cocaine had been found on the *Moonstruck*. The three of us swore that no one would find out before we had a chance to rescue you. And one of us sold out."

"That reminds me, does Maggie know I'm safe now?"

"I called her earlier," Hank said.

"But why would Leon endanger Elaine's life?" Dan felt he was missing something.

"I think he thought that, at the very least, Ron would be taken in. He had no idea that Elaine would tell a different story, not point a finger at Ron and demand he be arrested. He may have even wished that there had been gunfire— possibly fatalities. I think Leon is needing a scapegoat."

"But why, Hank?" Dan asked.

"I'm afraid I don't have the answer."

"Maybe I do. I think I was beginning to get in the way. I honestly think I may have been hired and given Rick as a client so that Leon could know exactly what was happening with the investigation into Hannah's death. I believe that he has more than a vested interest." Elaine quickly looked at Hank. "Do you know that video has surfaced that proves she was killed?"

Hank nodded.

"I also have new evidence, actual video, that puts the company truck at the Beaufort residence at the exact same time of her death. Perhaps, more circumstantial and not conclusive, but there's a match to the make of the truck and a partial plate insignia. And, Leon is the person who left in the truck and returned it to his office later that evening."

"Incriminating, but I see what you mean not exactly rock-solid proof of wrongdoing. Guess we better put this discussion on hold. Looks like the inspection's over." Hank turned away from the window, "That was quick. Ron and the officer are on their way here."

"Hope it's good news or maybe I should say no news at all." Dan stood while Hank held the door open, and Ron and the officer stepped inside.

"Sorry to keep all of you up so late, but I'm satisfied that there wasn't an incident. We get far too many crank calls anymore. Per usual, they didn't give the dispatcher a name. Ron filled me in on what you're doing here, Mr. Beaufort. I wish you well. I'm glad to see the old SeaTrac property put to good use and new job opportunities coming our way."

"We've got an open house slated for January—join us."

"Thank you. I'll keep that in mind."

Hank remained by the window until the cutter pulled away from the dock, then turned to Ron, "I'm thankful the *Nomad* was clean."

Ron simply nodded before pointing at the pot of coffee. "Is there another cup around here somewhere?"

"I'll get one." Elaine walked back to the kitchen and returned with an extra mug, plus a bowl of sugar packets, putting everything on the table before sitting down herself. "I feel that I should tell you the police know that Ian Fredericks and Ron Carter are the same person."

Ron shrugged and continued to doctor his coffee before looking up. "I should probably have a lawyer before sharing what I know."

"I'm assuming you're not going to call Stanley and Stanley."

A smile, then, "No, I don't think so."

"Eric Scott in Jacksonville is a good friend. I trust him, he plays fair and will go to bat for you if needed. I'll give him a call in the morning if you want."

"Thanks. I'd appreciate it."

"Think your guys would mind staying here with the *Nomad*? When I know what we're doing in the morning, I'll text everyone. We might want to meet back down here. Ron, I'll give you a ride back to town. I can even offer you a bed if you don't mind a sleeping bag. I'm bunking down in my office until my condo is finished. Things have been held up because of the storm."

Elaine paused a moment, but Ron *had* saved her life and had been gentlemanly about it. "We have a free guest room. You're welcome, Ron—you, too Hank."

"Naw, I've got work to do. But if I were you, Ron, I'd take 'em up on a hot shower and clean sheets. Much better offer than a sleeping bag on the floor."

"That had dawned on me. I'm in, thanks."

"Sounds like a plan then. Elaine and I will pick up her car tonight and be ready to go in the morning. Ron, if you need to get anything off the *Nomad* before we leave, just meet us in the parking lot. We'll wait for you."

* * *

One-forty-five in the morning but her car was in the garage, she'd remembered to put out a fresh stack of towels for Ron, the alarm was set for seven, and she was finally crawling into bed.

"I'm kinda glad this day is over. I never want to be that scared again. Are you going to tell Maggie that you were a stand-in for her?"

"Probably not. Hank may tell her. I'm just glad that Ron didn't let things get out of hand and was willing to trade me for a schooner. I mean, how many women are worth a schooner?"

Laughing, Dan pulled her closer. "I only care about this woman, and I'd maybe go as high as two schooners." He ducked a playful jab to his shoulder.

"Oh, damn." Elaine sat up in bed then pushed her legs over the side and stood up.

"Where you going, babe? It's almost two."

"I left my phone in my jacket. I've got to charge it. The battery's going to die before morning; I've got to do it now. I'll be right back."

"I'll be here."

She blew a kiss over her shoulder and, opening the bedroom door, she walked across the hall.

The closet was a walk-in. Wasted space was Elaine's reaction when she first saw it. Then, as it came in handy for storage—a box of Jason's books and electronics, photos that couldn't be stored in the humid garage, a mattress for the daybed, a box of clothing waiting to be picked up by a local thrift shop—now, she couldn't imagine being without it.

Leaving the door open a crack, the light from the hallway offered shadowy assistance. She slipped her jacket off of a hook beside the door and grabbed her phone out of a front pocket. As much as she relied on technology, it could be a drag, always making sure it was ready to go. She'd use the charger on the kitchen counter; it was just one less thing to worry about in the morning. She had just turned to leave when a voice coming from the guest room caught her attention. A fresh air vent connected the two rooms, and she was suddenly privy to one side of a phone conversation that sounded heated.

Without hesitating, she put her phone on record and scrambled to stand on top of the linen chest directly below the vent. On tip-toes, she held the phone to the grate.

"I'd think one million was cheap, Leon. We're talking life, maybe the death penalty. You want to risk that? I've been there. I don't see you enjoying the State pen."

(Muffled answer)

"No, I wouldn't think so. I'm clean here. You offered me a hundred thousand to get rid of her and when I turned you down, you did it yourself. I think the cops will be real interested in hearing about that. Pushing a woman off a widow's walk? My silence has got to be worth a million to you. "

(A pause)

"One more thing. Don't forget, I'm the one who set up your drug deals. According to my math, I've made you a lot of money. I should be worth a little investment now, don't you think?"

(Muffled answer)

"Well, I'm sorry to hear that. I never thought you were dumb, Leon. Guess I was wrong. Give it some thought. You know how to reach me."

It was obvious that the call had ended because the next conversation had Ron ordering an Uber—to take him back to the *Nomad*. Elaine silently sat in the near dark. She'd wait until Ron had left. The last thing she needed was to be found eavesdropping in the closet.

Finally, she heard Ron open and shut the guest room door and moments later the front door opened and closed.

She was safe now. She quietly left the closet and connected her phone to the charger on the kitchen counter. Headlights in the drive seemed to indicate that Ron's ride had arrived. Was he running away? Probably. It wouldn't surprise her if he sailed to the Bahamas and simply got lost.

But what she had recorded was dynamite—literally the glue that stuck everything in place. Questions answered right down to the probable need for money mules and laundering of drug cash. The question was, what should be done now? This couldn't wait until morning; she'd have to wake Dan.

Oblivious to what was going on around him, her sweet husband was snoring softly. She closed the bedroom door behind her and walked to the bed. Sitting on the edge, she quietly called his name and caressed his shoulder.

"What's wrong?" He pushed up on his elbows.

It never failed to impress her at how quickly he could wake and have all faculties thinking clearly. She told him about the recording and the fact that Ron had left.

"We have the answers—explanations finally."

"You work with him. Do you think Leon will spring for the big bucks to keep Ron quiet?"

"Leon doesn't like being told what to do. I can't imagine that he'd roll over easily. But a threat to expose him might make a difference."

"I hope Ron stays safe. Everything depends on his testimony. The recording won't be admissible in court because he didn't consent to being recorded. We're going to need him in the flesh. Makes me worry about what Leon might do. I'm going to call Hank now. I think Ron needs someone to have his back. If Hank was telling the truth about working tonight, he'll still be up."

Dan reached for his phone on the bedside table. Hank

answered on the first ring.

"Hey, thought you two had better things to do than call me at 2 a.m."

"Need your advice, gotta minute?"

"Shoot."

Dan filled him in on the overheard conversation and the fact that Ron was on his way to the *Nomad*. "We need his testimony."

"Yeah, that's a given. Let me handle this—trust me this time. Call the chief in the morning or better yet just show up on his doorstep around eight. I'll meet you there. In the meantime, I'll make sure Ron stays safe. And, Dan? Thanks. I appreciate the two of you getting involved with all this. As painful as it is, I'm glad we're finally getting some answers."

* * *

Morning, with sunlight streaming in the window, was a jolt. Elaine nudged Dan awake and got up to make coffee. She hated the groggy, sluggish feeling that was the result of not dozing off until almost four. Even Dan spent extra time in the shower, but still complained of mental cobwebs.

"Do you remember pulling all-nighters in college? How'd we do that?" Dan was sitting at the kitchen counter hunched over a mug of coffee.

Elaine laughed. "For starters, I think we were younger."

"Oh, I was hoping you wouldn't say that. As much as I hate to move, we need to leave in the next ten minutes. I left a voicemail for the chief just to give him a heads-up and indicated we had some game-changing information. Told him we'd be there by eight."

* * *

Once again, the chief met them at the door to his office, looking like he'd enjoyed a full eight hours of rest.

"C'mon in. I'm relieved that this case is coming together. We've all waited long enough. I think you know Hank Beaufort and Ron Carter." The third man at the conference table stood up.

"I'm Eric Scott. I'll be representing Mr. Carter and Mr. Beaufort." Dan stepped forward and shook hands.

"Take a seat. I want to make certain we're all on the same page." The chief pulled out a chair for Elaine. "Now, how about some coffee orders? I think some of you had a pretty eventful night last night—or should I say this morning?"

The chief pressed the intercom button and ordered five coffees, extra cream. "I'm also going to set up the recorder. Keeps us honest."

By the time the recorder was in place and tested, the receptionist had returned with a pot of coffee and five cups and a small wicker basket with containers of half-and-half. "Looks like we're ready to go. I'd like to start by questioning Mr. Carter. I'm assuming your legal counsel, Mr. Scott, will advise you?"

"Yes."

"Let me say that my client and I haven't had a chance to discuss all aspects of the situation and may need some time here and there to discuss particulars. Will there be a problem with that, Chief Mitchell?"

"No, I've pretty much cleared my calendar for the morning. Shall we start?" The chief pressed the recorder's On button. "I'd like to say that our state lab has viewed the videos taken by the Beaufort's neighbors on the night of Ms. Beaufort's death." The chief opened the folder in front of him. "They have determined that the suspect is left-handed. He is using his dominant hand to push the victim and there is the hint of a silver band, most probably a watch on the assailant's right wrist, just noticeable at the edge of his shirt cuff. We all have a tendency to wear a watch on our non-dominant arm."

He glanced around the table, "As far as I can see, we appear to all be righties at this table." He acknowledged the polite laughter before continuing. "We also tested a pair of black gym gloves and a baseball cap brought to us by Ms. Mahoney for DNA matching. These clothing articles had been found in the possession of Rick Beaufort and were removed from his office at Stanley and Stanley. Miss Virginia—Ginny—Akers, Stanley and Stanley's office assistant, provided items containing the DNA of various office members. DNA on the cap and gloves was a match with DNA from Leon Stanley. And, yes, we have it on good authority that Mr. Stanley is left-handed. We also have video placing the company pickup in the Beaufort driveway at the time of the murder. I think you'll agree, however, that as damaging as it may sound, the evidence I just mentioned remains circumstantial until Mr. Carter has given us a sworn statement that Mr. Stanley had offered to pay him to kill Ms. Hannah Beaufort and, shortly after Mr. Carter refused to get involved, Mr. Stanley bragged to this individual that he had taken care of it himself. Do I have that correct?" The chief glanced at Ron, but his attorney interrupted.

"May I interject something here?"

"Yes, Mr. Scott, you have the floor."

"I just want to say that Mr. Carter has agreed to testify if, and I expect when, Mr. Stanley's case would come to court. The prosecution's case will rely on his testimony. I am confident that, combined with other evidence, it gives conclusive proof of Mr. Stanley's culpability in Ms. Beaufort's death. I am suggesting that Mr. Stanley be jailed and held over without bail until his trial."

"I should have mentioned that Mr. Stanley was arrested this morning at approximately seven-thirty a.m. and will appear at an arraignment at ten. It was also my recommendation that he be held without bail due to possible obstruction of justice or interfering with a witness and that he should be detained in police custody."

"Good, I'm glad that's taken care of." Eric Scott paused to open his briefcase and put a folder on the table. "As the prosecuting team in this case, we are in a position to offer immunity to Mr. Carter. Let me explain the situation. In this instance we are relying on the exchange of information— the actual testifying against Mr. Stanley in exchange for immunity from prosecution involving several instances of drugs being trafficked under Mr. Carter's direction. We are asking for transactional immunity which will safeguard Mr. Carter from any current or future charges based on or related to testimony in this case in a court of law. Chief Mitchell, I'm asking that you will not detain Mr. Carter until said immunity can be established. I will vouch for Mr. Carter's willingness to remain locally under his own volition."

"Request granted."

"Is it possible to ask Ron questions?" Elaine asked.

"I'll advise my client if it's out of bounds."

Elaine turned to Ron. "Finding out that Rick had

died during the storm was gut-wrenching. Dan and I had so hoped that he was on the right path, turning his life around. Was his death an accident? I'm assuming that Leon had given Rick your cut for being a money-mule as well as Rick's and that you came by our townhouse during the storm to pick it up?"

"Yes, I'd left a note asking that he bring what Leon owed me and meet on the street behind your house. As he walked around the corner, he was struck and knocked off balance by a branch that also took down a powerline. His death was instantaneous. I saw it happen. There was nothing I could do."

"I certainly understand Rick's need for money, but it seems he had been on Leon's payroll as a mule for some months; yet, according to his bank statement, Rick had never withdrawn a penny of it. That seems so odd. Frankly, it doesn't make sense. Here's a copy of Rick's bank statement that I found at our house. You'll also notice that all deposits were made by H&H Enterprises." Elaine held up a copy of the statement.

"Using H&H Enterprises was just Leon covering his tracks, trying to point a finger at someone Rick would suspect of wrongdoing. Or maybe Leon was hoping to improve the relationship between the two. Maybe Rick assumed his stepdad was bankrolling him. I'm not surprised that Rick hadn't used any of the money. He had his heart set on opening a restaurant. That was his dream; it's all he talked about." Ron added, "I think that was the only reason Leon could even talk him into being a mule in the first place and establish himself on the streets. That's where I met Rick. I had to protect my identity by assuming a different name."

"I don't mean to interrupt, but who stole fifty-five thousand dollars from me and blew up the *Moonstruck*?"

"Ah, I will only give you my opinion. I do not have the facts, but I do know that the six men that you hired to guard the *Moonstruck* during the storm were being paid by Leon Stanley. I'm familiar with them; they are from the islands, part of a criminal gang—well known drug traffickers operating out of the Bahamas. The Eye of Horus is their insignia. I can't tell you why it seemed necessary to destroy the *Moonstruck*. To cover their crime of stealing money? Seems overkill. But why did Leon feel he needed to kill Ms. Beaufort? That also seemed unnecessary."

"I can probably answer that," Hank said. "It's no secret that Hannah and I each had our little indiscretions. Leon was simply my wife's most recent playmate—an affair of a few months that Hannah rather unceremoniously ended by dumping Leon when he didn't expect it. That, and I owed him two million that I was having trouble paying. He'd drawn up our wills. He knew Hannah had a two-million-dollar policy that would pay in full at her death. I was sinking anything and everything I could beg or borrow into Boatarama. He got tired of waiting and being put off. He's been pressuring me to pay up ever since the insurance company cut me a check."

"Spurned love and greed—time-worn explanations for criminal acts," Dan added. "Any feel for what a jury might decide? A man in his early seventies, apparently with no prior record, having recently suffered the loss of his wife and then a companion—I'm assuming he'll get more than a slap on the wrist. My guess would be life. "

Eric Scott spoke up. "Obviously, I'm not at liberty to even hazard a guess. My team and I are eager to work with

Mr. Beaufort and Mr. Carter. I will say that I believe their case is strong, but we're a long way from the finish line."

"I had a bit of good news last evening," Hank added. "The salvage crew working on the *Moonstruck* has given me an estimate to rebuild her. I hadn't thought that was even a possibility, but I'm intrigued. I talked to Ron this morning and offered him a half interest in the tourist business in St. Augustine. And that mother of yours," he turned to Dan, "she is one computer whiz. Take a look at the website she set up for Boatarama. I know she could help us get the tour trade back up and thriving. Hell, Ron, you could get so busy you'll want to turn the *Nomad* into a second tourist schooner. Elaine? What about you? I'm assuming you're fresh out of a job; want to join us?"

"I'm going to hang a shingle on my own. Maybe, if the opportunity arises, I would consider working with this guy." She pointed to Dan. "But then again, we'll have to see."

"Hey, I like the idea of a family affair. Is it too presumptuous to tell UL&C that you're available?"

"Hmmmm, maybe not. Family affair has a nice ring to it."

Thank you for taking the time to read *Widow's Walk*. If you enjoyed it, please consider telling your friends or posting a short review. Word of mouth is an author's best friend and is much appreciated.

Thank you,

Susan Slater

Watch for Dan Mahoney's next adventure, and in the meantime you can catch up on Susan's other books, including the internationally bestselling Ben Pecos series.

CHECK OUT *FIVE O'CLOCK SHADOW*, A STANDALONE THRILLER.

Newlywed Pauly Caton watches, horrified, as the hot air balloon—the one she should have been riding in—falls from the sky. She races to the wrecked basket to discover both the pilot and her husband Randy dead in the fiery crash. The lone survivor appears to be an unknown child, who runs from the scene, naked and fearful, and disappears from sight. Shocked, Pauly turns to her Grams, a flashy grande dame and carnival owner, and a source of comfort for her pain.

Soon, Pauly learns that nearly everything she knew about her new husband was based on lies and deception. As Christmas approaches, she attempts to pick up the pieces of her life and uncovers a host of other surprises about Randy—things that make her question everything about her choice to marry him. She senses she can trust no one, not even the police, and learns that there are secrets which threaten to put her own life in danger.

Books by Susan Slater

The Ben Pecos Mystery Series
The Pumpkin Seed Massacre
Yellow Lies
Thunderbird
Fire Dancer
Under A Mulberry Moon
The Thaw
Ghost Dust
Paper Arrows
A Way to the Manger (a Christmas novella)

The Dan Mahoney Mystery Series
Flash Flood
Rollover
Hair of the Dog
Epiphany

Standalone Novels
0 to 60
The Caddis Man
Five O'Clock Shadow

Visit Susan's website at http://susansslater.com
where you can sign up for her free mystery newsletter
and a chance to win some very cool stuff.
Contact Susan: susan@susansslater.com
Follow Susan on Facebook